Erotic Adventures

Carl East

Published by Carl East, 2013.

This is a work of fiction. Similarities to real people, places, or events are entirely coincidental.

EROTIC ADVENTURES

First edition. July 18, 2013.

Copyright © 2013 Carl East.

ISBN: 978-1393959663

Written by Carl East.

The Sorceress and Her Apprentice

My mother always told me that my naïve trust in men would get me into trouble someday, and she was right. I don't know what I was thinking when I went into the woods that morning with Frank and Steve. They told me it would be fun hunting with a woman, so I fell for their words of encouragement. I was dressed in shorts, T-shirt, and running sneakers, while they were wearing their hunting gear. I knew nothing about hunting, or how to dress, and they didn't go out of their way to tell me.

I knew something was up when we'd walked at least four miles into the wood, and they hadn't said a word – I just didn't know what it was. It wasn't until they both started to paw at me, and pinned me to a tree that I realized what they were really after. The first thing Frank said was "This is what happens when you tease men and don't put out," to which they both laughed.

I think they expected me just to stand there and let them take me without question, but they were mistaken. I quickly pushed them off and grabbed a small, dead branch that I spotted on the ground and swiped the pair of them before making a run for it. The trouble was I had no way of knowing where I was, or which direction to run. I'd gained a few seconds head start, at best, and I had to make the most of it.

I could hear them shouting profanities and coming after me, but as I ran through all the trees, I realized that the hunting clothes they wore were slowing them down as I was quickly pulling ahead of them. In fact, it wasn't long before I realized that I was safe, at least from them. In my haste to get away though, I'd ripped my shorts and T-shirt on branches and various other obstacles that were in my way. I tried to remember which direction we'd come in, but in my anxiety I'd gotten completely turned around. I was still in trouble, but I tried not to panic.

I walked for miles and came to a river, which I thought was a good sign. I followed the flowing water, knowing that it would eventually lead me back to civilization. However, by the time it started to get dark, I still hadn't found a safe haven. I was just starting to wonder what would become of me, when I spotted a light through the trees on my side of the river. I didn't really have much of a choice, so I headed cautiously towards it.

When I finally reached it, I discovered that it was coming from a cottage. It seemed completely out of place here, but I couldn't afford to ignore the fact that someone lived in the woods. I knocked on the door and stood back.

"Who is it?" said a stern female voice.

"Um…I'm sorry to bother you, but I'm lost and I need help," I replied.

For the longest moment, there was silence and then the door opened. I'm going to take my time in describing what I saw, because it was something I truly didn't expect to see. The most beautiful and stunning of women stood in front of me. She was about six-foot tall and wore a long, red, low-cut dress, with a very distinctive looking blood-red gem hanging on a golden chain above her chest. Her breasts were perfect. In fact, I suffered a moment of jealousy just staring at them. I thought I had nice breasts, but hers put mine to shame. Her hair was jet-black and silken, and shone from the light coming from inside the cottage.

"Are you going to stare at me all night or are you going to come in?" she said, standing to one side and allowing me to pass.

"I'm sorry. I was taken aback by—"

"By what…no wait, what's your name first?" she said, interrupting me.

"Oh…right, my name's Cherry. Pleased to meet you…um," I replied.

"You can call me Sonja. Now then, why were you lost?"

"I was chased into the woods by a couple of men and got turned around. I couldn't find my way back to the path and spotted your light when it was getting dark," I replied as I watched her looking out of the window.

"They didn't follow you here, did they?"

"No, I lost them quite a few hours ago and have been walking ever since."

Sonja closed the curtain and told me to take a seat. She then went about making us both a hot drink. While she was doing that, I glanced around the cottage. It felt homely and warm but sparsely decorated. On the table in front of me were scrolls, scattered around a crystal skull. I ignored the skull and glanced at one of the scrolls, but I couldn't read the writing.

"Have you lived here long?" I said for want of something better to say.

"I was born in this cottage; it's all I know," she replied.

I found myself staring at her figure from behind and once again suffered a bout of jealousy. She looked perfect in every way. The thing is, I'm as straight as an arrow, but she actually turned me on. I shook that thought from my head when she turned around and placed a warm drink in front of me and then sat down opposite.

"Drink that, it will keep out the cold. Now then, what to do with you? You realize that you're a good hour away from civilization, don't you?" she said.

"If you could just let me sleep on the floor here for the night, I'll be on my way in the morning, and you'll never see me again," I replied.

Before she could answer me, we both heard male voices approaching the cottage. I recognized one of them as Frank's.

"Damn it, they must've tracked me," I whispered.

Sonja looked at me suspiciously, but then stood up and walked towards the door. I could hear her muttering something to herself, but I couldn't make out what she was saying. She opened the door to find Frank and Steve coming towards the cottage.

"Can I help you gentlemen?" said Sonja.

"Hi, we're tracking a friend who ran off earlier and were concerned for her safety," said Frank.

"Well, you need not be concerned any longer; your friend is safe with me for the night," replied Sonja.

"I'd like to see her to confirm that if you don't mind," said Frank.

"Well, I do mind and you're not welcome here," replied Sonja.

"Now, what sort of way is that to talk to a complete stranger," said Frank as he reached for Sonja.

I was watching from the window, and I swear I couldn't believe what I saw. When his hand touched Sonja, I witnessed a bright flash of light and saw Frank being thrown through the air. He came to a halt when he hit a rather large tree and fell stunned to the ground. Steve stumbled backwards, holding his rifle menacingly, but seemed a little more concerned about his friend than with Sonja. He ran over to Frank and helped him get to his feet.

"Are you okay buddy?" I heard him say.

"Yeah, she just knocked the wind out of me. What the hell did that witch do to me?" replied Frank.

"I don't know and I don't want to find out, now let's get out of here."

Frank agreed with him and they both left. I watched as Sonja returned to the cottage, and felt fear for the first time that night. When she came in and closed the door, I thanked her for helping me. I then sipped my drink and sat quietly for a while, before blurting out what I was dying to know.

"Is it true what Frank said, are you a witch?"

At first she laughed, but then turned to me with a serious look on her face.

"No, I'm not a witch; I'm a sorceress," she replied.

"You can't tell her that, she's now in danger," said a voice that seemed to be coming from the skull on the table.

"Who said that?" I asked sitting up straight and peering around the room.

"No need to be concerned, it's just a demon," replied Sonja.

"Just a demon; I think I'd better go," I said, getting to my feet, "Thank you for all your help," I added as I backed towards the door.

"Tell me, Cherry, have I tried to hurt you at all?" asked Sonja.

I stopped dead and looked at her before speaking.

"Um...no, you haven't tried to hurt me."

"Then why are you suddenly afraid of me; do you know something about sorceresses that I don't?"

"Well, no it's just that...you consort with demons for one thing," I replied weakly.

"Stay or go, it's entirely up to you. You're welcome to sleep on the couch for the night, but I fully understand if you wish to leave."

I suddenly felt bad for assuming the worst, and instead of leaving I decided to sit down again. I couldn't seem to take my eyes away from what I thought was just a crystal skull.

"You needn't be afraid of him; he's trapped within the skull until I either release him or die, whichever comes first. He's bound by my incantation and has to do whatever I ask of him," said Sonja reassuringly.

"Huh, listen to her, the all-powerful sorceress," mocked the demon.

"Does he have a name?" I asked.

"I call him "Dee," replied Sonja.

"Will he respond to me if I talk to him?"

"If he wants to he will, but he doesn't have to. He has to respond to me because it's in the rules."

"What rules?" I replied.

"The contract between a demon and a sorceress is binding; if I asked him to quote me Shakespeare all day, every day, he'd have to obey," said Sonja.

"What would you need a demon for in the first place?" I asked, genuinely curious.

"At this moment in time, I'm a high-level sorceress thanks to the answers to my questions, given to me by Dee. Of course, there is a penalty for such an arrangement. Upon my death, I will lose my soul to him, which is what binds us together."

"I will savor your soul with relish upon that day," commented Dee.

"Aren't you afraid of being damned and going to Hell?" I replied.

"The way I see it, you have one life so you'd better make the most of it," said Sonja.

She then noticed the state of my clothing.

"You have rips and holes in your clothes," she said.

"I know. I messed my clothes up when I was being chased in the wood. It's okay though; I have more clothes back home."

"Why don't you go and get cleaned up in the back, and I'll find something better for you to wear," said Sonja.

I didn't refuse, mainly because I felt dirty and badly in need of a good wash. I decided to take her up on the offer and walked towards the door she'd indicated.

"Throw your clothes out here when you've undressed, and I'll have something ready for you when you've finished," added Sonja.

I entered the room to find a shower, and wondered how she got her hot water out here in the middle of nowhere. I quickly stripped and then threw the clothes out as requested, before turning the shower on and standing underneath the warm water. It felt so good to get clean, but I didn't waste too much time in the bathroom; I simply washed myself and then wrapped the large and only towel on the rack around my body. When I opened the door, I could see a short black dress hanging over the back of a chair near the door.

"Try it on; I'm told it will fit perfectly," said Sonja.

She had her back to me, so I removed the towel and quickly slipped the dress over my head. It reminded me of a gothic dress I'd seen at a party not so long ago. It fit snuggly and had tiny silver buckles down the center, but was low-cut, revealing a good deal of my bust. I liked it though. Sonja turned to see me wearing it.

"That won't do; come over here, girl, your hair looks a mess."

I didn't reply; I simply walked over to her and sat down as indicated. She then mumbled a few words as she waved her hands over my head, and suddenly my hair was not only dry, it was styled in loose flowing curls that fell past my shoulders. She showed it to me in a hand mirror.

"Wow, how did you do that?"

"You clean up quite nicely," replied Sonja, ignoring my question.

"Thank you for the dress, Sonja, it looks amazing," I said.

"You're welcome, oh and here, I see that you need a pair of panties," replied Sonja handing me a pair of cotton ones.

It was then that I realized she must have seen my bare pussy from where she was sitting, which made me turn bright red as I took the panties from her hand.

"Nothing to be embarrassed about Cherry, you have a nice body," said Sonja matter-of-factly.

I didn't reply; I simply stood up and quickly put the panties on.

"Sonja, don't you ever get lonely out here?"

"I prefer the solitude; besides, there's no place for me in a modern society. Too many rules and far too many people who worry about where their next meal is coming from," replied Sonja.

"How do you survive out here; I mean, there are no stores, yet you seem to have everything you need?" I said.

"Instead of answering that I'll show you," replied Sonja.

She asked me to follow her, and we went into the kitchen. She told me to sit down, and muttered some more of those words that I didn't understand, while waving her hands over the table. Suddenly, the table was crammed with all kinds of goodies, from cooked meat to ripened melon slices.

"How is that even possible?" I said staring at all the food in awe.

Again, she didn't answer; instead she told me to tuck in. I didn't need to be asked twice as I was very hungry. All the food tasted amazing, and once we were finished, she waved her hands over the remains and it just vanished.

How does she do that? I thought for the umpteenth time.

We went back into the sitting room and sat on the small sofa in front of the open fire to talk. Without saying a word, she suddenly began to brush my hair. By the time she'd brushed it a dozen times, I was closing my eyes to enjoy the soft touch of her hand as it followed each swipe of the brush. When she stood up in front of me and placed one of my legs between hers, she was so close that I could smell her scent. I couldn't help but admire her breasts once again as they pushed against the fabric of her tight dress. She continued to brush my hair, only now it seemed more sensual. Her fingers were gently moving over my scalp with each stroke of the brush, and with the close proximity of her gorgeous body, I was actually getting turned on. Then I suddenly felt the silver buckles at the front of my dress unfastening, and she wasn't even touching them. One by one they unfastened, until the front of my dress was open and my breasts were no longer pushing against the fabric.

She had discarded the brush and was using her hands to move through my hair. I felt my nipples hardening from the attention, and then something invisible was touching them. I could feel them being pushed around and tugged, and with the teasing attentions to my nipples I could feel my pussy getting wet. She then stopped and placed her hand under my chin to pull my head up to face her. As soon as our eyes met she leaned down and kissed me on the lips. I returned the kiss, and then felt her pussy resting on my leg as she got down lower.

Her hips moved back and forth, with her pussy pressing against my bare leg as my dress fell from my shoulders. She stepped back, and her dress fell to the floor in front of me. She was completely naked and had a figure to die for. She reached down and pulled my dress off the rest of the way, before pushing me back onto the sofa and spreading my legs. With a flick of her wrist, the white cotton panties she had given me earlier disappeared, and she got down onto her knees and licked her way up the inside of my thighs, until she reached my pussy.

The first touch of her tongue on my wet lips was electric, and as she pushed her tongue inside me, I could feel something moving my clit around. It wasn't her fingers as she held my legs apart with both hands, so she must have been using magic. Whatever it was, my clit was responding by popping out of the tiny hood as if on command. My body felt incredibly hot and the more she licked the closer I came to experiencing an orgasm.

Then she stopped what she was doing and turned me around to kneel on the sofa. She grabbed my butt cheeks and held me firmly. She'd stood up, so I wondered what she intended to do, when I felt the hard bulbous end of what seemed like a cock spreading my pussy lips apart and entering me. I gripped the end of the sofa as she slowly pushed it into me.

It can't be a cock, perhaps she's wearing a strap-on, I thought as she continued to push forward. Within moments, she pulled back out and then slowly started to fuck me. After that, I didn't question any further because all that mattered was the sheer bliss of that moment. When she picked up speed, I began to scream that I was coming. She ignored me and moved faster. Within seconds, her lower stomach was slapping my ass cheeks as she pounded me from behind. At the height of my climax, she suddenly called out that she was coming as well, and I felt something spurting all over my ass cheeks. I was too exhausted even to look around, and by the time I did, she'd covered herself up and was sitting down on the sofa next to me.

"That felt amazing," I said as I sat up straight.

"I enjoyed it too; perhaps I owe you an apology though for taking advantage of you in such a manner," replied Sonja.

"No apology necessary, I enjoyed it every bit as much as you did."

We talked for a while after that, before finally calling it a night and going to sleep.

****

In the morning, I was feeling completely refreshed and ready to take on another day. However, I still didn't know where I was or what direction to take in order to get home. When Sonja finally surfaced, she could see me getting ready to leave as I was wearing the tattered clothing I arrived in.

"Good morning, Cherry, I trust you slept well?" she asked.

"I did, thank you. I'm ready to leave and get out of your hair, but I'm still not sure which way is home. Could you point me in the right direction?" I replied.

"Before you leave, I have a proposition for you."

"Oh, and what would that be?" I enquired.

"At some point in my life, I need to take on another apprentice, preferably someone who wants to learn magic. Would you happen to be that someone?" she said.

I had to stop and think about that for a moment, but the more I thought about it, the more the idea appealed to me.

"I would love to learn magic, but am I the right candidate for such an undertaking?"

"I believe so; otherwise I wouldn't have asked. However, before you decide, you need to know that there is danger involved. I can teach you all you need to know, but nothing is easy in this life."

The idea of being able to perform real magic was very appealing to me, but what if I failed? Then, as I was thinking about it, I had an idea.

"Would it be possible for me to stick around for a while to see if it's something that I could do? I mean, what if I'm really not adept at magic, and you find it impossible to teach me?" I said.

"I could evaluate you over the course of the first week, and let you know at the end of that week whether or not I believe you have what it takes," replied Sonja.

"In that case, I'd like to give it a try."

"Okay; well, the first thing you have to learn is that I will now be known to you as Mistress. The one thing any apprentice needs to learn is respect for their master. Do you have any problem with that?" said Sonja.

"No, I have no problem with that."

We had breakfast and then my training began. At first, she had to tell me all about magic and how she was able to use it.

"Mother Earth is truly amazing. She provides us with everything we need, from food to magic and everything in-between. Anyone can perform magic if they know how. Unfortunately, the art of magic was lost to most people hundreds of years ago, when religions hunted those who possessed the knowledge out of existence. Back then, the only way to save the knowledge was to go underground, both literally and figuratively. I come from a very long line of sorceresses and have learned a great deal."

"What is magic though?" I asked.

"Magic itself is an invisible force that comes up through the ground. There are many such invisible forces, such as the wind or electromagnetic charges, to name just a couple. We call it Mana, and it is a force that can be stored within your body if you know how. Mana passes through everything all the time, but as yet science hasn't discovered it, or at least doesn't realize its significance."

"Who did discover magic, and for that matter, how did they know how to use it?"

"That's where the demons come into the story. The tale I heard as a child explains the very beginning of magic, but whether it's true or not is another thing entirely," replied Sonja.

"Oh, it's true, it just seems to get embellished as time goes by," added Dee.

Sonja looked at the skull with a pained expression and then turned back to me.

"Anyway, a demon promised to give great power to a sorcerer, in exchange for his soul. The sorcerer agreed, and was then taught everything there was to know about magic. Fortunately, this sorcerer decided to teach others, who then went on to teach others themselves and so on. It is said that this sorcerer had an incredible memory, and was able to learn vast amounts of information pertaining to the use of magic from the demon."

"Is it easy to perform magic?"

"It's easier than you think, and I'll teach it to you, which reminds me. From this moment on, Dee, you will answer any question Cherry has for you; is that understood?" replied Sonja.

"I understand; I would welcome another potential soul," replied Dee.

"Her soul is not under discussion, and you have no claim to it," responded Sonja.

"Not at the moment, but things change and she might very well bargain with me in the future."

"That's between you and her, but for now I expect you to follow my orders," said Sonja sternly.

Sonja then turned back to me.

"I'm going to start you off with a simple spell, Cherry; something that I learned a long time ago. Try to remember the following words: Stri-to-loth Ignitra and then look at the candle on the table in front of you. Now, take a deep breath and hold it while staring at the wick in the center of the candle and then speak the words," said Sonja.

I took a deep breath and held it, and then looked directly at the candle and spoke the words. Nothing happened. I exhaled and took another deep breath before trying once again. This time I stared at the wick sticking up in the center of the candle, before saying the words. Still, nothing happened.

"Am I doing it right?" I asked.

"I believe you are. I also believe you're not holding any Mana as it passes through your body. Take this and place it around your neck," replied Sonja, as she handed me the blood-red gem necklace that had been around her neck.

I put it on and then turned to the candle again; this time the wick flared up and the candle was lit.

"Why did it work with the gem, but not without?" I said.

"The gem is special. It's the only thing in this world that can store Mana and release it on command. It's also very rare and can only be found in the depths of the earth. As to why you couldn't summon the energy without the gem, I would have to say that you need to practice on this one exercise over the coming days, without the gem," replied Sonja.

She then left me alone to practice, and I tried as hard as I could for the next hour to light that candle. I felt frustrated that I couldn't do it, and when Sonja left the room to do something at the back of the cottage, I turned to Dee.

"Dee, why can't I do this?"

"I suspect that the Mana is passing through you too quickly to tap into. Try this; breathe in and out quickly for several seconds and then hold your breath," he replied.

I tried it, and although I didn't light the candle, I did see a wisp of smoke coming from the wick. I tried it again and then again, but it simply wouldn't light. Then Sonja came back into the room naked. I tried not to stare as she worked on something, but I failed miserably. It was too hard not to notice her perfect figure, and of course I kept remembering the night before. Suddenly, I realized that I was getting wet just thinking about it.

Concentrate woman. Forget what she did to you and how it made you feel. Light the god damn candle, I thought, trying really hard to block the memory of her breasts from my mind.

Then I felt my clit moving and let out a sigh of approval. *Is Sonja doing that?* I thought as my body reacted to the stimulation going on in my nether regions. It was when my pussy lips parted that I knew Sonja was doing something to me, and just before I looked up to ask, I tried lighting the candle one last time, and it burst into flames.

"I DID IT!" I shouted.

Sonja turned around and smiled. Then I felt my pussy opening up as I lay back onto the sofa. My pussy lips seemed to be moving around on their own, and my clit was being touched as I closed my eyes.

"Oh god, what are you doing to me?" I muttered.

Then it all stopped, and I opened my eyes to see Sonja standing in front of me.

"It would seem that we have found your center. Unfortunately, it complicates things somewhat," said Sonja.

I looked at her with a puzzled expression.

"Let me explain. My center is in my chest. Most people's center is in their gut, but some, who are very rare, have a center in their womanhood. Lie back and relax; I need to verify this with you, just to make sure my hypothesis is correct," she said.

I lay back as instructed and watched her sit down next to me. Then she placed a hand on my leg and moved it up until her fingers were stroking my wet pussy. She pushed a finger inside me, and once again my clit began to move around.

"Look at the candle again and when I tell you, light it with the spell."

I looked at the candle as she began to move her finger in and out of me. My nipples hardened, and my clit was on fire. I couldn't help closing my eyes for a brief second and then heard her say, "now."

I opened my eyes and said the words, and the candle lit up instantly.

"It's as I feared," said Sonja, stopping what she was doing.

After a second or two, I composed myself and sat up.

"You need to be stimulated before you can center the energy for the most powerful spells, which is not always possible in the heat of the moment."

"Great, now I have an overactive sex drive," I replied half-jokingly.

"It's not all bad. Judging by how quickly you lit the candle, I would say that you show some promise in becoming a powerful sorceress. You've felt the things that I can to you with just my mind, but there is far more that you can accomplish as far as sex is concerned. For instance, watch this," said Sonja as she stood in front of me naked once again.

Her body was incredible, and her bald pussy begged to be touched. I sat staring at it, wondering what she was about to show me, when I saw a bulge appearing from inside her. I watched with fascination as the bulge got bigger, and then suddenly a cock popped out and started to grow in front of me.

"Oh my god, it really was a cock that I felt last night," I said, watching it intently.

I watched it growing and standing up straight. I had an overwhelming urge to reach out and touch it. When I did, it jerked in the palm of my hand. It felt solid, and I could feel that it hadn't stopped growing yet as it slowly slid over my fingers. I was getting wet just stroking it, and when it stopped growing, I leaned forward and opened my mouth. I sucked the end and felt her pushing it forward. I had to hold her back with one hand as I couldn't take it all, but she placed her hand on the back of my head and began to pull me onto it.

It hit the back of my throat several times and I gagged, but I tried harder until I could take more inside my mouth. Then I pulled it out and looked up at Sonja.

"What is the spell for stimulating someone's clit?"

"Stri-to-loth cliteronus," she replied.

I then put her cock back into my mouth and muttered the words to myself, as I reached down and stroked her pussy lips with the tip of my finger. I knew that it was working as she started to squirm and became even more sexually aroused. Her moans of pleasure were getting louder, and I was getting wetter. Then I felt my own clit moving and my pussy lips parting. She was clearly reciprocating the attention that I was giving her. I was so excited when I recited the spell again that she suddenly screamed she was coming. I felt the end of her cock shudder, and then tasted the salty substance as it exploded onto my tongue and hit the roof of my mouth.

She held the back of my head tighter, and I felt another load of semen shooting into the back of my throat. I couldn't take it all as I felt some of it seeping out the corner of my mouth. She then pulled it free, and another spurt of seed hit my cheek and neck as I carried on stroking it. She was arching her back enjoying the final sensations until I pushed my finger deep into her and muttered the spell again. She ground her hips onto my hand and then started to climax. Her moans of pleasure were now louder, and I started to experience my own mini-orgasm. When it was all over, she sat down heavily next to me and tried to compose herself.

"That was incredible," she said eventually.

All I could think about was the cock I'd seen.

"How did you produce a cock?" I said excitedly.

"I'm not sure you're ready for such a spell, but if you want to know that badly I'll tell you," replied Sonja.

"I'd love to know."

"The words "Stri-to-loth internus adulescentulus auctus" are what is needed. However, you have to be sure that you pronounce it correctly otherwise it could cause major problems," she replied.

I said the words to myself repeatedly. I knew that because I wasn't being stimulated, the spell wouldn't work, but I wanted to memorize it. We had something to eat after that, and she told me some of the spells that would come in handy over time, such as the one to create food. I also got to learn about the clothes spell, and was told to go into my bedroom to practice that one. It felt strange having to play with myself before I could make any spell work, which is what made me think of my sex toys back home. I had one in the shape of two balls that vibrated when inserted inside me, and that would be perfect for stimulating my body without having to think about it.

I went back into the sitting room and asked her if it were possible to obtain the balls without leaving the cottage. She told me to describe them, which I did, and then she spoke the words that I'd now come to expect and suddenly the balls appeared on top of the table.

"What are they?" she said.

"You insert them inside you and they vibrate, which would be a perfect way to stimulate myself without having to think about it," I replied.

"Okay, that sounds like a good idea. Try them now and use the candle spell to see if they're good enough to produce the desired power."

I couldn't get over how forward she was. It was as if sex was an everyday thing and nothing shocked her. I took hold of the balls and discretely inserted them after turning them on. I knew what to expect as I'd used them several times in the past. As they began to work their own particular magic, I looked over at the candle and spoke the words. It lit up instantly, which made me smile. Sonja then went on to teach me other spells and by the end of the day, I was amazed at how much I'd learned. We both went to our own beds, but after lying there for an hour, I simply couldn't sleep. I was too excited about the events over the last two days. In the end, I got up and got myself a drink.

It was when I sat down on the sofa and remembered what we'd done there that I suddenly had the urge to wake Sonja up. I went to her room with the intention of doing just that, only to find her sleeping naked on top of her bed. I stood at the end of her bed and looked her up and down. She had an amazing body, and as I stared at her breasts, I started to think about being naughty. I'd left the vibrating balls in my room, so I slipped my hand down and started to stroke my pussy. Then I used the spell to move Sonja's clit around, and she immediately began to moan softly in her sleep.

I began to experiment by using the same spell on her nipples and watched them as they became erect. I could see her eyelids moving rapidly, and realized that she was probably having an erotic dream as I continued. I then used the spell that spread her pussy lips apart and moved them around. By now, I was so turned on that I didn't need to touch myself for the spells to work. The more she moaned the hornier I got, until finally I decided to try the cock spell on myself.

I'd gone over it repeatedly during the day until I'd memorized it. I spoke the words quietly and felt a strange sensation beginning behind my pussy wall. I then felt the bulge just as I'd witnessed on Sonja, until the head of my cock popped out and began to grow. My spells were still working on Sonja as my cock was growing, and her moans were becoming more pronounced. Within seconds, it was already bigger than Sonja's had been, and it started to worry me.

Have I done something wrong? I thought as it grew and spread my pussy lips further apart.

Fortunately, it stopped growing, and I stroked it in front of Sonja. Then, Sonja woke up and felt what was happening before seeing me holding a huge cock in front of her.

"Girl, you're insatiable," she said with a smile.

I moved around to the side of the bed and nearer to her head, where she suddenly grabbed me and pulled me closer to the bed. She opened her mouth and surrounded my huge cock. I couldn't believe how much she was taking in, but it excited the hell out of me. I now knew what it felt like for a man to have his cock sucked, and it was no wonder they enjoyed it so much. My spells were still working on Sonja, but I decided to reach down and stroke her pussy as she carried on sucking me.

Within minutes, I began to feel this strange tingling sensation at the base of my cock, and then an overwhelming and fantastic moment of release as the seed exploded inside Sonja's mouth.

"Oh god, oh that feels amazing. Ah...don't stop...please don't stop," I called out.

I needn't have bothered, because Sonja didn't even slow down. She was swallowing every last drop and kept sucking me long after I'd finished coming. When she did finally stop, I was still hard, and she quickly got up onto her knees with her ass facing me. I grabbed her butt cheeks and pushed my cock into her. She screamed out as it slid inside, and I began to fuck her.

I could feel every inch pass by her tight and sopping wet pussy, and the more I felt, the faster I got until I was literally slamming it into her. She gripped the bedclothes and screamed out for me to fuck her harder. I was pounding her when she suddenly came, and as I felt her pussy muscles tightening around my cock, I shot the last load of the night into her. When it was all over, we both collapsed onto the bed.

"I don't think I've ever been woken up in such a delightful manner," said Sonja after a while.

I laughed and thanked her for teaching me the spells that I'd used. We actually fell asleep together that night and when we awoke we had sex again.

At breakfast, Sonja talked about acquiring a gem stone for me, in order to make the spells easier and more convenient to use. However, she also told me that to get such a stone we would have to go to the lower levels. I didn't know it then, but I was about to go on an adventure I would never forget.

****

On my third day with Mistress Sonja, we were getting ready to head out to the lower levels in search of a bloodstone for me, and my mistress was explaining what the lower levels were.

"The lower levels were created and sealed by God. There are five levels in total. The top level is ruled by vampires," said Mistress Sonja as if it weren't really that big a deal.

"Vampires exist?" I said, not meaning to interrupt her.

"Oh, of course; I momentarily forgot that you know nothing of these things," replied Sonja.

"I always thought that vampires were made up, fictional characters, something from a Bram Stoker novel."

"Who's Bram Stoker?"

"It doesn't matter. He was just an author who wrote about a vampire by the name of Dracula," I replied.

"Dracula existed; he was the first, but how would a human know of him?" asked Sonja.

"I have no idea; until today, I thought it was all fictional."

"Oh well, it isn't. Anyway, the second level is ruled by goblins, the vilest of all level dwellers. They will cook and eat you if they get the chance, but they're not going to get the chance, so don't look so concerned."

"Could I ask? When did God imprison them all?"

"A thousand years before Christ was born. Vampires, demons, goblins and all the other creatures that dwell in the depths were deemed unworthy of God's love because of their unrepentant nature. However, because He is a merciful God, he banished and sealed them in the lower levels, rather than destroy them. On the third level, he placed werewolves as well as other shape-shifters. On the fourth level, dwell mythical creatures. On the lowest level is where the demons rule."

"Wow, this is so much to take in," I replied as I felt my mistress tying something to my upper right leg.

I looked down to see a knife in a scabbard strapped to my upper thigh.

"For protection only, and be aware that if you throw it, it will come back to you," said Sonja.

She then placed a similar one on herself, before conjuring up another dress to wear. This one was all white with a low-cut top. It was joined by a silver belt, which looked more decorative than functional.

"I noticed that you put Dee into your bag; how is he able to be out here when his kind is banished to the lower levels?"

"Dee is only here in spirit form and isn't free to wander the lands. In addition, the only way a demon can be out in the real world is if a human makes a bargain with it as I did with Dee. You might one day want your own demon, especially when you come to realize how valuable they can be. With that in mind, it is best for you to know where they originate and why they're so happy to receive such a bargain," replied Sonja.

"Which level can the bloodstones be found?" I asked, feeling that it was important information.

"The only place the gems can be found is the lowest level," replied Sonja.

"Why did I know you were going to say that?" I replied rhetorically.

"It really isn't as bad as it sounds, Cherry. You'll not only have my protection while you're there, but also that of the vampires, who are by far the most intelligent of lower level beings," responded Sonja.

"This is all amazing to me. Until I met you, I didn't even know magic was real, and now I'm learning that a lot of the mythical creatures I once thought came from ancient stories, truly exist," I said.

"You will learn a lot more before this adventure is over," replied Sonja.

After that, we set out towards the mountain range, specifically, the largest of the mountains. It was known as God's Cradle to my mistress, but I only knew it as Flat-Top. It took three hours to reach it, and when we did, Sonja wasted no time. She stood in front of the largest boulder I'd ever seen and spoke a few words. Suddenly, the boulder, which turned out to be an illusion, changed into a huge iron gate and slowly opened. As soon as we stepped inside, the gate closed behind us with a large bang. For a few moments, it was dark. Then our eyes adjusted to the lights that were coming from further inside the mountain, and I could see movement up ahead.

"Sorceress, this is an unexpected pleasure," said a voice from a dark figure that was closing in on our position.

"Ah, Jacob, I trust you're well?" replied Sonja.

My mistress then produced a light, seemingly out of nowhere, and I saw Jacob for the first time. I stood there with my mouth open, and wasn't even aware of it until my mistress coughed and made me realize that I was staring. He was drop-dead gorgeous. Then I heard another voice coming up behind him.

"Mistress, I wasn't expecting you," said a female vampire.

"Greetings Rose; I have another apprentice, and we're here to get a bloodstone," replied Sonja.

"You couldn't have chosen a worse time. The goblins are massing, and the elders think that they're going to try another attack on the city. We just don't know when," said Rose.

"Well, I'd better speak with the elders then. Oh, and this is Cherry. Cherry, this is Rose; she was my first apprentice until she fell in love with a vampire, and now she's trapped here for the rest of eternity."

"Pleased to meet you, Rose," I said as I reached for her hand.

She was stone cold to the touch, but I ignored it as we shook hands.

Rose led the way into the city, and because it had been so dark, it wasn't until we drew nearer that I realized there was a large wall with a single opening in the middle. When we passed through it, I could see light everywhere and the city sprawled out in front of us. It was huge.

"Are all the levels this big?"

"Yes, some are even bigger," replied Sonja.

The buildings themselves were made of stone, and I could see at least ten watch towers around the city. My mistress was talking to Jacob as we walked towards the city, which left me with Rose.

"Are you happy here, Rose?" I said by way of a conversation starter.

"Believe it or not, I am. It was a hard decision to stay here as I enjoyed being an apprentice to the mistress. However, the more I saw of Dale, the more I wanted to stay with him," replied Rose.

"Dale is the one you fell in love with?" I said.

"Oh yes, sorry, I forgot you didn't know. I met Dale the very first time we came here looking for a bloodstone, and each time we left I missed him more and more. I told the mistress that I'd fallen in love, and she gave me her blessing. Of course, once I was turned into a vampire, I could no longer leave the lower levels, but I've never regretted it."

"I'm glad you found what you were looking for, but I don't think I could stay here; I think I'd miss the outside world too much," I replied.

Just then, we were joined by what I later found out were a couple of elders. They greeted Sonja with open arms, and we were all led into a large hall with huge stone pillars that were capped with silver at the top and bottom.

"I hear that the goblins are massing; is it serious?" asked Sonja to what was clearly the spokesman for the elders.

"Yes, our scouts tell us that there are tens of thousands massing a mere mile from the ramp to the second level," replied the elder, "they also seem to be getting help."

"How so?" replied Sonja.

"They're wearing armor, which as you are aware is not something they're known for."

"Can I see this armor?"

The elder turned around and was handed a bundle from a lesser vampire. Sonja took it from him and felt the texture.

"You're right; they do have help, and it's no ordinary help. They have a witch on their side," said Sonja, "this armor is made from an organic material, something a witch would find very easy to do."

While they were talking I couldn't help looking around, only to be made aware that I was being flanked by two male vampires. I didn't even hear them approach me. They both smiled at me, and I looked back to hear my mistress introducing me to the elders.

"This is Cherry, my new apprentice," she said before turning back to talk with the vampires behind me, "Why don't you guys show her around? Oh, and I don't have to tell you that she is under my protection, do I?" said Sonja menacingly.

"She is quite safe amongst my people, Sonja," said the elder.

I was then led away by the two vampires, who quickly introduced themselves.

"I'm Vincent, and my companion here is Claude. The hall you are standing in is called the Great Hall. This is where the biggest decisions are made. It was created thousands of years ago and is the largest building in the city. Most of the buildings you saw when you entered the city were simply homes for each of the 1,001 vampires that live here."

I couldn't seem to stop staring at their eyes, they seemed almost hypnotic.

"Um, have you had trouble with the goblins in the past?" I asked, for want of something better to say.

"Yes, they tend to mass at least once every five years. They also breed at an alarming rate. We could stop them from multiplying, but we feed on their blood, so destroying them completely is out of the question. We can show you a few if you'd care to see?" said Vincent.

I followed his lead, and he took me to a one-story building. Inside, there were cells and in each cell was a goblin. They hissed at me as they sniffed the air around them. I guessed that they very rarely came across a human in their lives. They stood about five feet tall and had growths on their faces. Then I blurted out what I thought they looked like, "Orcs."

"Sorry, but what's an Orc?" said Vincent.

"Oh, they look a lot like a fictional character from one of my favorite novels that were called Orcs," I replied.

Just then, one of them made me jump when it suddenly darted forward and tried to grab me through the bars of its cell. Vincent intercepted the hand in a flash and pushed the goblin back into the cell.

"I apologize, this one has probably never seen a human before," said Vincent.

"Do you kill them to feed?" I replied.

"No, we actually look after them and feed them. The better fed they are, the better the taste of their blood. We also realize that without them, we wouldn't last very long," said Vincent.

That's when I caught Claude checking me out from head to toe, with a look of lust written all over his face. I actually blushed, which was unusual for me. I smiled at him and he smiled back, before drawing nearer.

"I hope I'm not offending you when I say that you have an incredible body," he said.

I was stuck for words, so I just said, "Not in the slightest...but thank you."

Next, they showed me their living quarters, which all looked pretty much the same. They each had a single bed in a small room. I half expected a coffin, but then realized that they had no need to hide from the sun as it never shone down here. As I stood in that room listening to Vincent, I could see Claude checking me out again. It was making me hot, and for whatever reason, I slowly and discretely unfastened the bustier that held my breasts in check. Then I remembered how my teasing in the past had gotten me into trouble, but being in the presence of these two vampires made it all seem justifiable.

"Do you all have partners down here?" I said suddenly.

"A third of us do, but the rest don't," said Claude, "why do you ask?"

I looked up and took a step closer, directly in front of them both.

"I was just curious as to what making love to a vampire would be like," I said as I pulled the laces on my top further apart.

My breasts were hanging loose but still slightly covered by the top of my dress. Vincent and Claude stood their ground watching my every move, undoubtedly wondering what I was going to do next. It was far too late to back down now, and I think I shocked them both when I suddenly shrugged my shoulders and allowed the fabric to slide down to my waist. I raised my arms to lift the hair back over my shoulders, and flaunted the rosy tips of my voluptuous breasts to their gaze.

"Little lady, you don't know what you're getting yourself into," whispered Vincent.

His eyes narrowed with lust as he gazed at the creamy mounds of womanhood before him. Vincent's eyes caught fire as he watched my hands lower to the fabric caught at my hips. I teased them both, swaying my hips slightly back and forth as my fingertips played with the loosely held fabric. Both Claude and Vincent seemed mesmerized by my hands as I ran them back up my toned abdomen to cup my breasts for their enjoyment.

Looking deeply into their eyes, their gaze was so intense that I found I couldn't hold it. My eyelids drifted shut for only a moment, to blink, and when they opened I found them both standing directly in front of me, close enough to touch.

Seeing the erections pressed against their pants, I couldn't resist dropping my hands down to cup them both. My fingers ran up and down the length of their manhood's, playing and squeezing the hardness that lay behind the fabric.

They moved in closer, their arms surrounding me as they rubbed against me. Thrusting their manhood's into my hands and brushing their upper bodies against my stiff nipples, their movements caused my dress to fall to my feet, and I stood naked before them.

By now, moans of lust were escaping my lips as I felt the heat of arousal filling my very being. My body was wet with need as I moved my hands to their zippers and caressed the bulges that lay beneath. Then they moved as one and removed their clothing. Their erections sprang out, making me gasp in anticipation. Vincent literally picked me up and placed me onto his hardened cock. I let out a gasp as it entered me and slid all the way inside. Then Claude pulled me backwards as Vincent held onto my thighs and began to pound away at my soaking womanhood.

I was pulled back until I was in a horizontal position, and I could see Claude's cock moving towards my mouth. I didn't hesitate, opening my mouth to allow it in, and he teased me a little by rubbing my lips with the tip of his cock. Then he slid it inside and I felt his hot meat on my tongue. Claude held my hair and started to use it to pull himself into my mouth. I could feel it sliding all the way to the back.

I moaned aloud as Vincent picked up speed and started to slam his cock into me. When I started to climax, I felt a spurt of Claude's seed hitting the back of my throat, but he didn't stop. Then Vincent came deep inside me but carried on as if nothing had happened. Suddenly, they were both like animals. With my head leaning right back, it was a perfect position for Claude to go deeper, and before I knew it, he was doing just that. I was starting to feel his balls hitting my upper lip as he fucked my mouth.

When I came for the second time, it seemed to last for minutes as opposed to the usual few seconds, and I loved every second of it. However, I could sense that something was amiss. They seemed to be getting rougher, and their voices sounded guttural as they continued to fuck me harder and harder. I'd never experienced rough sex before, and I knew that I should be scared, but instead, it was exciting me to the point of exhilaration.

Then Claude pulled his cock from my mouth, and I watched his seed explode from the end of his cock. It hit my chin and neck and I could feel it running down my face. Moments later, Vincent came as well, only he stayed inside me. My last orgasm was huge and made my thighs shudder with excitement. Then I witnessed Claude leaning over me and suddenly felt a sharp pain on my right breast. He was biting and sucking me.

I didn't feel Vincent pulling out as I was too concerned with what Claude was doing, when I felt another bite on my inner upper thigh. They were feeding off me, and again I knew that I should be scared, but I wasn't.

"That'll be quite enough of that," I heard my mistress say from the doorway.

I was unceremoniously dropped onto the ground, and the two vampires moved away from me. I looked up to see my mistress looking down on me.

"I hope you're having fun," she said, before waving her hands and mumbling a few words.

I suddenly found the wounds had healed, and that I was dressed once again. I stood up feeling ashamed of myself and unable to make eye contact. Then I heard the voice of an elder.

"Is this how you protect our guests?" he said.

I looked up to see Claude and Vincent leaving the room with their heads bowed in shame. I found myself wanting to thank them for such a wonderful time, but thought better of it.

"I apologize for the way they treated you," said the elder as he followed them out the door.

"There was no harm done, so don't punish them too severely," replied my mistress.

Once they had gone Sonja turned to me.

"I think it's time to teach you a new spell. It's one that has saved my life on a number of occasions," she said.

I stood up straight and awaited her command.

"The spell I'm about to teach you isn't all that powerful. However, it is extremely useful, especially down here. Say after me, 'Stri-To-Loth Tamquam Me,' which simply means, 'like me.' Whoever you direct this spell to will instantly like you and won't want to harm you," said Sonja.

Having an excellent memory meant that I now knew another spell, and couldn't help but agree that such a spell would come in handy down here.

"Okay, it's time we moved out. We have a group of vampires that will accompany us as far as the third level. They're coming to watch over us while we travel through the goblin territory."

I followed her out and saw the vampires she was talking about, ready and waiting.

"If we're all ready, I suggest that we move out. As you all know, the goblin level isn't something to take lightly. However, I believe that they now have a witch in their ranks, and although witches aren't as powerful as a sorceress, they are still formidable characters. Be on your guard," said Sonja, before leading the way.

When we arrived at the lower-level tunnel, I was amazed at its sheer size. The roof had to be at least fifty feet high, and the tunnel opening was over thirty feet across. There were six vampires with us, all dressed in silver armor, which made them look extremely impressive. Torches were lining the walls as we ventured downward at a slight incline, and as we got nearer to the next level, there was a distinct and very unpleasant odor coming towards us.

"What you're smelling child, is goblin. They rarely bathe and number in the thousands," said Sonja, as she noticed that I'd covered my face with a scarf.

After walking for thirty minutes, we eventually arrived at the second level. It opened up into a vast landscape, with valleys and mountains ahead of us. We could see a huge river cutting through the center of this impressive place, which was when I realized that we could see it all.

"Why isn't it pitch black down here?" I said.

"Look up and you will see your answer."

I looked up to see the roof glowing.

"What you're looking at is a florescent moss that clings to the roof. In effect, it makes it perpetually daytime on this level as well as all other levels," said Sonja.

The moss let out a soft but strong yellow light. It made you feel as if you were standing in a dimly-lit room, with just enough light to see everything. We then had to walk down a steep slope until we arrived at the base of level two. As yet, we hadn't seen any signs of life. That was about to change, when a large horde of goblins suddenly appeared three hundred feet away.

"That's very strange, milady; I wouldn't normally expect to see goblins this brave," said the head vampire.

"Um, I know what you mean. I'm guessing that with their new ally, they believe that they're stronger than normal. Be on the lookout for a witch, because the sooner I see her, the sooner I can do something about it," replied Sonja.

No sooner had she said that, and everyone could see a spell coming directly at us. The last thing I remember hearing was my mistress shouting that we were up against a sorcerer and not a witch. Then I blacked out.

When I awoke, I was on the edge of a ledge and could hear a huge rasping sound below me. I turned onto my side and looked over the edge. There below me was, well, I couldn't actually tell what it was, but it was asleep and huge. I looked around to discover that I was alone. The smell had gone, so I knew I was no longer in the goblin realm. I also knew that I had to get out of there and find my mistress. I sat up and saw a slope below my feet. I slowly inched my way down until I was on the same level as the snoring, whatever it was, a few feet away from me.

I crept towards what I thought was the entrance, and then foolishly stood on a large twig which snapped and echoed throughout the room. I looked around to see the beast stirring and then sit up. I couldn't believe what I was seeing. It was a Cyclops. A one-eyed giant and that one eye, was looking straight at me. I started to run and then heard heavy footfalls behind me. I knew long before I reached the exit that I wasn't going to make it. I felt two large hands gripping me, and as I was turned around to face it, the only thing I could think of doing was casting the very last spell my mistress had taught me.

"Stri-to-Loth Tamquam Me," I shouted.

Suddenly, it stopped moving me towards it and stared at me with awe, before placing me gently onto the ground.

"Can you speak?" I said.

"Me speak, I like you, will you be friend to Gruff," he replied as softly as he could.

"Gruff, is that your name?"

"Yes, me Gruff, what name you?"

"My name is Cherry, and I would like to be your friend," I said, feeling a little safer.

Just then, we could both hear a horrendous roar coming from the exit of what I now believed was a cave. Gruff suddenly grabbed me and threw me over his shoulder, before running deeper into the cave. I didn't know what was the most frightening; the sound we could both hear or the fact that Gruff, a Cyclops, was afraid of whatever was making it. He ran deeper into the cave until he reached a large circle of what looked like bushes and large sticks of wood scattered around in a huge circle. He walked through the one and only opening I could see until we came out into the center. It turned out to be his bed.

Gruff placed me on the floor gently and then checked the corridor we'd just run down. Fortunately, whatever it was didn't seem to be coming after us. Gruff turned around to sit next to me. He had to be ten feet tall, and all he wore was a loin cloth that seemed to be made of sheepskin and two metal homemade armbands. He had a pleasant face once you got over the fact that he only had one eye, which was just above his nose. I then suddenly realized where I was. This had to be the mythical realm.

"What was that?" I said.

"Dragon, big one sounds like," replied Gruff.

I now knew for sure that I was on the mythical level. I also knew I was just one level away from the demon realm, which was below the mythical one and two below the goblin realm. I tried to think what my mistress would do, but nothing obvious came to me. When I turned to face Gruff again, he was sitting cross-legged in front of me. I was going to ask him another question, when I caught sight of his rather large cock dangling just above the ground. I turned away, not wanting to embarrass him, but then I doubted that he would even care.

"You pretty, where you come?"

"Where do I come from, you mean?" I said, trying to clarify.

"Yes, what land your home?"

"I come from the surface, a few levels up. Have you ever been there?"

"I have seen goblin land, but Gruff not like. Too many goblins try to hurt Gruff, so I return to home and stay."

I could see him being out of place in all the other levels as I looked up at him. I couldn't help feeling sorry for him. He must be all alone down here, and I could see by the scars on his arms that he'd had to fight to stay alive.

"I need to find my friends, can you help me?" I said.

"Gruff help, if you tell Gruff what this," he said tugging on my clothing.

"What is this?" I said, correcting him, but then with hindsight, regretted doing so, "this is clothing, to keep me warm."

"Let Gruff see," he replied as he tried to tug it off me.

"Wait, I'll show it to you."

He stopped pawing at me, and for a minute I hesitated. What should I do? I mean, you don't argue with a Cyclops, do you? In the end, I unfastened the buttons on my blouse and took it off to show him. At first, he seemed more interested in the material he was holding than me. Then he looked down to see me covering my breasts with my arms. He reached down and pulled my arms apart with ease.

"You pretty, Cherry," he said.

He then gently stroked my breasts with the tip of one finger and watched them jiggle about. He looked at them for a while and stroked them again.

"What are you doing?" I said trying to sound offended.

"Gruff like's sacks of meat, they make Gruff feel funny," he replied as he carried on fondling them.

That's when I saw his cock moving and realized that he was getting hard.

Oh shit, he's getting excited, I thought as I watched it grow, *I wonder if he's ever had sex*.

By the time it had stopped growing, his cock was twice as big as any I'd ever seen before and twice as thick. Then it suddenly dawned on me that I was wet.

Shit bitch, you can't be seriously turned on by that thing, I thought as my nipples hardened from all the touching.

"Cherry reminds Gruff of wild women," he said.

"Wild women, who are they?" I replied.

"They sometimes attack Gruff from the rocks and throw stones at him," he said rubbing his head as if remembering such an event.

Once again, I felt sorry for him. *He must be chased away by every creature that comes into contact with him*, I thought.

"They don't sound very nice," I quickly added, as I didn't want him to think that I was one of them.

"Not nice, but nice to look at. Gruff sometimes watches them in the water."

Typical male, I thought.

Then, just as I thought he'd gotten his mind off me, he suddenly pulled my skirt up. He stared at my legs and stroked them with his hand.

"Smooth skin, not rough like Gruff's," he said.

I didn't know whether to thank him for the compliment, or shout at him to stop pawing at me. I looked down at that point to see that his cock was fully erect. I was clearly exciting him, but I don't think he knew why. His fingers stroked my inner thighs and brushed against my panties. I let out a deep sigh, which made him do it again. He soon discovered that if he rubbed between my legs, I would let out a slight moan of pleasure.

I tried to pull away, but he pulled me back. Then he ripped my panties off simply by pulling them slightly with both hands. I was now almost naked, with just a skirt that was pulled up around my waist. One of his fingers was as large as a man's cock back where I came from, and once he discovered that I was wet between my legs, he started to use one to stroke the inner folds of my pussy lips.

I couldn't help letting out a moan of pleasure, and suddenly grabbed his hand and pushed the finger into myself.

"Oh...oh god...that feels so good," I said, wanting him to go further.

He must have been enjoying this game, as he pulled me nearer and pushed his finger deeper inside me. I was now lying on my back with my head mere inches from his cock as he continued to finger me. I looked up to see his cock again, and it just made me wetter. Then he did something I wasn't expecting. He grabbed both my ankles and pulled me off the ground, and I was dangling upside down with my head hovering right next to his huge cock.

I felt his tongue sliding around my pussy lips and let out a loud groan of satisfaction. From that point on, I couldn't help myself. I suddenly reached for his cock and began to stroke it with both hands. He was fucking huge. I heard him groaning as I slid my hands up and down his shaft, and it had the added benefit of him licking my pussy harder with his rough tongue.

"Oh my god, don't stop, Gruff. Keep licking me there," I shouted.

As he picked up speed, I had an intense desire to suck the end of his cock. So I pulled myself over to it and opened my mouth as wide as I could and began to suck the bulbous end.

"Ah, Gruff enjoy that," he groaned, in between licks.

I was managing to get the first three inches of his cock into my mouth, but I didn't think I could do more. As it was, I was stretching my mouth as wide as I could and the cock itself had to be a foot long. Then I felt his tongue delving deeper, and I started to climax. The sensations coming from my pussy were driving me crazy. I sucked harder and faster, when he suddenly groaned the words out.

"Gruff feel strange, he not understand," he said.

At first, I didn't know what he meant, but then I felt his huge cock pulsating and knew that he was about to ejaculate. I took it out of my mouth just in time as his first explosive seed made an appearance. He shot a huge load all over my neck and breasts, and as I continued to stroke it a second one shot out. He was breathing heavily and groaning with excitement as he lowered me to the ground.

We both lay on the ground trying to compose ourselves. When I looked up, his cock was still hard, and I just had to know. I walked over to him as he lay on his back and climbed onto his stomach. He looked up at me and smiled, and then must have wondered what I was doing, because I suddenly squatted over his cock and began to lower myself onto it. I was so wet that I had no trouble slipping the end of his cock into me. However, the more that entered the tighter it felt until he was stretching me like never before.

He was watching me intently, but not trying to stop what I was doing. After a while, I started to feel a little more comfortable and felt at least half of it penetrating me.

"Oh shit, that feels so good," I said as I rocked back and forth.

I must have been exciting him, because the next thing I know he's gripping me and pulling me down onto him.

"AH...Gruff, slow down," I shouted.

He was too keen to feel these new sensations though, and continued to pull me up and down onto his meat. Before I knew it, his entire cock was entering me, and I was experiencing the best orgasm of my life. I felt like a rag doll as I was continually manhandled, until finally he started to cum for the second time that day, deep inside me.

"Ah, that is good, Gruff enjoying you," he shouted as I felt his seed pouring out between my legs.

I collapsed onto his chest and was still feeling small aftershocks of the orgasm I'd just experienced. I couldn't remember ever coming so intensely. By the time we were both recovered, I felt it was time to move. I asked him if he could lead me to the upper level so that I could rejoin my friends. He told me he would guard me and show me the way.

I re-dressed, minus my panties as they were shredded, and we walked out of the cave. Once outside, I was amazed at my surroundings. We were surrounded by snow-covered mountains, and fifty feet away was a large lake with a huge waterfall. I would've enjoyed it even more if it hadn't been for the sound coming from behind us. We turned around to see a dragon perched above the cave entrance and staring intently at both of us. Gruff lifted his large club as we stared back, but I didn't feel that the dragon was that impressed or intimidated as we backed away. Gruff then pushed me aside.

"Run Cherry," he said.

I didn't need to be asked twice. As I started to run I looked back to see the dragon pushing off from the rocks and heading straight to Gruff. I heard the clash, but I didn't see what happened next, and then suddenly two hands grabbed me and pulled me into the bushes. I squealed and looked around me to find that I was being held and told to stay quiet by two very tall women. I guessed that these were the wild women Gruff had told me about.

They poured some foul-smelling liquid on me and then stayed hidden. Moments later, I could hear the dragon stomping around and sniffing the air, before wandering off in another direction. I then realized what the nasty smelling odor was for. The only thing I wanted to do now was to go back and see if Gruff was still alive, but the wild women had other ideas. They gagged me, and tied me to a large wooden pole before heaving me up onto their shoulders and carrying me away.

I must have been either tired or the foul-smelling stuff they put on me put me to sleep because the next thing I know, I'm waking up completely naked inside a wooden hut. I was dangling from a wooden beam, being tied with what was clearly an organic twine of some sort. I looked around to find a single bed made of animal skin and covered with fur. There were a few pots scattered around the bed and some sharp knives on a rack on the wall. Then two wild women came into the hut carrying a pail of water and a rag. They didn't say anything, and because I couldn't use my hands, I couldn't direct any spells in their direction.

They began to clean me up, presumably because of the smell that still lingered. They seemed very interested in my body and more than curious about the fact that I had no hair between my legs. They were at least two feet taller than me, but apart from that they looked completely human. Their large breasts were perfect, and they were gorgeous women. It was when they began to clean between my legs that an idea occurred to me. I remembered the spell my mistress had taught me when we first met, the one that could grow a male cock.

The only thing I needed to perform the spell was a little stimulation between my legs, and as they rubbed me down there, I started to feel what I needed and muttered the words.

"Stri-to-loth internus adulescentulus auctus," I said.

I didn't need my hands for this particular spell as it was being cast on myself, and as they carried on washing me, I could feel the bulge getting bigger behind the wall of my pussy. Suddenly, the wild woman who was cleaning me down there stepped back and let out a squeal. The other one took notice, and they both stepped back to watch. Then, the head of my cock popped out, and it started to grow in front of them. One of them called out someone's name, and within seconds, their leader entered the hut.

My cock was still growing, and when it finished my cock stood up erect and proud. The leader walked over to me and placed her hand over the shaft before stroking it.

"Ah, that feels good," I said.

She stared at me as her hand slid up and down my cock and then touched my breasts.

"What are you?" she said.

"I'm a woman just like you, but I'm not a wild woman. I come from the surface and am trying to get home," I replied.

"Wendell, taste this and tell me if it is the same as the wild men," she said, clearly talking to one of the other girls.

Wendell walked over and reached for the cock before dropping to her knees and placing it into her mouth. She began to suck it, and before I knew it, the end of my cock was hitting the back of her throat.

"Oh Christ, that feels so good," I said.

Wendell picked up speed, and then was interrupted as the leader wanted to take over. I looked down to see my cock being handed over to her and felt it sliding deep into the leader's throat.

"Could you untie me now?" I asked hopefully.

Without stopping, the leader indicated to the others with the wave of her hand that I should be set free. I watched one of them taking a knife to the vines that held me, and once my hands were free, I used the 'Like Me' spell on all five of the women who were now inside the hut. In hindsight, that turned out to be a mistake. Suddenly, they all wanted to take part in what they were witnessing. Their hands were all over me, and my nipples were standing out fully erect from all the handling and sucking that was going on.

I couldn't believe how much of my cock was going into the back of the leader's throat, but I knew that it wasn't going to be long before I started to cum. Before that happened though, the leader stopped and stood up in front of me.

"Give me child," she said, before turning around and backing onto my still rock-hard cock.

She then started to work me like a pro, as she moved her butt back and forth engulfing my cock with each backward motion. I now had a mouth covering each breast as my cock was entering the leader as far as it would go. After just a couple of minutes, I began to call out that I was going to climax, but she carried on fucking me until she felt the seed spewing into her pussy. Then she held me as deep inside her as I could go, until she was satisfied that I'd cum my load.

I loved all of this attention, but it was going to be short-lived. I'd just finished ejaculating, when a huge club took out the opening of the hut and Gruff grabbed hold of me. It all happened way too quickly for me to protest, and the wild women simply weren't ready for the attack. Fortunately, Gruff didn't hurt anyone; he simply grabbed me and started to run with me over his shoulder. I did try to shout out that I was fine, but there was so much commotion that I doubted anyone could hear me.

He must have run for at least three miles before slowing down, with a good lead on the wild women. Then he put me down and I could see that his shoulder was burned, undoubtedly from the attack of the dragon earlier. I thanked him for rescuing me, although I didn't really need rescuing. I didn't have the heart to tell him that though, as I knew that what he did was out of kindness, plus he'd suffered because of me.

He walked me to the start of the next level, and then told me that he'd see me safely to the top of the slope before going back home.

****

Gruff had walked with me for just ten minutes when we spotted my mistress and three vampires coming down the slope towards us. I ran to her, thanking God as I did so that she was all right. I could hear Gruff lumbering up behind me and quickly told him that she was my friend.

"Oh heavens, child; I'm so glad that you're okay. When I discovered that you were in the mythical realm, I hurried to catch up with you," said Sonja.

"What happened, Mistress? One moment I'm standing by your side, and the next I find myself waking up in Gruff's cave?" I replied, "Oh sorry, this is Gruff, by the way; he saved me from a dragon."

"Thank you Gruff, for looking out for my apprentice. Wait, I see that you're injured," said Sonja.

She then went into her spell-casting mode, and we could all visibly see Gruff's wounds healing.

"As to what happened back there, we were fooled into thinking that the goblins had a witch in their ranks, when in fact it was a sorcerer. However, that deception was as clever as he got because he was no match for me. I knew that it was sorcerer magic as it approached; it's very distinctive. But, I only had time to protect myself with a shield spell before his spell hit us. It was a travel spell. When it hit our party, everyone was sent to different levels, with you being sent to the mythical realm. We still haven't found the other three vampires, but we probably will soon," said Sonja.

"You look tired, Mistress. I know of a camp not too far away where you can rest. It's the home of the wild women," I replied.

"Thank you, child; lead the way and I'll follow. I could use a rest and something to eat. I can now relax a little knowing that you're in one piece."

Twenty minutes later we were walking into the wild women's camp. As soon as they saw us they grabbed their spears, but then the leader recognized my mistress.

"You know these women?" I said.

"Yes, we've met before on another expedition," replied Sonja.

"Mistress Sonja, you are welcome here. However, we do not associate with the likes of him," said the leader pointing to Gruff.

"Gruff saved my apprentice from a dragon and in doing so, became my friend and ally. I would deem it a favor if you could halt all hostilities towards him," said Sonja.

"So be it; I welcome him into our camp as long as he's with you."

After that, the leader asked if I were okay from being so rudely taken away without much warning. I told her that I was fine and that my mistress needed a place to rest. However, no sooner had I said that, than my mistress was casting a spell on the leader's hut. Suddenly, it was much bigger, and completely repaired from the damage that Gruff's club had done on the entrance. The leader showed the way and told her girls to fetch refreshments.

When we entered, the room was much bigger, and the bed was huge. Sonja sat on the edge of it and then decided to lie down. The vampires stayed outside guarding the entrance. Gruff stayed by my side and was wary of any of the wild women. They were going to bring in food and drink, but Sonja created a feast for everyone, including Gruff.

"So what's the story with you and Gruff," said Sonja in my ear.

"I woke up in his cave, and when he chased after me, I used the 'like me,' spell on him. He started to get really curious about me though, and before I knew it, we were having sex. I think it was his first time, but after all that happened, he wanted to protect me until I reached the upper level," I replied.

"What was the sex like?"

"In a word, incredible; his fingers are as big as a man's cock, and his cock is a foot long," I replied smiling.

Sonja laughed, but took a good look in Gruff's direction, eyeing the loin cloth at his hips. After the feast, which everyone enjoyed immensely, they all started to talk about their plans.

"We have one level to reach now, but it's by far the most dangerous one. Finding a gem that would suit you is the easy part, but getting out in one piece is the hardest. I suggest that Gruff stay here as he's too big a target and probably wouldn't fair well with the demons, no matter how big and powerful he is," said Sonja, "For now though, I'm in the mood for some fun."

With that, Sonja walked over to where Gruff was sitting and began to talk to him.

"Gruff, I hear that you're a ladies' man," she said as she laid a gentle hand onto his massive shoulder.

Gruff stared at her with a puzzled look on his face.

"Gruff no understand," he said in his guttural voice.

I then saw Sonja reaching forward and sliding her hand down his muscled chest to the loin cloth below. Her fingers lingered at the edge for a moment before they slipped over the ties at the sides and then below to find the prize beneath. Her eyes widened at the first touch of the growing girth below, before taking hold of Gruff's rapidly lengthening cock.

"I'd like to experience this for myself," she said as she firmly took hold and began to stroke it.

Gruff looked around the room, and when he saw me encouraging him, he turned back to Sonja.

"You pretty like Cherry," he replied.

I couldn't believe how forward Sonja was, but it seemed that if she wanted something, she didn't let anything get in her way. A few whispered words from her lips and the ties holding the cloth loosened, and as I watched the material fall from his body, I leaned forward to see his cock growing in her hands. Sonja gasped as it reached its full length.

"My god, Gruff, you have a wonderful cock," said Sonja as she stroked the full length of it.

I saw her saying some words to herself, and I knew that it was a spell – I just didn't know what one. What I saw after that defies belief. Sonja leaned forward and took his entire cock into her mouth and throat. Gruff lay back to enjoy the sensations and all the wild women were watching the show. I was getting wet watching it myself, so I knew how the other women would be reacting. At one point, we could see Gruff thrusting his cock up into her mouth, and it wasn't even fazing her.

I later learned that she'd used an accommodation spell, but before I found that out, it all looked incredibly impressive. Gruff was moaning aloud, throwing his head from side to side with the sheer bliss of the moment. It was during the moment he came for the first time that impressed me. Sonja took it out of her mouth at just the right time and stroked it with both hands. His seed shot out and almost reached the ceiling before dropping back down again. At that instant, the leader of the wild women tapped me on the shoulder and asked me if I would take her once more.

I immediately undressed and leaning back, allowed her to start licking my pussy. I still had the picture in my head of Gruff coming, so it was easy to use the spell that would produce my cock. When it popped out the leader didn't hesitate; she covered it with her mouth and started to suck it all in. We witnessed some of the girls bringing the vampires into the hut, and suddenly there was an orgy going on. People were moaning with pleasure all around me, and then we all heard Sonja screaming in ecstasy. I looked over to see Gruff taking her from behind, and the image of all that meat penetrating her will forever be burned in my mind.

It made me grip the leader and turn her onto her back. I then climbed on top and spreading her legs wide, I thrust my cock into her. She let out a squeal of approval as I began to pound her moist pussy with every inch I had. Within minutes, there were sounds of arousal filling the hut from every corner. Once again I looked over at my mistress, and this time Gruff was standing and holding Sonja in the air in front of him as he repeatedly thrust her down onto his cock. Her face said it all as she screamed with her first orgasm of the day. Below me, the leader threw her legs up into the air and spread them wider before telling me to fuck her harder.

I thrust forward again and again until she began to scream out with joy. When I eventually came, she held me inside her as deep as it would go as I pumped my seed into her. As I rolled off with sweat running down my face, I caught sight of Gruff, exploding all over Sonja's naked body. Sonja was running her hands through it and smiling up at Gruff. I then looked around the room and watched as each of the vampires finished off the rest of the wild women.

I thought it was all over when suddenly I felt a mouth surrounding my cock and looked down to see that the leader still hadn't had enough. I sat up and gripped the back of her head before pulling it onto my cock. She took it all with seeming ease as I began to fuck her mouth. She was like an animal. My thrusts didn't seem to be enough for her as she gripped my ass cheeks and pulled me into her violently. I could feel the end of my cock sliding down her throat, and the sensations were unbelievable.

When I came she sucked me dry, which was when we realized that everyone else was finished and watching us perform. The talk and laughter in that hut after all that, was something I will never forget.

****

In the morning, after a good night's sleep, we set out for the lowest level. Gruff accompanied us to the entrance and then said his farewells. I told him that we'd meet again soon. The demon slope turned out to be the longest of them all, and I learned some important things on the way down. First, demons were the only beings that couldn't come up to the other levels. Apparently, there was a strong invisible barrier that was deadly to demons. Sonja guessed it was placed there by God. Second, demons could possess a weak soul, so I had to prepare myself with rituals and protection spells.

The one important rule I had to remember was that no demon ever told the truth, unless it was in the service of a human, like Dee was with Sonja. I also learned that they were masters of seduction, which intrigued me.

"Have you given any thought to possessing your own demon?" said Sonja.

I hadn't thought about it, so I asked what the benefits were.

"One of the biggest benefits is their ability to answer any question you pose. That is the one sole reason I'm as powerful as I am," said Sonja, "Normally, it would take a sorceress most of her life to learn what I have learned in the short time I've been practicing magic."

"Doesn't that mean that I could learn as much with just your guidance?" I replied.

"That's true, and I'm willing to teach you everything I know. However, that's just one thing the demons are useful for. Another is their ability to protect against magic. As long as the contract stands between you and your demon, they are obligated to protect you, even if all that protection consists of is advice. They can also grant you a longer life. You see, a demon has one thing above all others that stand out in my mind – the ability to be patient. They know they will get their soul eventually, and will offer you anything in order to get the contract signed, sealed and delivered."

"Well, I'm still young. Don't you think I should wait for a few years at least before making this decision?" I replied.

"I can see that this is something you don't want at the moment, so I would suggest that we leave it for now," said Sonja.

That was the point when we reached the base and passed the giant posts and line that the demons couldn't cross.

"Okay, everyone be on the lookout. We have a ten-minute walk to the water's edge, and we're looking for a red gem. We should find one easily, but the demons will stop us if they can," said Sonja.

"How many times have you been down to this level, Mistress?"

"This will be my third visit, and I was lucky to return at all the second time I was here. If it weren't for Dee, I wouldn't be alive today."

I looked around and found it to be a lifeless mass of emptiness. There were no trees or mountains, just ditches and dry mud for as far as the eye could see. The moss that glowed was all over the roof of this vast expanse, so it was easy to see anyone approaching. We walked for just over ten minutes until we reached a wide river. I could see dozens of gems just lying on the bank, but none of them were the red kind.

"Okay, you three go that way, and we'll go this way. As soon as you find one, we'll be getting out of here," said Sonja.

The three vampires agreed, and off we went. We must have walked for another ten minutes when we spotted a gem. It was slightly bigger than Sonja's, but size wasn't the issue. I picked it up, and we started back towards the vampires. By the time we caught up, we discovered that they too had found a gem worthy of taking back with us. I wondered why the gems were just lying on the ground, but I didn't bother to ask.

We'd almost gotten back to the ramp without seeing anyone, which I thought was a bit of an anticlimax, when we spotted a dozen demons blocking our exit.

"Let me do the talking," said Sonja as we approached them.

"The Master wishes to see you," said one of the demons.

"We haven't got time for that; please let us pass, and I will only ask once," replied Sonja.

If that were meant to intimidate them, it wasn't working. They stood blocking our way and began to spread out.

One of the demons ventured forward, and suddenly he began to scream. After a moment, we discovered why. There were roots growing out of his feet and embedding themselves into the mud, making it impossible to walk any further.

"We know how powerful you are, Sonja, but we either die here trying to take you with us or die from failure to do so," said the first demon.

"I prefer the latter part," replied Sonja.

I wondered what they were going to do next, when suddenly their master appeared before us.

"I've been monitoring this conversation and I must say, Sonja, you're being very rude. I simply wanted to talk with you," he said in a deep voice.

"As I told your minions, I have no time for talking; I'm in a hurry."

He was about to talk again, when Sonja got us all to hold hands. Once we were holding each other, she spoke the words of a spell, and suddenly we were standing on grass.

"What happened and where the hell are we?" I said.

"I used a travel spell with the aid of that spare gem we found. As to where we are, we're in the shape-shifters realm where the werewolves can be found. He was about to cast a spell on us, and I doubt that I could've stopped him; so I did the next-best thing – I got us all out of there. He'll probably be pissed right about now, but I don't have to worry about him anymore. At least, not until I need to venture down there again," replied Sonja.

The contrast between this level and the demon one was staggering. There seemed to be life everywhere, from the trees to the many different species of flowers that grew wherever you looked. Sonja led the way, and as we walked I had a question.

"I always thought that werewolves needed a full moon to change," I said.

"That's a myth. Werewolves can change whenever they want to, although it would be fair to say that their senses are heightened during a full moon."

"You mentioned shape-shifters. Does that imply that there is more than one kind?" I asked.

"Oh yes, you didn't suppose that the werewolves have this realm all to themselves did you?"

"I didn't know, but what other humans can change then?"

"There are some shape-shifters that can change into anything, although they are quite private and don't like to be disturbed. There are were-horses and bears, as well as the little folk who prefer to turn into birds."

Sonja had just finished telling me all this when we spotted at least four horses galloping across the meadow.

"Are they all human?" I said as I watched with fascination.

"Yes, they are."

"It's incredible, but how do they produce so much mass from such a smaller creature such as a human?"

"That's where magic comes into it. It's believed that magic is infused within a shape-shifter from birth, and is continually recharged from the magic that comes up through the ground. It is also the strongest magic, because even though we can do it ourselves, it takes a great deal of concentration and a fair amount of magic," replied Sonja.

It all fascinated me, and as we walked further, I suddenly realized that those same horses were coming our way. When they arrived, the lead horse suddenly began to change into human form. It seemed like a seamless change as the snout went back to form a human face, and the legs aligned to become a pair. The last part was the shrinking and standing straight. That all sounds complicated, but the fact was the horse changed within three seconds of turning. However, that wasn't the most impressive thing. The fact that a naked man now stood before us and that man was hung like a horse really got my attention.

"Greetings Mistress," was the first thing he said.

I wondered if there was anyone my mistress didn't know.

"Hi Fletch, I didn't recognize your mane until you changed otherwise I would've waved," replied Sonja.

"What brings you to the shape-shifters realm, milady?"

"We've just been to the lowest level to acquire a gem, and now we're on the way back home. We're heading towards the upper-level slope right now."

"Would you care to ride?"

"That would be a nice change of pace. Thank you, Fletch; we'll take you up on that offer," replied Sonja diplomatically.

He suddenly changed back into a horse, and Sonja indicated that I should climb on. I held his long mane and kicked off from the ground, and with a little help from Sonja, I was now sitting on his back. Everyone else got a horse, and we started to trot towards the furthest mountain range. It was a very pleasant ride, and within an hour we reached the domain of the were-horses.

When we dismounted, Fletch offered us refreshments, which my mistress didn't refuse, and we were escorted into a large tent. There were naked men and women everywhere, and it made me wonder if they ever wore clothes. It was nice to be able to sit down, because even though the ride was pleasant, my ass felt sore. I'd only ever ridden three times in my life, and they were all with saddles.

"Is there a reason they never wear clothes?" I whispered to Sonja.

"Yes, a very good one. Although this looks like a friendly place, there are creatures in this realm that would kill and eat them. With that in mind, they need to be able to change into their alternate forms quickly, and clothes just get in the way," replied Sonja.

I could see the need to be quick under such circumstances. Our hosts laid out a spread consisting of sandwiches and iced tea, which was much appreciated. I asked if someone could show me around their camp, and was pleasantly surprised when three of them asked to be my escort.

It was very hard not staring at their equipment as we walked around their camp, mainly because they were all hunks in more ways than one. They showed me their main hall first, where they held important meetings to determine their future. Then I was shown to their stables and hadn't realized that they would have one. I asked why they would need one, and was told that many of their kind preferred the state of a horse as opposed to being human, which meant that having a stable was a necessity.

We were then joined by another man, who was hung just like the others. I was starting to feel a flush in my cheeks with so many huge cocks surrounding me.

"Whom do we have here?" said one of the newer faces.

"Cherry is my name, sir. With whom do I have the honor of addressing?" I replied.

"I'm Clifton, the leader of the horse clan. It's a pleasure to make your acquaintance. Aren't you hot in those clothes?" he replied.

"Now that you mention it, I am quite warm."

"Then allow me to help you out of those garments. It's the least I can do."

Before I could agree or disagree, I suddenly felt hands removing my clothes, both in front and from behind, and within seconds I was standing as naked as they were.

"I must say milady, you have a beautiful figure," said Clifton.

I felt my cheeks flush with so many eyes looking me over. I also couldn't hold back anymore, because I found myself reaching forward and gently taking the leader's limp but very large cock into my hand.

"I must say, I like what I see," I said as I stroked it.

That must have been their cue because suddenly there were hands all over me. I could feel the cock in my hand growing, and when I looked down I was shocked to see how big he was getting.

"Oh my, I do hope you know how to use that?" I said as I squeezed it with the palm of my hand.

He didn't reply; instead, he reached down and ran his fingers gently through my already moist pussy lips. I let out a moan of encouragement and felt a finger penetrating me. My nipples were hard, as my breasts were being fondled by two other guys. Then I felt an erect cock touching my ass cheeks, and was suddenly lifted up from the sides. The leader quickly positioned himself at the front, and I felt the bulbous end of his cock probing for the entrance to my now sopping wet pussy. When he entered me, I let out a loud moan of pleasure as his cock stretched my delicate skin. Then I felt pressure from behind and suddenly a cock was sliding into the back door.

"Oh Christ...oh fuck that feels incredible," I muttered as I felt their lengths filling me up.

I reached down to stroke the cocks by either side of me as they strained to hold me in place. Then the leader and the one behind started to lift me up and down as well, and each time they did I could feel their entire lengths penetrating me. Each inch stretched me, and I felt so wet that I knew I was soaking their cocks with my juices. When I climaxed for the first time, my entire body shuddered with excitement.

They carried on for another ten minutes making me cum once more, and then I felt the seed from each of them filling me up and pouring down my inner thighs and butt cheeks. I screamed with pleasure as they pulled out and sprayed their second loads onto my sweating body. Then I was lowered onto the floor, and another one stood in front of me. He took me down to the floor with me on top of him, before penetrating from beneath. I was then taken from behind by the other guy who held me up from the side. The leader stood to one side stroking his still rock-hard cock in a taunting manner. I bade him forward, and he moved within reach so that I could take the end of his cock into my mouth.

I then felt my right hand being lifted and placed onto the last cock on my left side. I stroked it while sucking the leader, and allowed the other two to do the real work. I could only imagine the scene if anyone had been watching, but it must've looked extremely erotic. The leader was now pushing his cock deeper into my mouth as I could feel the end brushing the back of my throat as the onslaught continued.

When I came for the third time, I couldn't tell you how long it continued. I seemed to be experiencing wave upon wave of pleasure coming from my pussy. Then I experienced a moment of sheer bliss as the leader pulled his cock free of my mouth and his seed exploded onto my face and neck. I looked around to the guy I was stroking, and as I did so, he came as well, with a large amount of semen shooting onto my back and ass cheeks. The two inside me came shortly afterwards, and when it was all over, I was literally covered in manseed.

I was then picked up and taken to a large shower, where I was cleaned up and dried. My clothes were handed to me, and after getting dressed, I turned to the leader.

"Thank you for giving me the most intense experience of my life, and believe me, I've had a few," I said.

The leader led me back to my group, where I sat to eat something and drink copious amounts of iced tea.

"Did you enjoy the tour?" said Sonja.

"Immensely," I replied with a smile.

Shortly after that, we were thanking them for their hospitality and walking once again towards the upper level. When we reached it, we had another climb to look forward to. It wasn't so bad though, as we could see the shape-shifters land in all its glory when we'd nearly reached the top, and it was breathtaking. Soon, we were in the tunnel that led to the goblin realm.

"Do we have anything to worry about in the goblin level?" I said.

"No, we have nothing to worry about since I dealt with the sorcerer and sent the goblins scurrying for cover. I'd be surprised if we even see a goblin," replied Sonja.

It turned out that she was right. We didn't see anyone, even though we knew that the goblins numbered in the tens of thousands. When we eventually arrived at the vampire level, all the tension seemed to fade away. We soon found out that the three missing vampires had been returned to their own level, and had decided to stay there in case the goblins managed to break through. Sonja informed the elders that our mission was over, and thanked them for their assistance.

****

Once back in Sonja's cottage, Sonja formed and shaped the gemstone that we'd found and placed it onto a chain. She then put it around my neck and informed me that the real work could now begin. Dee was placed onto the table in the center of the room. When Sonja went to have a lie down, I started to ask Dee a few questions.

"Dee, would you mind if I asked you some questions?" I said, trying to keep it civil.

"I am under command to answer any question you ask, so fire away," he replied.

"Is there a quicker way to travel between levels, using magic?" I said.

"Yes, there are several ways that are quicker than walking," he said not volunteering what those ways were.

I knew from that point I'd have to formulate my questions a little more carefully.

"If you were me, what would be your choice of travel between levels?"

"My choice would be a portal, one that connects between every level," he responded.

"Does Sonja know about such a thing?"

"No, she only knows about the travel spell."

"Why haven't you ever informed her?" I said.

"She didn't ask. I'm obliged to answer any question that I'm asked, but I don't have to volunteer information that isn't enquired of me."

This seemed too good to be true, yet I knew that Dee wouldn't lie to me.

"Is the spell to create a portal between levels a difficult one to master?"

"It's not difficult to master, but it is difficult to remember."

"Could you teach me the spell required, and will you?"

"I could and I will. I think you'd better write this down," replied Dee.

I grabbed a piece of paper and a pen and told him to begin. He was right; when I'd finished writing it, I could see that it was three sentences long. However, I had a photographic memory and could picture every single word. I wondered if I should try it out, but then thought better of it in case something went wrong. I was itching to tell Sonja about it all and with that in mind, I entered her bedroom.

Sonja was asleep on her bed, and because it was a large one, I decided to sleep next to her. I think I was asleep within seconds and started to dream. I was awoken some time later, when I felt a tongue sliding through the folds of my pussy. I lifted the bed covers to find Sonja buried between my legs. She had a very gentle touch about her, as the tip of her tongue repeatedly stroked the end of my clit.

"Oh, that feels wonderful," I said softly.

She responded by pushing a finger inside while still licking me. I arched my back, wanting to feel it going deeper.

"Oh god...I'm going to cum...oh yes...please don't stop."

When I started to cum, Sonja crept up the bed and positioned herself between my legs. Her cock was already out, and she thrust it inside me. My orgasm continued as I felt her full length deep inside me. She then used her hands on each side of me to rise above me, and started to fuck me hard. I pulled on my nipples to add another sensation to the mix, and then felt her coming inside me. Instead of stopping though, she began to pound at my opening until I was almost screaming out with sheer ecstasy. By the time she came again, I was exhausted.

It took a while to get composed after that, but eventually I told her what I'd learned from Dee. She seemed very interested in this new finding, but annoyed with herself for not discovering it earlier.

She made a decision to try it out, so we both got dressed and went back into the sitting room.

"Dee is there anything I should know before attempting this portal spell that you divulged to Cherry?" she said.

"The only thing you need to know is that it will be exhausting. Your natural magic, which you store within your body, will probably be depleted upon arrival at your destination. You will need to replenish that magic before you can return," he replied.

Once again, I hadn't asked all the questions I needed to ask and was thankful I hadn't tried the spell on my own. I would probably have believed that it was a one-way trip and walked back.

"Can this spell be cast by two people at the same time?"

"Yes it can. In fact, I'd suggest you use it in that fashion."

"Okay, I think we need to concentrate on teaching you a few useful spells, Cherry. You need to know how to protect yourself. The first one that I'm going to teach you is a shield spell. It's the one I used to ward off the spell that the sorcerer threw at us," said Sonja.

A few hours later, I had memorized all the spells she wanted to teach me. However, that didn't mean I was capable of using them. I still had to learn to summon my magic for the more powerful spells. I didn't seem to have any trouble with the smaller spells, but the bigger ones took more energy.

"I've made a decision Cherry. I've wanted a place to call my own in the lower levels for some time now, but until today, I didn't think it wise. Now that we have an easy way to escape any trouble that might come our way, I feel more inclined to make it happen. Of all the levels you saw, which one do you want me to choose?" said Sonja.

"There are two levels that I really liked, the mythical and the shape-shifters. I thought that they were both beautiful places and interesting to visit. If I had to choose one of the two, then it would be the mythical level," I replied.

"It would make sense to create another home there, as we've already made quite a few friends and would be welcomed," responded Sonja.

That turned out to be the final decision. All that was left now was to use the portal spell and see if it would work. At first, we practiced the spell together until we were sure that we knew it by heart and then after gathering up a few things, including Dee, we cast it together. It has to be said, it was the strangest spell I'd seen so far. We seemed to shrink within the field that surrounded us, and then expanded as we appeared on a slope overlooking the mythical realm. We also both collapsed onto the ground once we'd fully materialized.

"Oh my god, I feel exhausted," said Sonja trying desperately to sit up.

I just lie there unable to move, and thought; *Thank god we didn't try this on our own*. It had depleted all the magic energy from both of us, even though we both wore a gem to magnify our abilities. As I lie there, I knew one thing for sure, and that was that Murphy's Law was still working. If something could go wrong, it would. As proof of that, I suddenly felt a couple of spears touching my ribcage. I opened my eyes to see that we were surrounded by what I believed to be elves.

Even when they tied us up and began to carry us, we could do little about it. In fact, it wasn't until we were being carried into their village that I was able to hold my head up and look around. A huge waterfall dominated the back of the village as it cascaded from the mountain that acted as the fourth wall. The other three were wooden slats with a large gate being the only way in and out. There were huge trees down the center of the camp, and above I could see tree houses of various sizes. I also saw rope bridges going from one home to the next.

We were taken to the tallest and thickest tree I'd ever seen, and I've seen some big ones in my time. This one was so immense. It had a large door in the center of it. We were taken inside and unceremoniously dumped onto the floor just inside the doorway.

"Who are you and what are you doing here?" said a voice behind us.

Sonja managed to turn around and sit up.

"I will answer all of your questions once my friend and I are released from these bonds," she said.

I could hear footsteps approaching us when she said that, and suddenly a knife was slicing through the vines that bound us. We both sat up and faced our captor. He was an old man, but by the way he walked back to his seat, a spritely one.

"The question stands," he said.

"My name is Sonja and this is my friend Cherry. We're humans looking for a place to build a home and aren't looking for any trouble," said Sonja.

"You forgot to mention that you're a sorceress," he replied.

"I didn't think it was relevant, because as I said, we aren't looking for trouble."

"Wait a minute; why would you treat us like this if you knew that Sonja was a sorceress?" I said.

"I didn't know until you turned around and I saw the blood-red gems around your necks. Those can only be found in the demon realm, and only a sorcerer would venture to that place, or a sorceress, in your case," he replied.

"Well, if you would show us the way out, we'll be leaving your territory," said Sonja.

"You're free to leave at any time, but I would ask that you stay, at least for the night. I'd like to make amends for this happening, and I would also like to ask a favor, should the night prove us to be worthy. My name is Brant; I'm considered by my people to be an elder. Elders are held in high esteem with my people, as we believe that wisdom comes with age."

"How old are you, if you don't mind me asking?" I said.

"One hundred and thirty-five years I have lived in this village, the village I was born in," he replied.

I swear he didn't look older than sixty.

"We'll stay for the night if that is your wish," said Sonja.

We were then shown around the camp and into the dining hall which was situated behind two enormous gates within the mountain. This place was massive, and the roof was supported by giant pillars of stone with intricate artistic carvings around each one. A feast was being prepared, and we were the guests of honor. I couldn't help but notice while we were waiting for the food, that there were more male elves than there were female ones. I didn't think it relevant, so I didn't say anything.

When the feast started we were sitting next to Brant at the head of the table. The food was incredible, and as we ate, Brant told us what the favor was.

"A little over six months ago our females began to disappear. At first, it was one a day, then two, until finally we had to stop them from leaving the village. We sent out scouting parties of our bravest warriors, but they always came back with no news and no females. We're at a loss as of what to do, and if you could help in any way, we would forever be in your debt," he said.

"Bring me an item of clothing from each of the females who are missing, and I'll locate them for you," replied Sonja.

Brant clapped his hands, and two servants appeared from behind him. He whispered in their ear, and they ran off to do his bidding. Moments later, they returned with several items of clothing and laid them on the table in front of Sonja.

"Stri-to-Loth inveniet dominum," she said aloud while holding one of the garments.

"It pulled me to the north, and in the morning I'll head in that direction and return your females," said Sonja.

Brant was overjoyed, as were his people, and the wine flowed freely that night.

****

In the morning, we set out and headed due north. Sonja revealed to me as we walked that she'd never explored the northern region of the mythical level, and didn't know what to expect. We saw some incredible things along the way, dragons flying in the distance, a huge ogre chasing a deer, and three harpies. Fortunately, none of them saw us.

Sonja had to use the location spell on the clothing several times to home in on where the female elves had been taken, and it eventually led us to small valley between two small mountains. However, that was where the trail went cold. The spell was insisting that we'd reached our destination, but there was nothing there. Just then something strange happened. Dee offered up a suggestion.

"It might be hidden behind an illusion," we heard his muffled voice say from within the bag that Sonja was carrying.

Sonja used a show illusion spell, and sure enough, there to the left of us was an entrance into the side of the mountain.

"Whoever we're dealing with knows how to use magic. I don't want to jump to conclusions this time as to whether or not it's a witch or a sorcerer; so we're just going to have to enter and find out," said Sonja.

We walked in slowly after placing a shield spell on ourselves, and found that it led to a huge tunnel. As we walked, we could hear banging from further along, and knew that somebody was hard at work making something. When we came to a bend in the tunnel, we took a peek, and there were literally dozens of goblins building what looked like ramps. When we looked further, we could see elven women carrying drinks and looking dazed.

"They're under a spell and clearly being used as slave labor," said Sonja as we hid around the corner once more.

"Could this possibly be the lair of that sorcerer you killed?" I said.

"Quite possibly, but the goblins would know that he's gone by now. So why would they keep working? Those ramps are probably meant to scale the vampires' walls, but without a sorcerer on their side, they don't stand a chance," replied Sonja.

"Could it be possible that he was in league with someone else?"

"That's just conjecture, and until we see evidence to the contrary, we should assume that they do have a master whom we haven't seen yet. The question is what to do from here?" said Sonja.

"It's a shame that we can't use disguises and mingle with them to learn their plans," I replied, thinking that wasn't very useful to the situation at hand.

"Yes, that's a good idea," replied Sonja to my surprise.

She then mumbled a spell and cast it onto me. I looked down at my own body and was shocked to find that I looked like a goblin.

"Be careful not to talk or touch anyone, or the game will be up. I haven't actually changed you; what you're seeing is an illusion. I'll do the same thing to myself, and we'll just walk in and mingle, okay?" said Sonja.

Once she cast the spell on herself, we walked in and over to where the work was being done. Sonja took the lead.

"Where's the boss?" she said in the deepest voice she could muster.

"Where she always is, with the elven bitches; I swear that woman's perverted," replied a goblin who looked in charge.

He'd pointed to some carved-out stairs in the rock, and we could see a platform up there. We headed straight to it, and when we reached the top Sonja turned to me.

"Okay, we now know there's a woman in charge. I'm guessing another sorceress, but she could also be a witch so be on your guard."

We walked into another room to discover we were on a balcony overlooking a circular room, and that the balcony went all the way around to steps on the other side. I peered over the edge and couldn't believe what I was seeing. There were at least twelve naked elven women all dangling and chained to a wooden beam. Among them was a very tall and well-endowed man, who was in the process of fucking one of the elves from behind. We couldn't see the bitch in charge. Sonja grabbed my arm, and we went back into the corridor.

"I could take him out and free the elven women, but that doesn't get us past the goblins. I'm also not happy that we can't see the leader of this motley crew. I'd like to know where she is before I act," said Sonja.

"Why don't you turn me into an elven female and take me down there as your prisoner? Once you get close enough, take him out, and we'll come up with a plan of escape after that. We can't just leave them there like this," I replied.

Sonja agreed, and suddenly I was naked and looked just like an elven female. She marched me back into the room shouting for me to move it. I played the damsel in distress and stumbled forward. We walked down the steps, and just as we reached the bottom, the guy fucking the chained elven female came all over her backside. I saw it dripping off her and felt pity for her plight. Sonja then moved me up nearer to the wooden beam.

The big guy turned around to look at what we were doing, and suddenly Sonja threw a spell on him. Unfortunately, the spell didn't work, and the big guy suddenly changed into a woman. I guessed that she'd had a shield spell activated and the spell had been deflected. Sonja dropped the entire pretense after that and we were both ourselves, standing in front of the bitch.

"So, you've found me at last. I was wondering when I'd get the pleasure of your company," she said to Sonja.

"How do you know of me?" replied Sonja.

"The goblins know all there is to know about you," she responded.

"I seriously doubt the goblins know half of what they think they know. Who are you and what are you doing here?"

It was at that moment that I discovered just how powerful Sonja could be. Her enemy didn't answer the question. Instead, she threw a spell, which Sonja deflected. She then threw another one, which missed. Sonja didn't ask any more questions – she threw her own spells. The first was deflected; the second froze her enemy and the third disintegrated her. She then went about unchaining the elves as if nothing had happened. I stood there in awe and started to help her.

There was still a problem though. As we set the females free, they all started pawing at our bodies and telling us to fuck them.

"Dee, what is this?" said Sonja.

"If I had to guess I'd say that they're under an arousal spell, which doesn't have a counterspell to stop it. However, it's the type of spell that has to be applied once a day, and will probably wear off in a few hours' time," replied Dee.

"Damn it, we haven't got time for this. I'd better seal the entrance up there so the goblins can't see what's going on in here," said Sonja.

I then watched her throwing a spell up at the entrance to the room, and a wall appeared at the entrance. I swear, the more magic I saw being used, the more I wanted to learn it. After we'd unchained all the elven women we spoke to them, trying to make them see that they were under a spell, but it was no use. They were of one mind, and sex was the only thing on it.

"What if we give them what they want, would that help?" I said.

"It couldn't hurt, and besides we'd have to wait for the spell to dissipate anyway, so we might as well have some fun while we're waiting," replied Sonja.

She conjured up a couple of beds, and we both stripped our clothes off. Half the elven females descended onto Sonja, and the other half onto me. It wasn't hard to get aroused as they were all very attractive, not to mention naked; so I used the male sex spell and as expected, a cock burst out and started to grow. They saw it appearing and descended upon it.

I had three elven females licking it while three others were kissing every inch of my body. The same things were happening to Sonja. One of mine sat astride my face while facing my cock and licking it from that direction. I buried my tongue inside her, which made her squeal.

One of the others was hungrily licking the ridge of my cock, which was driving me crazy. Another one was lower down and licking my slit, just below the cock, that was protruding from it. I had a mouth on both breasts sucking my nipples, and it all felt amazing. The thing is they were all insatiable. The strongest of the three and the tallest managed to sit on top of my cock and was quickly sliding up and down on it. All the others were either touching or licking various parts of my body. It all made me wonder what the spell they were under felt like. Once the female who was fucking me started to climax, she was pushed off and replaced with another. That's how it continued until there was just one left. I decided that I wanted to be in control for this one, so I forced her onto her back and jumped on top of her. As soon as I slid my cock in, she grabbed my butt cheeks and started pulling me into her.

I came before her, so I continued until she did as well, and then it all seemed to calm down. I looked over at Sonja, and she was still working on two of hers. The others had either collapsed onto the bed or on the floor. The two left were sharing her cock with each other.

One would suck it and then hand it over to the other. I watched Sonja ejaculating, and they both licked her clean before carrying on again.

I got off the bed and walked over and quickly grabbed one of them. I then positioned myself behind her and pushed my still-hard cock into her pussy. She was soaked and very eager to feel something inside her. I fucked her hard while Sonja finished off the other one. When we'd finished we were both exhausted.

Two hours later, they all started to wake up, and fortunately, we found that the spell had worn off. Sonja had had time to figure out a strategy for getting out of there without a fight. First, she ordered the goblins to send in the rest of the female elves as she remembered seeing some among the goblins when we came in. Once they were all there, she placed an illusion over them all, and they simply walked out of the cave. They all looked like goblins.

****

We arrived at the elven village through cheers and applause. The elder came out to greet us and couldn't thank us enough. He then offered to build the home that we wanted to set up in this level, and Sonja decided to take him up on his kind offer.

****

You wouldn't believe it if you saw it, but an army of elves constructing a building is a sight to see. They moved like a well-oiled engine and within the first day, they'd finished the shell of the structure. This was to be our new home, as we felt more welcome here than we did back on the surface. The location was chosen by Sonja, and it was breathtaking. We were above a meadow with mountains in the background and a river a few hundred feet away.

Sonja finished off the inside of our new home, and it even had running water. Food was never going to be a problem, and we decided to celebrate with all of our friends when it was finished. There were elves, wild women, vampires, and even a couple of werewolves that Sonja knew. My favorite guest though was Gruff. I was very pleased to see him again.

The drinks flowed freely that night, and everyone had a great time. Sonja put on a show, with magic of course, and soon it was all over and people were drifting off back to their own homes. As I was saying goodbye to them all, Gruff asked if he could talk with me. I told him of course, and led him out to the back where the elves had constructed a barn to store things in.

"What's up, big guy?" I said once we were alone.

"Gruff miss friend and wanted to enjoy friend once last time," he replied.

I didn't quite cotton on to what he meant at first, and then the penny dropped. I was wearing a short dress as I walked over to him and looked up.

"I'd like to feel this thing inside me again," I said as I slid my hand beneath his loin cloth and stroked his limp but massive cock.

I felt it growing almost instantly, and the way it spread out on the palm of my hand was a real turn-on for me. He unloosened the cloth and allowed it to fall to the floor, making his shaft spring up as it continued to grow. Then I remembered that Sonja had taught me the accommodation spell the other day. I quickly used it on myself and leaned forward. I didn't know what to expect as I'd never used the spell before, but I was in for a shock.

I covered the end with my mouth and started to suck, much to Gruff's delight. Then I allowed a bit more in then a bit more. When it started to hit the back of my throat, I couldn't believe it. I wasn't struggling in the slightest, so I decided to see how far I could take it. Suddenly, his entire length was disappearing inside my mouth and down my throat, and he was groaning aloud with pleasure. He began to swing his hips back and forth and nothing he did bothered me.

I was getting extremely wet from doing all of this, and I don't think Gruff could believe that it was happening. At one point, he started to get too excited and I knew what would happen next.

Sure enough, I felt his cock pulsating, and suddenly he was shooting his load into my mouth. His groans of pleasure were turning me on and making me want to please him as much as possible. I carried on sucking him until he was drained but still hard, and then allowed him to pull it free. He didn't say anything. Instead, he grabbed me and pulled me up into the air. I was so high I could grab the wooden beam above me, which I did. The next thing I knew, he was ripping my panties off again.

What is it about panties that he objects to? I thought and smiled to myself.

Suddenly, his tongue was swiping the opening to my pussy and making me grip the beam even harder. He licked me long and hard for several minutes and then pushed his huge tongue inside me. I started to experience my first orgasm of the day, and it made me tingle all over. Then he pulled me down and positioned me on the end of his cock before pulling me down onto it.

With the accommodation spell still in effect, I had no trouble taking him. What made it so good though was that he was doing all the work. I was being pushed and pulled onto his meat, and before long I was literally screaming with pleasure. When he came again, I hadn't had enough, so I grabbed his neck and carried on pounding him. I was lifting my butt up and dropping it down as hard as I could. I could feel every inch of his meat as it penetrated me, and then started to enjoy my reward.

I must have stayed with him buried inside me for quite a while until he eventually placed me gently onto the floor. He asked me in his own clumsy way whether he'd ever see me again, and I assured him that he most definitely would. By the time he left, I wondered what else life had in store for me. I re-entered our new home and caught sight of Sonja smiling to herself.

"What's so funny?" I said.

"Oh nothing, I just can't believe how far you've come. You seem to fit in here like no one I've ever known," she replied.

"To be honest, Mistress, I've never felt so at home in my life. I feel that I belong here, and I'm so glad I got to meet you. Magic is incredible and I can't imagine life without it now," I said.

We discussed our plans after that and Sonja was determined to explore this land, so that there were no surprises in the future.

****

By mid-morning of the next day, we were a good twenty miles from home. We were entering a large forest, and Sonja wanted to see how big it was. Within ten minutes, we knew that someone or something was following us. We just couldn't see them. Suddenly we were surrounded by fairies. At first, they were the small variety with perfect human bodies with wings, all flying around us. Then they suddenly grew to our own height and looked more menacing. There were about twenty of them and the eldest of them all approached us.

"You are trespassing in this forest; please turn around and go back the way you came," he said.

"No, we're exploring these lands and aren't looking for trouble. If you see us as a threat, then you don't know us. We are peaceful people and are no threat to you or your kind," replied Sonja.

"Then you give me no choice but to use force," was the response.

Suddenly, they were all chanting a melody and walking around us in a circle. Sonja quickly threw a spell out to cover both of us and the chanting stopped.

"What happened?" I heard one of them say.

"I cancelled out your magic, and furthermore, you'll not be able to perform any magic for at least another hour," said Sonja getting their attention again.

"You're a sorceress?" said the elder.

"Yes, but not an evil one. If I so wished I could destroy you all, but as I said we're peaceful people ordinarily and mean you no harm," replied Sonja.

"We have perhaps been a little hasty in our actions, and I take full responsibility. If you have to punish anyone, please let it be me," he said bowing his head.

"What part of "peaceful people," don't you understand?" I said, stepping forward.

Sonja moved me back with a wave of her hand.

"Perhaps we could start back from the beginning and forget all of this. My name is Sonja, and this is my apprentice Cherry. With whom do I have the pleasure of addressing?" said Sonja softly.

"I am Oak Shield the Wise, although I do seem to be having an off day as far as wisdom is concerned. Come into our camp, where we can welcome you the way we used to many years ago," he replied.

Oak Shield led the way, and soon we were walking into a clearing with dozens of tiny homes scattered around a large fire. I was surprised to see the male fairies wearing pants of a kind as they only came down to the knees. As for the females, they wore tiny skirts that looked very tight. It was their wings that fascinated me though as they seemed to shine in different colors depending on the lighting.

"We would've preferred you dine in our great hall, but your size discounts that notion," said Oak.

"We can follow you," said Sonja.

I just thought, *'we can?'*

Oak led the way to the largest of the small buildings and then appeared to disappear. He had, in fact, shrunk to his more natural size and was entering the hall. Sonja turned to me.

"Use the accommodation spell," she said.

I watched her use it on herself and then put a hand inside the building followed by her arm, and I noticed that with every section of her body that entered she shrank more and more until she was physically inside.

"So that's how the accommodation spell works," I said aloud as I placed it on myself and did the same thing.

Soon we were both entering what Oak had called the great hall, and I had to admit it was pretty cool in there. We then discovered how many fairies actually lived here. There were literally hundreds of them. The funny thing was that even though I knew we had shrunk, it still felt normal somehow. The great hall was decorated with golden leaves and artistic representations of the forest on every wall; it truly was a great hall.

I couldn't help noticing how beautiful the female fairies were. Most of them were stunning, but I tried not to stare. Sonja and the elder talked about the history of the fairies, but I found that to be boring. I, on the other hand, was more interested in talking with the females. They seemed to want to please me in every way they could, yet the males seemed indifferent. What I couldn't understand was why the females were turning me on. I mean, I knew they were beautiful, but I'm normally a straight woman. I guessed it was because I had the ability to act like a man, what with the gender spell and everything. That's when I overheard a conversation between Sonja and the elder.

"We're happy here, but we do have our problems from time to time. At the moment, we've had to abandon the east side of the village as we take care of a couple of fairies that were enchanted," said Oak.

"Enchanted in what way?" replied Sonja.

"Two of our females were cursed by a witch. The curse is that of being a siren. Whenever they sing, which is most of the time, the males can't ignore the message. However, once in the clutches of the enchanted females, they are made to copulate. That may sound wonderful to some folk, but they're unable to stop making love. In time, the males become exhausted and collapse."

"How do you care for them if you can't get near?" said Sonja.

"We simply cover our ears, and we use magic to keep the sound they make confined to their room. I feel sorry for them as they do know what the effect of the singing does; they simply can't stop themselves," replied Oak.

"I'm going to let my apprentice figure something out for you," said Sonja.

"You are?" I replied without being addressed.

Sonja leaned towards me and whispered something in my ear.

"To get rid of this curse is very easy. You simply tell them to forget the past. If they can't remember being enchanted, they won't remember how or what the enchantment consisted of. A witch's curse depends on the memory of the victim, so if the victim can't remember it, the curse has no effect."

"I never knew that; so all I have to do is use the forget spell and they'd be free of the curse?" I replied.

"Yes and no; they'll be able to come back into the village without harming anyone, but the curse will still be on them, they simply won't know it," said Sonja.

"There's just one more thing. Why are you getting me to do this?"

"I've seen the way you look at some of these females, and I thought you might enjoy this assignment."

Was I that obvious, I thought as I smiled back?

"Okay, if someone could show me the way, I'll help these fairies to return to their people," I said aloud.

A young female fairy came forward and told me that she would be happy to show me the way. I followed her after telling everyone

I wouldn't be long. All the fairies looked skeptical as I left, but I knew that it would work. Sonja was too confident for anything to go wrong, and besides, I was actually looking forward to it. The female who was showing me the way was clearly flirting with me. Her name was Felicity Greenacre. She was very attractive and wore a short skirt with a low-cut top to match.

"Tell me, Felicity, does the singing affect the females as well?"

"Oh yes, it makes us want to please those that are singing. However, we can carry on indefinitely provided we have food. The males, on the other hand, are physically exhausted if left for too long, so they stopped the entire male population from entering the building," replied Felicity.

It didn't take long to reach the building in question, and Felicity told me to be careful, and that I could find the females at the end of the corridor. As soon as I entered the building I could hear the singing. I'd always wondered what a siren song would sound like, and how it would affect me. It turned out to be the most enchanting sound I'd ever heard. It made me want to follow it. I had the foresight to try and stop myself, but found that I couldn't do it. The sound made me want, or rather need to investigate.

When I reached the room that the sound was clearly coming from, I opened the door and stepped inside. There were three female fairies inside, but one of them had her ears covered. She was clearly there to watch over them. I asked her to leave, which she did, and then turned to the females as they carried on singing.

They were both incredibly beautiful, and I found myself wanting to go to both of them at the same time. The strange thing about it all is that I was aware of everything I was doing. I knew I could cast a spell if I wished to, and I could even talk to them. However, I was being urged to embrace them, and that was something I couldn't fight. I stripped my clothing away and then placed the male gender spell onto myself. They watched intently as the bulge appeared, and gave me a surprised look when my cock suddenly popped out and started to grow in front of them. They didn't stop singing though. It was as if they were compelled to do it.

"Come out from behind those covers," I said as they were covering themselves up in their beds.

They immediately dropped the covers, and I discovered that they were both naked. Their bodies were a work of art. They both had slim waists and large breasts, but their faces seemed to glow with beauty. I walked up to the beds and eventually chose one of them.

"Get onto your friend's bed," I said as I reached out involuntarily to stroke her breasts.

She did as she was told, and I found myself looking at two visions of beauty sitting side by side on the edge of the bed. The singing hadn't stopped once and was driving me crazy with lust. They both reached for my cock and got down to their knees. I felt the lips of one of them covering the end of my cock as the other licked its length. I noticed straight away that the sounds that held me there were still audible, but now they were in the form of humming.

The lust was still driving me crazy, and I felt the need to be physical. With that in mind, I placed my hands onto the back of the fairy that had my cock in her mouth, and pulled her onto me faster. She seemed to take it in her stride, and soon I could feel the end of my cock hitting the back of her throat. The other one was still licking me whenever she could see my cock. I found myself wanting to fuck them both at the same time, even though I knew that was impossible.

Then I started to cum, and they pulled their mouths away as it shot out the end of my cock. They took turns in taking the seed as it appeared until I had completely stopped coming. Sonja had taught me another spell the other day, and it was one that I wanted to try out. It was the spell of strength. I quickly threw it on myself and then picked one of the fairies up from the floor. She stood up close to my chest as the other one carried on licking my cock back to life.

Even though the strength spell was activated, I didn't feel any different. Yet, when I grabbed her waist and pulled her off the floor, she felt as light as a feather. She threw her arms around my neck, and as I entered her, she started to fuck me. She was lifting her butt up and dropping it down again, as the other one carried on licking me below.

I felt as if I wanted to fuck forever, and realized that was what the males must feel like. I could see how it would affect the male population if they couldn't get free. I could feel her hard nipples pressing into my chest as she continued the onslaught. I also realized that I was getting more and more aroused. I started to cum again and she let it slide out. Next I felt the other one sucking it below us as I came the second time. I quickly placed the one I was holding back onto the floor and picked the other one up. I literally threw her onto the bed and turned her around, before entering her roughly from behind.

I knew then that the sounds were affecting my mind in all the wrong ways as I would never be so rough under normal circumstances. I gripped her butt and started to pound her with my cock. I carried on until she was screaming that she was coming. Then I had the presence of mind to put an end to all of this. Even as I threw the spell of forgetfulness over them, I wanted to carry on with what I was doing. Suddenly the feelings stopped, and they collapsed onto their beds. I put my clothes back on after getting rid of my cock and asked them if they were all right.

"Who are you?" they said almost together.

"Just a friend; now get dressed and we can go and see your people," I replied.

I waited for them and then took them back to the great hall. When they saw us entering, they all cheered as they knew that the spell had been removed, or in this case canceled out.

"How did you do this?" said the elder.

"I threw a simple spell of forgetfulness on them, which will stop them from remembering the past. However, they won't recognize anyone here. They need to be looked after until they're familiar with everyone and what their duties are," I replied.

Sonja thanked me for doing a good job and we enjoyed the rest of the night, as we were treated like royalty. The next day we said our farewells and continued on our journey. The adventures we had in the following days are now being written by me, and they are worth reading.

The End

Alex in Wonderland (An Erotic Parody)

Alex sat propped against the large oak tree, looking up at the puffy white clouds that hung in the magnificent blue sky. He lay there for some time and imagined all kinds of shapes, including a giant white rabbit. He smiled to himself and felt struck by all the magic around him. He felt nature was a wonderful gift from God and one that was not appreciated by many. He was a twenty year old daydreamer and a lover of peace and quiet. He had intended to read his book, but felt more content just to relax and take in all the beauty around him. He closed his eyes to take a deep breath of the intoxicating fresh air, but when he opened his eyes again, he witnessed the most astonishing thing.

There, standing a mere ten feet away was a large white rabbit. Under normal circumstances, seeing a white rabbit wouldn't be anything special, except that this particular white rabbit was wearing a brocade waistcoat. Alex watched it silently, in wide-eyed wonder, and then was struck with curiosity, as the rabbit produced a golden pocket watch from the breast pocket of its waistcoat. The rabbit took a quick look at the time and crinkled its face in obvious displeasure. It muttered a tsk, tsk sound, shook its head, popped the watch back into its pocket, and took off at a quick hop.

"Curious indeed," he said as he watched the rabbit run off.

Alex stood up and sprinted after it. His curiosity had gotten the better of him. He saw it dive into a thick hedge, but knew that he couldn't follow into the tight green foliage. Instead, he ran down to the end and then walked around to the other side to discover a hole at the base of a large oak tree. He got down onto his knees and peering into the darkness of the hole could swear that he heard voices. In an effort to hear what the voices were saying, Alex tried to lean further in and that's when it happened. The ground he imagined was solid suddenly gave way and he found himself falling into the hole.

His fingers desperately clutched at the tree roots in his downward flight, but they gave way beneath his falling weight. Clods of dirt and debris followed him as he fell faster and deeper into the hole, and he knew that he was in trouble. Seconds seemed to turn into minutes and he wondered why he hadn't hit the bottom yet.

"Surely, it can't be that deep?" he said to himself in disbelief.

There, ahead of his flailing arms, he saw a light. Brightness at the rapidly approaching bottom and thought, well, this is it. This is how my life will end. Yet, when he was mere feet away from the bottom, he felt a sudden strong upsurge of air, which was actually slowing him down. In fact, by the time he finally reached the bottom he was going no faster than you would if you fell off a three foot wall. He rolled with the impact and came to a stop a few feet away from the bottom of the hole. When he finally looked up from his resting place, he found that he was in a large round room, and that the room was lined with doors.

"Curiouser and curiouser," he said as he got to his feet.

One by one, he tried the doors but found them to be soundly locked. Glancing up at the gaping hole in the distant ceiling he knew he couldn't go back the way he came, so the next thing he tried was to knock on each of the doors. Nothing happened. Then to his surprise he saw a polished marble table, which he was positive wasn't there a minute ago. On the table sat an ornate bottle with a label on its face. Alex picked the bottle up and read the label.

One for the Ladies, and underneath in smaller handwriting was written, *Drink Me*.

He wondered what that could possibly mean, before returning it to the table. That's when he spotted the key, which had been placed next to the bottle. He picked it up and walked over to the doors once again. He tried the key in all of them, but again was frustrated by the fact that it didn't fit a single one. Then turning around, he spotted a door that had two rather large holes in it. He'd swear that they were not there a moment ago. One of the holes was at head height, so he cautiously peered through it.

He could see two of the loveliest women he'd ever seen playing hop scotch together. He placed his mouth to the hole and called out to them, but when he looked through again they hadn't heard him. He then spotted the other hole further down and upon investigation he discovered words scratched below it. They read, *Insert Cock Here*.

"That can't be right," he laughed as he read the words again.

He looked through the top hole again and they were still there. He couldn't help staring as they were incredibly beautiful and were both wearing the most revealing of short dresses. Whenever they played the game, Alex could see their breasts bouncing up and down in such a delightful manner. In fact, after watching for a few minutes he realized that they were making him hot and hard. It struck him, as he looked down at the growing bulge in his pants, that it matched the height of the lower hole.

Just a coincidence, he thought.

He was hot now and then he remembered the bottle and walked over to the table to retrieve it. He took the top off and smelt the contents and then poured a few droplets onto his tongue. It was deliciously sweet to the taste, so he decided to take a swig.

"Hmm, it's got a honey taste to it," he said as he put the top back on and placed the bottle into his pocket.

He then returned to the door and started to look through the hole once more to find that they were still there. He must have watched for another three minutes when all of a sudden he felt the strangest sensation. His cock was pushing his pants outward more than normal. In fact, it was starting to get uncomfortable. He had to quickly unfasten his pants and discovered that his cock was growing.

"Oh dear God, what on earth is happening?" he said aloud as his cock grew to over a foot in length before stopping.

Once it had stopped, Alex couldn't help but admire it. He grabbed hold of its thick girth and stroked its length. Then he remembered the hole in the door.

I wonder, he thought.

He took hold of his cock and slid it through the hole and then looked out through the one nearer the top. As if by magic, the girls noticed it straight away.

"Oh look, I wonder who left that there?" said one of them as they both skipped over to take a closer look.

Alex said hello through the peep hole, but they didn't seem to be able to hear him.

"It looks nice," said one of the women as she grabbed it and stroked its hardened length.

"Yes, I agree. Shall we have some fun with it?" said the other one as she grabbed it as well.

Moments later, Alex could feel a warm mouth engulfing the end of his cock. He let out a groan of approval and tried to see what they were doing through the hole at the top. All he could see were their backsides as they bent over in front of his cock. Then he felt his cock sliding out of the moist mouth and being handed to the other one.

"This is how you really do it," said the second one.

Suddenly he felt the back of a throat as she deep throated him.

"Oh God, yes that's it, right there," he murmured with pleasure.

This one was obviously an expert. He felt her lips and tongue moving along the entire length of his cock before sliding it back in again.

"I don't think I can do that," said the other one.

"Here, take it again and I'll show you what to do."

Alex felt the other one grab hold of it and then heard what the first one was saying.

"Relax, take a few inches inside your mouth, that's it, now open your mouth wider and bend down further. Now, take some more of it into your mouth and when it touches the back of your throat bring it out again straight away."

Alex was feeling everything that she was describing, and sure enough he could feel the end of his cock hitting the back of her throat. They then took turns again and within ten minutes Alex was unable to hold it any further. He shouted out that he was going to cum, but they ignored him and carried on. He felt his seed exploding inside the mouth he was in and heard her giggle as she swallowed and handed it over to her friend for the second blast. They carried on doing that until Alex stopped coming and then they both stood up licking their lips in satisfaction.

"I enjoy the taste of semen but I want to fuck it now," said the taller of the two.

Without a further word, Alex saw her suddenly lift her right leg to her shoulder and watched as she leaned forward. As he felt his cock sink into the depths of her tight wet pussy, he realized she had done an upright split and had come to a rest against the other side of the door. He gasped at the clutching tight fit as she started to slide off and on his meat.

"Of fuck yes, what a beautiful cock. Oh deeper and deeper," she called out as she moved faster and slammed her pussy onto his cock.

Alex could see and hear her slamming into the door as she swayed back and forth onto his cock. He was going in so far it felt amazing. He looked again and could see that she had pulled her top down as she pounded his cock and was gripping her breasts and pulling her nipples with each long stroke. This carried on for a while and then she moved her hips even faster.

"Oh fuck, I'm going to cum," she screamed out.

With just a few more lunges forward, Alex could feel her pussy tightening around his cock and felt it quivering as she climaxed. The ripples of her pleasure tantalized his rigid length. Then she pulled away and off his cock.

"Shit, I was almost there," shouted Alex.

Fortunately, he then felt another, even tighter pussy pushing its way onto his cock and looked through the hole again. The other female was bent over and taking his cock in from behind. As soon as his cock was all the way inside her, she began to pound away just as the first one had done.

"Oh yes, of fuck yes," he could hear her say as her rounded ass slammed into the door repeatedly.

"That's it Pauline, fuck it hard. It is so sweet, I don't think I've come that hard in quite some time," encouraged the first woman.

Alex could feel the end of his cock hitting bottom each time she travelled along its length and he also knew that he was going to cum for the second time that day. Within the next few thrusts from the other side of the door, Alex exploded inside her, but she continued to fuck him.

"Oh yes, I'm coming, oh God here it comes...yes...yessssssss, ah YES," she screamed.

Alex relaxed against the door with his rigid cock now deflating on the other side, until he heard them talking once again.

"Let's take it with us," said one.

Just then Alex felt one of them trying to pull it through the hole and as she did he banged his head against the door.

"It won't budge, have you got a knife," she said when she couldn't set it free.

Alex immediately pulled it back out.

"Oh shit, it's escaped," he heard one of them say, "oh well, let's go and play again."

Alex looked through the peephole to see that they'd all but forgotten about his cock and were playing as if nothing had happened. He quickly pulled his pants back up and only just managed to get his cock in, it was so big now. Then he spotted a tiny door across from the one with the holes in it.

"Now I know that that wasn't there before," he said.

He then remembered the tiny key and fetched it from the table. Sure enough, the key fit into this door. He opened it to find a large garden on the other side, but the door was way too small for him to get through. He propped himself up against the wall shaking his head. *This place is frustrating*, he thought.

He looked around and to his amazement he spotted a small piece of chocolate on the floor next to him with a label on it. He picked it up and read the label. It simply said, *Eat Me*. So, without stopping to think, he ate it. A few seconds later, he began to feel strange once again and then he began to shrink. He called out with fright as his clothes began to surround him but then stopped when he saw that he was the correct height for the tiny door he'd just opened. He crawled out from under his clothing completely naked. His cock was now the correct size for his body, but he felt exposed.

He immediately saw the white rabbit again in the distance as it checked its pocket watch, and gave chase. The garden he was running through had giant flowers and then he realized that they weren't giant flowers, but that he had shrunk. He stopped and leaned against a tall mushroom.

"You look lost sir," he heard someone say behind him.

He turned to see a huge caterpillar sitting on top of the mushroom and smoking something from a long tube.

"Did you just speak to me?" he said.

"I did indeed young man. I'm pleased that your hearing is intact," replied the caterpillar.

"Did you see a white rabbit come through here by any chance?" said Alex.

"I did not, but I saw a horse fly once. It had huge wings," replied the caterpillar.

"I bet it did," replied a confused Alex.

"You are rather small for a human, why is that?"

"Oh, I ate something that made me shrink. I needed to get through a tiny door you see," replied Alex.

"No, I don't see, but if you want to grow up, you should eat some of my mushroom. I'm told it makes a lot of things grow," replied the caterpillar.

Alex looked at the mushroom and decided to see for himself. He broke a tiny piece off and nibbled on the edge. Then, seconds later he grew to his normal size again. Of course, he was still naked but at least he was the correct height.

"Thank you caterpillar, I appreciate your help," said Alex looking down.

The caterpillar did reply, but Alex could no longer hear him. Instead, he ran off towards the last place he'd seen the rabbit. When he turned the corner he saw a strange bush. It was strange because it had little bottles growing on it, all with labels on them. He stopped and looked at a few. One of them just said *Drink Me*, while another said, *For the Ladies*. He recognized that one and quickly picked it from the bush. He then grabbed a few others and set off again.

He needed somewhere to put the bottles and as luck would have it he found an empty bucket on his travels. He placed the bottles inside and carried the bucket by his side. He walked further along the lane and just as he came to a cross roads, he heard voices coming from one of the other lanes. He decided to hide in the bushes and waited to see who they were.

"I'm telling you, I saw a white rabbit wearing a waistcoat. Why is that so hard to believe?" said one voice.

"Well, whoever heard of a rabbit wearing a waistcoat, it just sounds ludicrous," replied the other.

Alex moved to see where the two voices were coming from and couldn't believe his eyes. They were two of the most gorgeous young women he'd ever laid eyes on and they were identical. He quickly searched through the bottles in his bucket and found the one he was looking for. He took a good swig and sure enough, his cock began to grow. Once it stopped, he walked out from behind the bushes and walked towards the two beauties. He pretended that he didn't see them as they spotted him.

"Oh my god Trixie, do you see that?" said one of them.

"You couldn't really miss it could you Trixie," replied the other.

"Oh, hello ladies, it's a fine day," said Alex.

"It is indeed," replied Trixie One as she stared at his amazing cock.

"Where are you going sir?" said Trixie Two with her eyes transfixed on his cock.

"I was just going for a walk, oh and I'm Alex by the way. May I enquire as to your names?" replied Alex.

"Of course, I'm Trixie Dee and this is Trixie Dum. We're looking for a magic mirror. I don't suppose you've seen one?"

"Um, no I can't say that I have. I assume you're sisters?" replied Alex.

"Actually no, we're not related. It's kind of a long story. I was walking along the lane when I came across a magic mirror and Trixie Dum was on the other side," said Trixie Dee.

"You mean you saw your own reflection?" corrected Alex.

"No, that's the strange thing about it. We were able to talk to one another but when we both looked around the other side of the mirror there was no one there. Anyway, Trixie Dum told me that it was wonderful where she lived and I told her the same thing about where I lived. So, we decided to see if we could cross over to each other's side. We both stepped forward simultaneously to cross over into each other's land when the mirror shattered and we found ourselves together. I insisted that she was now in my land and she insisted that I was in hers. Now we're looking for another magic mirror, so that we can both go home," said Trixie Dee.

Alex had been staring at their beautiful cleavages as she talked and the inevitable happened. His cock started to twitch and grow. The girls noticed it straight away and couldn't seem to look away. Alex decided to tease them and suddenly took hold of his cock and began to slowly stroke it from base to tip.

"I need to find a naked woman for this thing, as it likes to bury itself inside their warm pussies. Therefore, if you'll excuse me, I'll keep looking," said Alex as he stroked its length one more time, enjoying the fact that they were staring at it with lust in their eyes.

"Um, before you go, maybe we can help you," said Trixie Dee.

"Yes, we would enjoy helping that," added Trixie Dum, pointing at his massive cock.

"I don't see how, neither one of you is naked. I'm looking for a good naked woman, someone who is not afraid to feel this giant pounding away at her sweet pussy," replied Alex.

Suddenly they both stripped their clothes away and stood in front of him.

"We're naked now, does that count," said Trixie Dee.

"Oh, indeed it does ladies, indeed it does."

Alex looked around and there on the verge at the side of the road was a giant mushroom, at least four foot in height. He led the girls over to it and then bent Trixie Dee over and under the mushroom canopy before lifting Trixie Dum onto the top. He told Trixie Dum to wait just a second, while he positioned his rigid cock below with Trixie Dee. Once the end of his enormous knob was lined up, he moved it around her opening to feel that she was already wet and then pushed forward, making Trixie Dee scream out with pleasure.

"Oh fuck that feels incredible," she called out as his cock travelled all the way inside her willing womanhood.

Once he'd gotten a good rhythm going he then turned his attention to Trixie Dum. He grabbed her legs and then spread them wide and leaned forward. As he buried his head between her parted thighs, his talented tongue licked at her sweet nectar, his hips were swaying back and forth faster and faster below the mushroom. Trixie Dee's calls of more were driving both him and Trixie Dum crazy. Trixie Dum gripped the back of his head in an attempt to get him to go deeper with his tongue.

Alex introduced a finger as he licked, but it still wasn't enough. She craved more and her hips were starting to move violently against his tongue as she begged him to fuck her as well. He then had an idea. He closed his fist with two fingers pointing forward and entered her while he carried on licking her swollen clit.

"Oh yes, that feels good, more, I want to feel you deep inside me," moaned Trixie Dum.

He then put three fingers in and began to massage the cluster of pleasure points deep inside. Then, with all her pushing and pulling, his hand slipped inside her and he was fucking her up to his wrist.

"Oh God yes, that's it keep going please don't stop," she cried out.

The same could be heard from below as he pounded Trixie Dee with everything he had. With them both screaming in ecstasy, he soon found that he was going to cum and tried desperately to hold it back. However, it was no use. He simply couldn't do it and suddenly with a rapid thrust of his hips, he exploded deep inside Trixie Dee. She let out a final scream of ecstasy and began to climax herself. Alex carried on pushing his hand into Trixie Dum and soon she too was experiencing a rippling orgasm. Still reeling with the last waves of her climax, she helped him pull his hand free and then slumped back onto the top of the mushroom to regain her composure, enjoying the aftershocks of her climax. Trixie Dee stood up after a while and saw Trixie Dum's collapsed state. She then turned to Alex.

"That was incredible sir, if you ever need another woman's help please find me," she said, before retrieving her clothes as well as her friend's.

Alex said his goodbyes and was off again, although he had no idea to where. He remembered his bucket before he left them and wondered what some of the other bottles did. He picked one out and read the label. It just said, *Speed*. He put it back and then after walking for another mile or so he spotted a castle in the distance.

"I wonder who lives there?" he said aloud.

By the time he got within reach of the castle it was getting dark. He quickened his pace and was soon approaching the castle gates. The whole place seemed to be deserted. At least, that's what he thought. Then he saw what looked like a dragon lying just inside the gates. It was clearly asleep as it was snoring puffs of smoke. There was room to pass on either side of it but it was risky. If it woke up and spotted him, he'd be toast.

He decided to go for it. After all, he needed somewhere to sleep. He slowly walked towards the dragon on tip toes and when he was close enough to touch it, he crept by one step at a time. He got past without it waking up and looked around the courtyard. There was no one to be seen and no lights were coming from the castle itself. He then walked over to the entrance and found that the twin doors were unlocked. He entered and explored the rooms on the main floor, but could find no one.

"There must be someone here. Perhaps they all go to bed early," he said aloud.

He walked up the large stairs that led to the upper level calling out for help and found several empty bedrooms. He then found another set of stairs leading upstairs to a single door. He opened the door and peered inside. There on the bed was a beautiful woman crying. He stepped inside quietly and walked over to her.

"Is something wrong?" he said.

"Ah...who are you and how did you get in here. In addition, why are you naked?" she shouted.

"Please, calm down, I mean you no harm. I came looking for shelter and found this castle being guarded by a dragon. I called out several times for help but got no response," said Alex.

"I am the only occupant of this castle and what you called a dragon was in fact the Jabberwocky. It is meant to stop me from ever leaving this castle, but how did you get past it?"

"It was asleep, so I crept past it and came in," replied Alex.

"You will surely be trapped within these walls now then. You were lucky indeed to find it off guard. The Queen of Hearts placed it there so that I may never leave and seek the crown. But again, I ask you, why are you naked?"

"Um, it's a long story but essentially I lost my clothes when I entered this land and haven't found any to replace them yet. My name is Alex by the way."

"I'm Princess Rebecca, the rightful heir to the throne. It's my stepmother on the throne at the moment. She acquired it after my father died under suspicious circumstances. She knew that my father was going to abdicate and hand the throne over to me, but she plotted and won the day. She even managed to turn the people against me and then locked me away, never to be seen again," replied the Princess while trying desperately to avoid looking at the huge cock dangling in front of her.

"I'm sorry to hear that. Is there anything I could do to help?" replied Alex.

Before she answered, Alex could see her pressing her legs together as if she was excited about something.

"You could look for Mad Harriet. She was the Court Hatter and has completely disappeared. She was also a close friend of the royal family," said the Princess.

"Where do you suggest I start looking?"

"Her closest friend was the Duchess and you can find her a mile down the road from my old castle in the North. Don't let the Queen's guards see you though, as they are suspicious of everyone," replied the Princess.

She looked at his cock again as she spoke and Alex could see that she was flustered over the sight before her. He felt she needed a push in the right direction. With that in mind, he started to stroke his cock. She saw what he was doing and blushed.

"My God, why is your cock so big?" she said as her eyes seemed transfixed by the motion of his hand as it slid along the length of his shaft.

Alex moved closer and was within a foot of her bed as his cock stopped growing. He didn't respond to her question, he just kept stroking. She sat up on the edge of the bed to watch more closely and Alex could see her licking her lips with her tongue as if hungry to taste what she was witnessing. He stroked faster and moved a little nearer. The end of his cock was mere inches away from her face and her tongue appeared again, as if to wet her overheated lips.

Then he moved just a hair closer and felt the end of his cock brushing her lips. Suddenly, she could take no more and leaned forward to surround the end of it with her mouth.

"Mmm...oh yes," she murmured as she sucked it in. Alex let go of it, allowing her to grip it with one hand. He watched her feed it into her mouth and felt her tongue licking the sensitive ridge when she brought it back out.

"Oh yes, suck it harder Princess," he said.

She swallowed even more in and began to stroke it at the same time. Then she moved faster and he felt the end of his cock brushing the back of her throat. After a few minutes of this she suddenly pushed him away.

"I want that monster inside me, NOW," she shouted out excitedly.

She then stood up and removed the robe she'd been wearing, before laying back onto the bed and spreading her legs wide. Alex jumped onto the bed and got into position and could see the gleaming wetness at her center. He pushed the bell end between her parted lower lips as she lifted her hips. He plunged deep into her hot wet center as she reached for his hips to pull him into her.

"Holy Mother of God, that fucking thing feels incredible," she yelled as he moved forward to fill her up.

Alex pulled back slowly and then pushed forward faster. Her screams of pleasure filled the room and the faster he fucked her, the louder she became. The bed was making a lot of noise as he pounded her, but neither one cared. She gripped his butt tighter, her nails digging into his flexing buttocks, to pull him towards her harder each time he pulled out and before long she was screaming that she was going to climax. Alex made a last supreme effort and gave a grinding twist of his hips to hit her pleasure center. When she came, she gripped his neck so tightly that Alex could barely move.

"Stay inside me, don't move," she whispered in his ear.

Alex could feel her pussy spasms as it tightened around his erupting cock and could feel her juices running down to his balls. He sighed in complete satisfaction as his cock began to soften. Then she let go of his neck and collapsed back onto the bed. Alex lay next to her to catch his breath.

"I have never experienced an orgasm that intense before," she eventually said.

"I could tell you were enjoying it," responded Alex.

She looked at him and laughed.

"I bet you could," she said.

"Can I spend the night in here now?"

"Yes, you might as well. I don't know how you're going to get out tomorrow though, but tomorrow is another day," she replied.

They both fell asleep shortly after that.

****

In the morning, Alex told the Princess that he'd try to find Mad Harriet. However, he first had to get past the Jabberwocky. It was wide awake when he entered the courtyard and Alex studied it from a discrete distance. He found that it tended to move around a lot and figured that its own weight probably had something to do with that. He knew that whales could die when beached because of their own weight and figured it was something like that.

He watched as the beast got up and walked around in a circle several times before coming back to rest. It reminded him of his old dog that occasionally stood up in its basket and turned around, only to lie back in the exact same position. This all gave him an idea. He waited patiently for the beast to move and then quickly got into its blind spot, behind. He followed it around until he was at the gate and ran to hide around the corner. It worked; the beast had no idea that someone had just left the castle grounds.

Alex proceeded North at a steady pace and soon saw another castle coming into view. He knew he had to get past it without being seen so he decided to use the fields and trees on the opposite side of the road to hide his approach. Until now being naked had been fun, but he was starting to wish he had some clothes. He'd asked the Princess if there were any old clothes in the castle but she said there were only women's clothes to be had.

He could now see the castle through the trees and it was an impressive structure. Once he'd gone by it completely he decided to use the road again and a couple of miles down the road he saw the large Manor. He headed straight for it and knocked on the door. A few seconds later, a butler opened the door.

"Yes sir, who shall I say is calling," said the butler.

"A friend of the Princess," replied Alex.

The butler closed the door leaving Alex outside and waiting. Alex could hear raised voices and moments later the butler came back to the door again.

"Come in sir," he said.

Alex entered to find the Duchess waiting for him.

"Why is this man naked?" she said, to no one in particular.

"It's a long story milady, but it can wait. Do you know where I might find Mad Harriet, the Princess is concerned for her welfare," replied Alex.

"I'm sure I have no idea," was the response.

"Oh, would you know where she might be. I promised the Princess that I would try my best to find her you see?"

Just then a door opened from across the hall and a rather attractive mid-thirties woman walked over to join them.

"It's ok Beatrice, I will take the chance with this young man, he seems honest. I am Mad Harriet sir, although, the Princess is the only one who ever calls me that," she said.

"Can we talk in private, I have something to ask and you might not be inclined to answer in company?" said Alex.

"Yes, follow me," she said and walked briskly off towards the same door she'd entered from.

Alex followed and she led him to a secret room. It was strangely decorated with whips, chains and all kinds of torture devices. At least, they looked like torture devices.

"What is so important to ask?" said Harriet.

"The Princess wonders if you know anything about her father's death. Did the Queen have anything to do with it?"

"The Queen had everything to do with it. I saw her adding the poison to the King's mead, but was stopped on my way to warn him in the hall, by guards who had been given orders to detain anyone wishing to gain an audience with the King. I knew that I would be next, so I fled. I heard what the Queen did with the Princess and was relieved that she was at least safe. I hear now that the Queen is becoming most unpopular amongst the people and it's only a matter of time before there's an uprising," replied Harriet.

"Thank you. I will relay this message to the Princess. Is there anything you'd like me to add?"

"Just that I'm sorry, her father was a good man. But, before you go, would you care to have a little fun?" replied Harriet.

"What kind of fun are you referring too?"

"Oh, the kind young men enjoy," she replied as she walked over to him and stroked his long limp cock.

He checked her over once again and although she had to be in her late thirties, she was still a striking woman. Her hair was thick and golden, piled high atop her head, while her creamy white breasts overflowed her bodice to the point where he could see the barest hint of pink areoles. However, before he could answer her, his cock did it for him. It was quickly growing in her hand as she continued to stroke it. The smell of her exotic perfume filled his senses as he unbuttoned her dress and she allowed it to fall to the floor. She stood barely a breath away, watching his reaction as she removed her undergarments. Standing only in stockings and heels, her pointed nipples brushed against the hairs on his chest while her parted lower lips glazed the length of his cock with her wetness. Standing there, face to face, she rode him back and forth coating him with her wetness before she moved off him and walked over to a bench with various tools and odds and ends resting on it. She picked up what looked like clothes pegs and brought them back over to where Alex was standing.

"I need a certain amount of stimulation at my age, I hope you don't mind?" she said.

"I don't mind," he replied, hoping that she wasn't coming anywhere near him with those pegs.

Instead, he watched her place a peg on each excited nipple and then handed him the third one.

"You can place that one onto my clit," she said, as he took it from her hand.

Turning around she led the way to a sumptuous bed, her rounded hips and smooth cheeks, issuing an invitation that his excited cock refused to turn down. She then lay on the bed and spread her legs wide. Alex could barely take his eyes away from her squeezed and painful looking nipples, yet, as he looked down at her pussy he could see her excitement gleaming wetly between her thighs. The very thought of what he was about to do was turning her on. She moaned aloud in anticipation.

"Do it, get that peg onto my clit and then fuck me as hard as you can," she urged.

Alex reached forward and moved the peg up to her erect clit and then clamped it onto her.

"OH FUCK...I want to feel that cock inside me," she crooned.

Alex got into position and pushed his cock passed the peg and into her sopping wet pussy.

"Oh...mmm...oh yes, deeper, I want to feel it deeper than that. Push it all in," she begged.

Alex pushed into her tight core and began to move his cock faster. Plunging deeply he felt her juices running out and onto his balls. Her writhing hips lifted with each plunge, as she clenched her inner muscles around his driving cock with each stroke. Her every moan and thrust enflamed his senses and he began to slam his rigid cock in to the hilt, his ball sack slapping her ass with every heave of his body and she screamed.

"More...give me more of that magnificent cock of yours."

He was now pounding her on the bed and shouting out profanities.

"I'm going to fuck you like you've never been fucked before," he yelled.

His entire cock was going inside and he was hitting bottom with each stroke. She began to scream that she was coming and he tried to move faster. Then she removed the peg from her clit and screamed that she was having an orgasm. Alex could then feel her gushing all over his cock and balls and as she tensed up around his cock he exploded inside her. He moved back and forth a few more times, draining the last few spurts of his cock, and then she gripped his butt cheeks and held him as deep inside her as she could. They stayed that way for another five minutes before they sat up on the bed. Harriet removed the pegs from her nipples and then turned to Alex.

"Young man that was the best fuck I've experienced for a long time. Thank you."

Alex had never experienced anything as intense as that, but he had to admit, it did turn him on. He then cleaned up at her sink and told her that he was leaving. She thanked him again and then showed him out. He walked until he saw the Queen's castle and fully intended to leave the road again to use the trees for cover. However, just as he was thinking about leaving the road he heard a voice behind him.

"Hey stranger, what do you think you're doing walking the Queen's highway naked?" he heard.

Alex turned to find several of the Queen's guards and had to think fast.

"I was robbed sir and they took everything," he replied.

"You were robbed you say, who by?"

"Um, I don't know sir, they wore masks."

"Well, we'd better get you some clothes hadn't we. You might scare a few of the ladies walking around like that. Come with us my boy," said the guard.

Alex didn't have much choice, he followed behind obediently. The castle gates were open and the castle itself was an impressive structure. It had four large towers on each corner and the drawbridge was a good fifty foot across. Once inside the courtyard, Alex could see hundreds of soldiers parading. He was quickly taken into the castle, with the intent of clothing him. However, just before they reached the tailor's work shop they heard the commanding voice of someone in charge.

"Why is that young man naked?" it said.

They turned around to see the Queen approaching them. She was tall and slender and Alex judged her to be in her forties. She wore a beautiful red and white robe and was flanked on either side by her loyal servants.

"Your Majesty, this young man was robbed on the road and everything was taken, even his clothes," said the guard as he bowed.

Alex followed suit and bowed as well.

"Do we have the ruffians in custody?" said the Queen.

"No your Majesty, we've only just discovered him outside the castle gates," replied the guard.

"Well, if you find them be sure to take their heads. In the meantime, come with me my boy. I wish to get acquainted with you and that gorgeous thing of yours," said the Queen as she pointed to his dangling cock.

Alex was ushered along to join her and he fell in dutifully behind the Queen, feeling more like a puppy than a young man. She led him into her throne room and made him sit beside her. Then, when everybody was dismissed she reached over and grabbed his cock.

"You have quite a specimen here young man," she said as she stroked it.

Alex didn't really want to react to her strokes, but found it almost impossible to stop the inevitable. His cock started to grow with her repeatedly gentle strokes and before long his cock was fully erect.

"Oh my, I think that's a bit too big for me. I wonder what the Tarts would say about it though."

She then stood up and called out.

"Fetch the Tarts, I wish to see them," she said and then sat down again.

Ten minutes later two beautiful young women came into the throne room and Alex recognized them both. They were the ones who had had their wicked way with him upon arrival in this land. They'd both sucked and fucked him behind a locked door.

"Girls, can you get rid of this enormous cock. I think it needs some attention," said the Queen pointing at the large cock in question.

"Oh my, that looks very familiar doesn't it friend," said the taller of the two.

"Oh yes, so it does. I think we can solve this little problem your Majesty," agreed the other.

They both got onto their knees in front of Alex and started to kiss his cock all over. Then, the taller one sucked the end of his cock and he felt the tip hitting the back of her throat. After three long strokes of her tongue she handed it over to her friend, who did the same thing. They swapped it back repeatedly until Alex could take no more. He called out that he was going to cum. When he did the girls moved their heads back a little and carried on stroking him. The Queen was watching all of this and saw the large string of man seed as it exploded from the end of his cock.

"That was quick girls, you know, you never cease to amaze me," said the Queen as Alex came for a second time.

After that, they cleaned him up and his cock started to deflate.

"Ah, that's better it's more manageable now," said the Queen as she stroked it again.

Twenty minutes later, the Queen was bored again and told her servants to take Alex away and find him some clothes. Alex was glad to get out of there as he hadn't said a word during his entire visit with the Queen. The servants took him to the tailor, who just happened to be a gorgeous blonde. Her hair flowed off her shoulders and the tiny dress she wore showed an incredible cleavage along with a long pair of slender legs.

"Oh my, what do we have here then," she said.

"The Queen wants him clothed," replied the guard.

"Ok, leave him with me."

The Guard left and Alex stood there watching as the tailor admired his body.

"I'm Alex, pleased to meet you," he said.

"I'm Victoria, and the pleasure is all mine," she replied.

She then bent down to take his inside leg measurements. Alex had an incredible view of her breasts as she placed the measuring tape against his foot and brought her hand up to his crotch. She was gorgeous and it was too hard not to think that way. Alex could feel his cock reacting and just as she was about to stand again, his cock twitched and started to rise.

Victoria remained where she was, staring at it like she'd never seen a cock before. She watched it grow until it was fully erect and then ran her tongue around her lips. Alex coughed, which brought her back to the moment and she stood up again.

"Um, I think we have a nice pair of pants that would fit you," she said.

She went over to a cupboard and opened it to reveal certain items of clothing, mainly for women. She then produced a pair of pants that looked too short for him.

"These should fit," she said.

She got down to the floor again and placed one of his feet into the pants leg, before doing the other one and pulling them up. When she reached his cock, she gently tucked it in, before pulling the pants over it. She fastened them and stood up again. They were the sort of pants that only came down to just below his knees, and they did fit. There was just one problem. His cock was causing such a bulge at the front that it was very distracting.

"I think we need to make that bulge go away. Maybe then the pants would look better," said Victoria.

She then got down onto her knees again and pulled the pants down. His huge cock sprang out, only this time Victoria grabbed hold of it and stroked its length.

"I have never seen such a nice cock," she said as she leaned forward and took the end of it into her mouth.

Alex let out a moan of pleasure and looked down to see her engulfing his meat. Her breasts were driving him crazy, which suddenly gave him a wonderful idea. He decided that this time he was going to take charge and immediately pushed her off and onto her back on the floor. He then gripped the thin material at the front of her dress and ripped it open to reveal her breasts.

"Oh my, what are you doing?" she moaned as he knelt down on top of her.

His knees were on either side of her slender body, but he was sitting up and placing his cock between her breasts. He then took hold of both her hands and told her to squeeze her breasts together. After she'd done that, he began to rock back and forth passing his huge cock between her compressed orbs. The end of his cock kept hitting her chin as it squeezed through, until he told her to suck the end. She immediately moved her head up and allowed his meat to enter her mouth whenever he moved forward. He moved up slightly and was able to go deeper into her mouth with each forward motion.

"That's it, fuck my mouth. I want to feel it going deeper," said Alex as he moved faster.

She was moaning aloud with pleasure and then moaned even louder as Alex thrust one hand down behind him and onto her sopping wet pussy. He quickly pushed two fingers into her womanhood and rubbed her clit with a third.

Mmm...oh...mmm," she groaned as the end of his cock touched the back of her throat.

He moved his fingers deeper and faster and could see her slobbering all over his cock with excitement. When she'd sucked him like this for ten more minutes Alex could feel his seed was about to make an appearance and quickly pulled his cock out to rest it on her chin. His man seed blasted her bottom lip and face. She leaned forward again and took his second load into her mouth to suck him dry. When she'd done that, Alex moved down and grabbed both her legs to pull up and spread, before placing the end of his cock into her now soaked pussy.

He pushed forward and she screamed with the pleasure of his entrance. He then wasted no time. He began to fuck her hard and fast.

"Oh god, oh shit I adore your cock," she shouted.

His strokes got deeper and her moans louder until she began to have her first orgasm. Alex had not had enough though he was still worked up by how gorgeous she was. He waited until her orgasm had finished and then quickly turned her over. He then grabbed her butt cheeks and lined his cock up with her rosebud ass.

"No not there, oh god I've never had it there," she shouted.

His cock was still soaked and as he pushed forward she let out a squeal of pain. He pushed a little harder and suddenly he was in. He started to fuck her slowly as she looked around. She then placed a finger onto her clit and began to rub it as he fucked her. She felt so tight and before long Alex could feel that he was going to cum for a second time. When he did Victoria was experiencing her own climax and collapsed onto the floor.

Alex pulled free and then stood up with his cock going limp between his legs. Victoria stood up shortly afterwards and spotted his now limp member. She cleaned him up and then tried the pants on him again. This time his cock tucked in nicely and he looked cute in his new pants. She then produced a shirt with puffy sleeves, which made him look princely.

"Ok, you're already to go. Oh by the way, take these slippers they look a lot like shoes and should do for a while at least. And please, come back again sometime, I would enjoy your company," said Victoria as she positively glowed.

Alex thanked her and then proceeded back into the castle. The guard was waiting for him and led him up into the higher levels. Apparently the Queen wanted him to see her land from the highest tower. He guessed that she probably wanted to gloat that she owned all the land. When he reached the highest tower, she was waiting for him.

"Oh my, you do look cute in your new clothes. I wanted to show you the amazing view from up here. Is it not breathtaking?" said the Queen.

It actually was a sight to see, but Alex was a little more concerned with the fact that the balcony seemed to be too old and unsafe. He could see that parts of it had crumbled away and fallen off. He was about to mention this fact to the Queen, when there was an almighty creaking sound from his extra weight and the balcony gave way. Alex grabbed the rail at the entrance to the balcony and tried desperately to reach the Queen with his other outstretched hand, but it was no use. He simply couldn't reach her and had to watch the anguish on her face as she fell.

Her guards came rushing over when they heard her scream, but they too were not in time. They helped Alex to his feet, knowing that he had nothing to do with the Queen's death. Alex took that opportunity to tell them what the Queen had done and to his surprise they had suspected the truth. Without the proof, they simply followed orders. They also told him that they would send out a contingent of guards to bring the Princess back home.

The news of the Queen's death was soon all over the castle and Alex was glad that the kingdom had been restored. Alex had to admit that the death of the Queen wouldn't have been his first choice in giving the Princess her rightful title back. He waited until the guards returned with her, as he wanted to share in her return to the throne. She was happy to see him and thanked him for all his help.

It was then that he told the princess where he came from and asked if there was any way he could get back home. She produced a bottle with a label on it that read, *A Return Trip*.

"Take a drink and think about where you'd like to return to and you will find yourself there," said the Princess.

Alex held the bottle and looked around him. He did think of staying, but he had a life back there and a fiancé waiting for him. He kissed the Princess' hand and said goodbye, before taking a drink and thinking of home. The crowd around him began to blur and suddenly he was waking up next to the tree he'd fallen asleep on.

"What an incredible dream," he said.

Then he noticed the clouds were getting darker and quickly gathered his things together. He started to run down the side of the river and then crossed the bridge and just as he reached the boat house the rain began to fall. He waited it out and then walked home. When he arrived, he found his fiancé waiting for him.

"Hi Natasha, I hope you haven't been waiting long?" he said.

"No, I just arrived. I have something important to say and I needed to see you," replied Natasha.

Alex showed her into his sitting room and they sat to talk.

"So, what's on your mind?" said Alex.

"Do you remember that conversation the other day about not having sex until we are married?" said Natasha.

"Yes, I remember."

"Well, I've been thinking. What if we get married and find that we don't make good lovers together. Not that we wouldn't, but what if we didn't. We might be happy with one another's love, but how long would that last without the physical connection to go with it?"

"Are you saying that you wish to make love to me, in order to know for sure?" said Alex frankly.

"Yes, I want my marriage to be perfect in every way Alex and I want that perfection to be with you."

Alex didn't say anything further he simply grabbed her hand and led her to the bedroom. They kissed passionately and Alex began to unfasten her dress, then he felt the strangest thing. His cock was growing, but it seemed all wrong. He then felt Natasha's hand resting on the bulge appearing in his pants.

"Oh my, what is this?" she said looking down.

The bulge was massive and Natasha stepped back to admire it. She then got down to her knees and unfastened his pants as her curiosity got the better of her. Once unfastened, she pulled them down and a huge cock sprang out.

"Oh my God Alex, you're huge. I had no idea," she said.

"How can this be, it was all a dream," he said.

"What was a dream?" replied Natasha.

"Oh nothing, forget it," said Alex with a smile.

Natasha grabbed his cock out of sheer awe and stroked its length.

"Holy fuck, it's enormous."

She then licked the end of it excitedly, before placing the bulbous tip into her mouth. She sucked on the end with sheer abandonment and then licked the ridge. Alex was looking down and watching her every move. He still remembered every second of what he thought was a dream and stood in awe of what he was witnessing. Then Natasha stood up sharply and began to pull her clothes off as quickly as she could.

"I want to feel that monster inside me," she said as she removed her undergarments.

She then grabbed his hand and they fell onto the bed together. Alex was on top, only this time, he wanted to take his time. He'd loved Natasha for as long as he could remember and had been over the moon when she consented to marry him. He gently rubbed the end of his huge cock between her legs and felt the end sliding through her womanly lips. She kissed him passionately when she felt the end of his cock probing her entrance. Then he pushed slightly and felt the end stretching her open. He let out a moan of approval and then pushed harder. Suddenly his cock was entering her and she grabbed his butt cheeks.

"Be gentle with me Alex, I want to savor this moment," she said.

Alex responded by slowing down but kept pushing forward. Soon, his cock was deep inside her and he was pulling it out again. Once he felt the tip at her opening he pushed it back, and she let out a squeal of pleasure as it sank deep inside her. Alex moved a little faster after that, making her clutch him even tighter. She was biting her bottom lip with every penetration and her face was flushed with color as she enjoyed each and every move that he made.

Alex could feel that he was stretching her and adored how tight she felt. Then she began to scream that she was coming and Alex could feel it getting harder to push in. When she did cum, she was swearing that she'd love him forever. Alex carried on and when he finally reached the moment of his own orgasm, he pulled it free. Natasha looked down to watch his seed explode all over her stomach and without saying a word she quickly got down the bed and placed his cock into her mouth to catch the second load.

"Ah, that feels so good," said Alex as she sucked him dry.

Once she'd finished, she sat up on the bed.

"How is it I knew nothing of this wonderful surprise?" she said.

"Well, it's not the sort of thing you go around mentioning to everyone, is it?" he replied.

He then looked up and mouthed the words thank you to the heavens, before making love to his future wife once more.

The End

Fairy Lore (An Erotic Adventure)

It had taken me over two months to get back to the States after being wounded in Afghanistan, but I was finally home. The only souvenir I brought back was the metal plate I now had holding my skull together, courtesy of the overseas military hospital. The surgeons there did an incredible job of saving my life. I was one of the lucky ones though. I'd been involved in a road side bombing and the other five men from my company, that had been in the truck with me, had all died.

I had a very restless sleep that first night in my bed. My home in the forest was light years away from the hot dry land I had come from. Maybe it was the sounds of the leaves rustling in the coolness of the mountains that kept me awake, but in the morning when I got up, I decided that I was going to take a walk through the woods to read at my favorite place in the entire world. I had found the secluded hollow shortly after moving to my home. About a mile from my house, deep in the forest, there was an oak tree the likes of which most people have never seen. The trunk had to be fifteen feet wide and it stood at least three hundred feet tall and dominated the place that I had named as Fairy Hollow. It was surrounded by a variety of wild flowers of every shape and color, the likes of which couldn't be found anywhere else. It was peaceful and a secluded place.

I always enjoyed going there whenever I was troubled and it seemed to take my cares away. When I arrived it was everything I could remember. There was one gigantic root that spread from the base of the tree and dove into the ground a few feet away. I always sat on the thickest part of that root and rested against the tree to read. It was a sunny day, so it was nice and warm when I started to read.

I must've reached the third chapter when I caught sight of something moving towards me from the corner of my eye. I glanced up and couldn't believe what I was seeing. I rubbed my eyes quickly, thinking that the light was playing tricks on me. But no, there, about four feet away was a fairy and she was coming towards me. I looked away, still believing that I was imagining it all. When I look back I realized that it was a female fairy. She was now resting on a flower, quite close to me, and collecting pollen.

It was also plainly obvious that she was a female, because she was completely naked. However, I think the best way to describe her would be to say that she looked like a perfect human female who had shrunk down to the size of a miniature doll. The kind of doll you'd see in a music box, one that would turn and dance when you opened the lid. In fact, the only thing that made her look different from a human was her pointed ears and the pair of wings coming out of her back and upper shoulders.

She seemed to be oblivious to me and I dared not move as I was completely captivated by it all. Then I spotted another one flying towards her, only this one was a male. When he came to rest beside the female he looked directly at me. It was then that I remembered why I appreciated this place so much, it was deathly quiet, so quiet in fact, that I could hear them talking.

"Is it my imagination, or is that human looking straight at us?" said the male fairy.

She looked up and caught my eye.

"No silly, he's probably looking at the flower we're sitting on," she replied.

It was then that I made my mistake. I said something.

"Um, I can see you both," I said still looking directly at them.

She turned her head quickly and looked up at me in horror, the male fairy took flight, grabbed her arm, and they quickly flew off and out of sight.

"Wait, I don't mean you any harm," I said as they flew from view.

I could've kicked myself. Why did I have to say anything? I might have witnessed their behavior for hours, but no, I had to open my big mouth. I stood up and walked around in the direction they'd flown, but I couldn't find a trace. In the end, I decided to go home. I couldn't stop thinking about that incident for the rest of the day. I wanted to tell others, but I knew that without proof, no one was going to believe me.

The next day I went back and sat on the root once more to read. I'd been there for well over an hour when suddenly I saw three fairies coming towards me. The two I'd seen the day before and an older one. This time I sat perfectly still and fully intended to remain quiet. They all flew up close and stopped in the same place as the day before. I was looking straight at them.

"Can you see and hear us?" said the oldest looking of the three.

The fact that he was addressing me made me answer.

"Yes I can see and hear you," I replied.

"See, I told you. This has to be the foretold prophesy," said the female.

"Silence child, I'm trying to establish that," replied the elder.

"Prophesy, what prophesy would that be?" I said.

"She mis-spoke, it is yet to be established as to whether you have anything to do with the foretold prophesy," replied the elder, "all we know for now is that you can see and hear us, when you shouldn't be able too."

"Why shouldn't I be able to see or hear you?"

"The power Orb Arkainia prevents humans from seeing or hearing us. However, the wizard who created the Orb also foretold that it would one day be destroyed. The destroyer would turn out to be our savior, although we don't know from what we will be saved. The prophesy states: One will come with the sight to see, destroy the Orb and set you free," said the old fairy.

"Well, I have no intentions of destroying anything," I replied.

"Arkainia's predictions were always vague," said the old fairy.

"Arkainia...I thought you said the Orb was named Arkainia?"

"Yes, it was named after the Great Wizard Arkainia."

"Oh, I see, well is there any way to find out whether or not I have something to do with this foretold prophesy of yours?" I said.

"Fairy Lore states that every possible avenue should be investigated, should the foretelling of the Prophesy be in doubt," said the elder, "with that in mind, I would like to take you with us and put you to the test. I will need your permission for this."

"You have my permission," I replied.

I was eager to find out where this would lead and I was still fascinated by the fact that fairies were real and not some story or myth. Then, suddenly the elder flew over and around me chanting some words that I didn't understand. The next thing I knew I was shrinking at an alarming rate. In just a few seconds, I was standing on the root I'd been sitting on and it now looked like the trunk of a huge tree. The two younger fairies grabbed a hand each and then we were airborne. The fact that they were both naked didn't seem to bother them. However, at this size I could barely stop looking at the female, she was perfect in every way.

I could see the flowers just below my feet as we skimmed over them and then turned sharply around the large oak tree. They flew down towards the opposite side of the tree and as we got nearer I could see a hole at the base. We flew through it and landed. We then walked along a corridor and when we turned the corner I could see lights and little huts everywhere.

'They have lived here all this time and I knew nothing about it,' I thought.

"Welcome to Fairy Grove, our home and sanctuary," said the elder.

We were all greeted by over fifty other fairies and it was hard not to notice that most of them were females. They didn't seem to own clothes, or at least they weren't in any hurry to wear them. I was starting to feel out of place, especially as some of them were looking and pulling at my clothes in an inquisitive way.

"Ok, leave him alone. You've all seen clothes before," said the elder.

"Why do you not wear clothes?" I said as he'd brought it up.

"We only wear clothing in the winter months. It saves on precious water in the summer, as we have no need to clean them. In addition, we feel less restricted and lighter when we fly."

'*That makes sense,*' I thought.

All the new fairies seemed fascinated by me as if they'd never seen a human before. Then one of the females, the one who helped to transport me, spoke.

"Elder, he needs to be cleansed, before we can test him," she said.

I couldn't stop staring at these delightful creatures. However, the fact that they were naked was very distracting.

"Yes, you're right. Ok, girls take him to the Holy Hall and cleanse him," said the elder.

I looked at him inquisitively.

"The water in the Holy Hall is blessed and any evil you may hold will be cleansed from your body," said the elder.

I just figured that we all have certain beliefs, so I should follow theirs while I was a guest. Suddenly, half a dozen female fairies ushered me along to a building that stood out from the rest of them. I figured it was their version of a church as there was a golden cross on the door. Once inside, I was directed to the back of the hall and into another room. There was a small pool in there, being fed by warm water from a tube coming from outside. They all tried to undress me and I resisted.

"I can take off my own clothes," I said.

However, they ignored me and continued to try and remove my clothes. I had to help them in the end as they didn't know how zippers worked, or how to take a shirt off without pulling off the buttons. I was fine with all of this until I got down to my underwear. It didn't help that a few of the girls were giggling about something. Then, before I could protest someone pulled my briefs down from behind. I quickly stepped into the warm water and sat down.

What I didn't count on was the fact that they were all getting in with me. They immediately began to bathe me, all six of them. I tried to close my eyes as I knew what was going to happen, but I couldn't keep them closed. I wanted to reach out and bathe them as well. When it came time for them to wash my lower parts I tried desperately to think of something other than them touching me, but failed miserably. The next thing I know, I hear a few gasps and look down to see that three of them are holding my cock as it stood fully erect. They were all sitting there just staring at it and I didn't know what to do.

"Um, I'm sorry, I tried not to let it happen but it was impossible with all you lovely ladies paying so close attention to me," I eventually said.

"Why is it so much bigger than usual?" said one of them to no one in particular.

"I don't know, but it's very nice," said one of the girls that were holding it.

She then rubbed the soap all along the length of it as if to demonstrate the fact that it was big. Of course, it looked the same to me as it always did, but I had no idea what they were used to. Then they carried on bathing me and giggling as they did so. Once that was finished, they dried me off and gave me my clothes back.

'That wasn't awkward,' I thought sarcastically as I dressed.

When I was ready they escorted me back to the elder.

"Before we take you to the Orb the girls will test you. They will then let me know if you can be trusted. If all is well at that point, I will show you to the Orb and we'll see how it goes from there. I have no idea whether you are part of the foretold, or whether this is all a mistake but one way or another we will find out. Do you have any questions?" said the elder.

"No, the only thing I've been wondering is why you all look human?" I replied.

"It is written in one of our oldest books that we are descended from humans. How or when this happened I cannot say. We do feel that magic was involved at some point, but we don't know when. Being fairies is all we know."

I wondered if other fairy communities knew the answers, but didn't ask. Then the girls led me off again and I just followed. I then wondered how they would test me, but again I didn't ask. This time there were at least fifteen females and each one was beautiful. I was led to a large hut and once inside I was told to sit on the floor in the center. They all sat around me and started to ask me questions.

"Have you ever killed?" said the first one.

"Um, yes but only in self-defense," I replied.

"Do you feel any animosity towards my people?" said another.

"No," I replied.

"I noticed in the bath that you were excited by us, are you attracted to us?"

"Yes, I find myself very attracted to you. I'm sorry if that is wrong, I just can't help it."

"Did you know before today that we existed?"

"No, I didn't."

After a few more questions they all drew nearer to me and placed a hand somewhere on my body, before chanting some unfamiliar words. The only problem with this was that they were all very close and I found my cock reacting to their bodies. I hated the fact that I couldn't control it, but within seconds my cock was standing up like a tent pole in my pants.

"We sense that you mean us no harm but that you have strong reactions to our touch. Is this normal for humans?" said the one directly in front of me.

"It's a human trait that goes back a long way. We're very easily stimulated and what is happening here and now wouldn't happen back home. Your people think nothing of being naked, whereas humans are nearly always covered by clothing. I find you all very attractive and nothing I do will ever change that view."

"We can all sense that you are an honest man. You have passed our test and we should now go back and see the elder," she replied.

I stood up feeling embarrassed that I was still hard, but they all seemed to ignore it. Once outside, the elder was waiting and after talking with the female fairies he told me to follow him. He led me to another hut and once we stepped inside I was struck by all the different colors lighting up the room. The streams of colored light were coming from an Orb that was sitting on an ornately carved wooden pedestal in the middle of the room.

"This is the Orb Arkainia. It is the means by which we are both invisible to humans and unheard," said the elder.

As I stepped into the room to get a better look, I found myself feeling drawn to it. The compulsion to move closer to it felt unnatural to me. My body continued forward, step by step, even though I hadn't intended to.

"It's making me want to get nearer, even though I'm trying not to, I'm feeling compelled," I said urgently.

The elder didn't respond he just watched and suddenly I was standing over the Orb. Then I reached for it with both hands and when I was cradling it, within the palms of my hands, I felt frozen in place. The light from the Orb then intensified to such a degree that I had to close my eyes against the brilliance and then suddenly there was an explosive burst of light and I was thrown backwards. I opened my eyes as I sat on the ground next to the wall and the Orb was no longer glowing. In fact, it was now a mere shell. I stood up and quickly helped the elder to his feet.

"What happened?" I said.

"I'm guessing the foretold prophesy just came about. What this means for my people is still unclear, but what I do know is that you are not to blame for this," replied the elder.

Then I was made to stand straight and suddenly I could feel another presence. I wanted to speak but something was stopping me and then I began to talk but nothing I said was coming from my mind.

"Elder, keep this man safe and take care of his every need. I am Arkainia and I will take possession of his body every day for one hour at a time. I will speak with you again tomorrow," said the voice.

I was then given back control of my own body and stood staring at the elder.

"I guess we have our answer, Arkainia has a plan for us," said the elder.

We then went outside where he informed his people as to what had happened.

"Sara Lee, you are tasked with looking after this human and giving him whatever he desires," said the elder to one of the fairies.

Sara Lee stepped forward as all her people stepped to one side. She walked up to me and took me by the hand.

"I accept this assignment," she said, before leading me off to her own hut.

She was the most beautiful creature I'd ever seen, her slender figure along with her large breasts, were a match made in heaven. When she smiled her teeth almost glowed they were so white. Yet, she felt delicate to the touch and seemed almost fragile. Her skin was soft and smooth and she seemed genuinely excited to be taking care of me. Once inside her hut, she asked me if I was hungry and as it happens I was. She immediately set about making a meal.

"What is your name?" she said as she worked.

"Brandon and yours is Sara Lee isn't it?" I replied.

"Yes, I must say I like the name Brandon."

"Thank you, I think Sara Lee is a very pretty name," I replied.

She seemed to blush from that comment and the more I was in her company the more I liked her. She had a certain-innocence about her that I found both charming and fun to be around. However, I do wish sometimes that we as humans could take our minds out of the gutter from time to time. As she worked with her back to me I could see her perfectly formed butt cheeks and whenever she bent down to get something from the cupboards below the sink I would get a sight that many men would die for. Needless to say, she was unintentionally turning me on. I was just glad that I was sitting at a table and that she couldn't see the rather large bulge that had appeared within my pants. When she served dinner it consisted of vegetables on the whole, or though there were a couple of things in it that I didn't recognize. However, it tasted delicious. She gave me a drink of something fizzy and again it was something I'd never tasted before.

"Is this satisfactory?" she said as she ate beside me.

"It's very nice, thank you," I replied.

The more time I spent in her company the more I wanted to stay. I'd never felt this way about a human female before and I don't think it had anything to do with the fact that she was naked. That was more a distraction than a draw, although I do have to add it was a very welcome distraction.

After the meal she cleared the dishes and then asked me to come over to the sitting area. Once we'd taken a seat, she fetched a bowl of water and a cloth and told me to remove my clothes. This was a fairy ritual. They washed thoroughly whenever they ate and as she was attending my every need, she felt that it was her duty to clean me from head to toe. I didn't object this time, as I knew that she was just doing her job and I didn't want to offend her. I stripped all of my clothes and stood in front of her.

"Oh my, why is your member so big?" she said innocently.

"Um, you're going to have to excuse me for that. You see, I find you attractive and that's the effect you are having on me," I replied.

"Oh I see," she replied and then just stared at it, like it was the first one she'd ever seen.

I coughed to clear my throat, which made her realize that she was staring. She then commenced in bathing me and I could tell that she was deliberately trying to look away from my cock. However, there came a point when she could no longer ignore it and I felt her hands surrounding it in order to clean me up.

I closed my eyes to the sensations as the soap was rubbed on and I swear it grew a little more as she handled it. When I opened them again, it was because she hadn't stopped. I looked down and watched her sliding her hands across its length and stare at it with almost a longing in her expression. The cloth fell to the floor with the soap now gone but both her hands still surrounded it. I could feel my cock pulsating in her hands and a drop of pre-cum appeared at the tip. She licked it, making me shudder with excitement. Then suddenly she leaned forward and took the end of my cock into her mouth.

'*Oh God, oh that feels so good*,' I thought.

I didn't say anything. I just watched her head moving back and forth as her tongue played with the ridge of my cock. I'd mistakenly thought that sex was something they didn't do with strangers, I was wrong. I stroked her hair as she continued and saw a few more inches pass her lips. She held it with both hands as she continued and I closed my eyes once more.

Then I felt one of her hands gently massaging my ball sack as she stroked my cock with the other. The overwhelming sensations were telling me that I was close. I'd been frustrated on a number of occasions, but now I knew that I was going to ejaculate. She carried on sucking, only now with a little more vigor. Moments later, I told her that I was going to cum and she pulled it from her mouth. It exploded from the tip, hitting her shoulder and cheek as she carried on stroking it.

She let out a moan of approval as the second load made an exit and then allowed the last few drops to come out onto the back of her hand. She reached down for the cloth and wiped her hand clean and then stood up in front of me.

"I need to feel that inside me," she said, almost urgently.

I grabbed her waist and picked her up. I then positioned her onto my cock and found that she was soaked. She then suddenly felt lighter and I realized it was because she was flapping her wings, which helped me to hold her in place easily. I felt the end of my cock spreading her pussy lips apart and then heard her moan aloud as it began to enter her.

"Oh sweet God, that feels wonderful," she said, looking me directly in the eyes.

I'd only gotten the end in, so I wondered what she'd think when it was all inside her. I pushed forward and her face said it all. She felt incredibly tight as I pushed a few inches inside her, yet she was bathing my cock with her juices. Her moans were becoming screams as my entire cock reached bottom and then I withdrew it and pushed forward again.

"Oh yes...oh don't stop...please don't stop," she pleaded.

I moved faster and began to pound her pussy and then I heard gasps coming from the side. I turned my head to see two other female fairies watching our every move from the other side of the window. I then turned back as I felt Sara Lee's pussy tightening around my cock and realized that she was about to have her first orgasm. When it came she let loose. Her screams of pleasure echoed around the room. Her nipples were fully erect and the sweat was dripping from her body. She then suddenly went limp as I continued to pound away.

I felt like changing positions at that point and gently put her down onto the floor, before turning her around. Again, I heard gasps coming from the window as they saw the size of my cock. I entered Sara Lee again only this time from behind and started to fuck her. Her wings flapped as the excitement built up and I could feel the breeze it was causing, wafting up into my face. I could go deeper in this position and I didn't waste any time. I started to fuck her hard and upon turning my head to see the spying fairies, I could see that they were both spell-bound by what they were witnessing.

It wasn't long before Sara Lee began to moan aloud again, only this time I wanted to cum at the same time as she did. I moved faster and faster and suddenly she screamed out again and I started to cum. Once I felt it exploding inside her I stopped with my cock buried as far as it would go. I saw her shudder with excitement several times and then a few minutes later I pulled out. I immediately knew that I had to hold her up and quickly picked her up to lay her down onto her bed. I sat beside her and then looked around to find that the voyeurs had gone. Minutes later, Sara Lee opened her eyes and looked up at me.

"I have never experienced anything like that," she said.

"I feel the same way," I replied.

She smiled and then sat up.

"Can we do it again later?" she whispered.

"I was kind of hoping you'd say that," I replied with a laugh.

We talked for hours that day and made love once more, before the elder came to get me. He led me back to the hut where the Orb had been and once inside, I felt Arkainia taking over my body.

"Elder, I will need a list of things. You must obtain them all, so send your best out, understood?" said Arkainia through me.

"Yes Great Wizard," replied the elder.

I then set about writing out a list and didn't recognize a single thing on the paper I was writing on. It felt incredibly weird being controlled by someone else, but I didn't mind. When the list was done the Wizard then got to work performing magic and by the time the ingredients had been found, the Wizard had another Orb ready.

'The Orb is necessary for my people, it keeps them hidden and unheard. It also has healing properties and is where my mind resides. I can come out every year to look over my people and I will need a vessel such as yours to do so. I'm hoping that you consent to such an arrangement,' I heard inside my head.

'I would be honored to do such a service,' I thought back.

'You are a good man Brandon. I think fate picked you wisely. I will be leaving you with a gift and also some needed information. So, until we meet again, farewell my friend,' was the reply.

I could sense him leaving me and then the Orb began to glow again. He'd performed a spell of some sort with the ingredients he'd been given and everything was as it should be. The elder thanked me for my part, which is when I informed him of what the Wizard had told me.

"What is this gift he talked about?" said the elder.

"I don't know, but I guess we'll find out sooner or later. I do know what the information was however. He informed me that you have too many females and not enough males. He wants you to instruct the people to produce more offspring and thinks that I might be of service to that end. I will gladly stay, at least until we find out what this gift is, if that is alright with you?" I replied.

"My dear friend, you can stay for as long as you wish. In fact, we're going to hold a party tomorrow night to celebrate the return of the Orb and to welcome our new honorary member," said the elder excitedly.

I found Sara Lee waiting for me outside and she took hold of my arm as we walked back to her hut. I informed her of everything that had happened, to which she was delighted. Once inside the hut we heard a knock on the door. Upon answering it, we found several female fairies all wanting to talk to me. Sara Lee let them in and they all looked at me star-struck, as if they'd never seen a male before.

"Can I help you ladies?" I said.

"The elder has just informed us that we need to produce more off spring and that you were one of the candidates and we were wondering if you'd be our partner for this endeavor?" said the spokes fairy for them all.

Before I could answer, there was another knock on the door. In fact, within the next ten minutes there were several such knocks on the door. It turned out that they all wanted the same thing. There were now over thirty-two females in the room and they were all staring at me with pleading expressions.

"Ok, I will help each and every one of you, but we have to do this by the numbers. I would suggest that you all write your names on a piece of paper and I will take two of you every day, until I have reached the end," I said.

They all started to talk with one another and quickly agreed. Then they produced some paper and a pen and began to write their names out. Once I collected them all, I placed them in a container that Sara Lee supplied and chose the first two.

"Um, Wander and Geisel," I said aloud.

The two girls mentioned came forward.

"Tonight, after the party I will come to your huts and we can begin," I said.

They both looked so excited, whereas I couldn't believe any of it.

****

The party was going well, until I found out what the gift left to me by Arkainia was. I was having a drink, laughing and talking with the elder when I suddenly passed out. When I opened my eyes again, I was on the floor. They all looked relieved that I was alright and then suddenly I realized what I knew. Arkainia had imparted all of his knowledge to me and the sudden release of all that information had been too much for my mind. I sat up and informed the elder.

"Oh my, that is great news indeed," he said.

I was then helped to my feet and felt full of life. I couldn't believe the things I knew and just how powerful Arkainia really was. The rest of the party went off without a hitch. However, I still had to visit Wander and Geisel as promised. Then I had an idea. I knew a spell that would help me achieve the task at hand all in one night. I decided to try it.

I cast the spell and there in front of me stood an absolute double of myself. I talked with my other self to see if he had all of my memories and sure enough, he was an exact copy. I decided to do it again and again, until I had thirty two copies. Then I instructed them on what to do and watched as they each walked off to find one of the females that I'd promised to make love to. After that, I went back to Sara Lee's hut to find that she was surprised to see me.

I told her what I'd done and she immediately realized that I was now hers for the night. However, as I stripped my clothes away, I suddenly had another wicked idea. I talked to her about it and she seemed excited enough to try it. I then placed a spell on myself and immediately fell to my knees. I had given myself a shape shifting spell and hadn't realized how painful the change would be. I felt my cock shrinking and moving inside my body and then my chest began to grow and within seconds I had large breasts. Then my face went through the change and it was excruciatingly painful. I also realized that I'd have to go through this again when the spell wore off in two hours' time. Once the pain had stopped, I managed to stand up and Sara held her hand over her mouth in awe.

"It worked, you're now a beautiful woman," she said.

I looked down to admire my handy work and immediately saw a pair of large womanly breasts. They were full and quite large and tipped by two rosy pink nipples. Raising one hand, I saw that it was also more slender and tipped with womanly fingernails. I gently reached for my breasts with both hands and felt their weight and fullness. Their size spilled over my hands and as I touched them with wonder I felt tingles of pleasure run through to the tips. Reaching out with the ends of my fingertips I managed to play with the sensitive tips and watched as they hardened into pointed ends of pleasure. I closed my eyes at the intense feelings running though my body and played with the orbs until I felt moisture gathering between my legs.

Looking down past the breasts I was playing with, I left them behind as I ran my fingers over the slender abdomen beneath them. Running my hands around my now slender waist, I reached behind me to feel the smooth globes of my rounded buttocks. In awe, I continued back to the front to feel the smooth front of my womanhood. No hair covered the delta there and the softness of the skin there entranced me. My fingers felt the split of my new lower lips and pleasure began to fill and inundate that area, as my fingertips ran over the split repeatedly.

Feeling moisture gathering there, I spread the lips with my fingers and gently touched the wetness that had formed there, and felt faint at that first touch. I looked up at Sara Lee in astonishment of the sensations and she just coyly smiled as she watched me discover the areas of my new body. Looking back down I touched the bud, and a shock of pleasure ran though my body, and as it did my mind began to spin with the possibilities.

I then looked at Sara Lee and quickly cast another spell. This one wasn't going to change her. Instead, it was going to include something very special, something this new body shamelessly wanted to experience. Suddenly we both saw a bulge appearing above her pussy and we watched it as it grew, until finally a cock popped out of her pussy and started to lengthen.

I'd always wondered what it felt like to have a cock entering you, as a woman. I could now find out. We came together and kissed lustfully. I placed a hand over her rigid cock and stroked it greedily as we carried on kissing. Then I had a sudden urge to drop to my knees. I didn't fight it and there in front of me was the cock I'd created coming out of Sara Lee. I held it as if in a dream, holding it, shaping it with my hands and then determinedly slipped my mouth over the end and began to suck it.

Sara Lee let out a moan of pleasure and gripped the back of my head. In the background we could distantly hear the moans of pleasure from the other female fairies as they were being serviced by my doubles. I greedily tried to see how far I could get the cock into my mouth and found out first hand just how hard it is. I could manage about two thirds of it before it was hitting the back of my throat. I sucked harder and faster when I heard Sara's moans of pleasure and then slipped a finger into her pussy, just below the cock. She let out a loud groan of approval and then could take no more.

She pulled her weeping cock out of my mouth and then pushed me onto my back on the floor. In one swift motion she straddled me and lay on top, our breasts grinding against each other. I could feel the heaviness of her cock resting between my legs and then felt the fullness of the bell-end as she moved it closer and rubbed it against my tender opening. I was bombarded with emotions. I was anxious, yet excited, wondering how it would feel when she finally pushed it in. Then I felt the pressure as the end of her cock slipped into me past the tight muscles at my entrance. I could feel it stretching me wider and it felt amazing. She coaxed it into me slowly, sliding it back and forth as the moisture gathered there. When she eventually stopped moving, it was as far inside me as it would go and then she began to rock in and out.

Each time it came out I desperately wanted it back in again. The sensation of fullness was incredible. She started off slowly and then picked up speed, until she was fucking me the way I fucked her the day before. She was using fast, long, hard strokes that seemed to last forever. I reached out and held her butt tightly to force her deeper into me. I started to feel an odd feeling of a slow building pressure deep within me. It felt so good and I shifted my hips to feel more of it. With that small adjustment of my bottom I felt my new pleasure bud press more firmly against the hard cock that was entering me and the feeling was like an electric shock that went through me. Each time I ground my pleasure point against the invading cock my insides wound up tighter. Widening my legs I feverishly tilted my pelvis upward, riding the wave of pleasure it created. My toes began to tingle and a wave of ecstasy travelled up my legs until it reached my pussy and exploded in a crest of pleasure so intense that I screamed aloud. Wave after wave of pleasure flowed over me until I felt almost faint with the knowledge that this must be what a woman feels when she's experiencing an orgasm. It was unbelievably powerful and made my muscles tighten up as Sara Lee continued to pound me. Then I heard her scream and felt the cock inside me pulsate and knew that she was about to cum.

When she did cum she held it inside me and collapsed onto my breasts. Moments later, I could feel her juices oozing out and running down my inner thighs. As we lay there arm in arm we could still hear the screams of joy coming from the other huts as they too started to experience an orgasm. I finally sat up, still feeling the lingering tingles of ecstasy as it passed through my body.

"So, that's what it feels like for you?" I said.

"Yes, and now I know how it feels for you as well. I think over all though, I prefer to be a woman. Cumming with a man's cock is incredibly powerful, and very pleasurable, don't get me wrong, but I think a female's orgasm is more intense and felt throughout the whole body," said Sara Lee.

We talked until the spell I cast had begun to dissipate and my change back started to happen. Again, it was very painful and when it was finished I couldn't help thinking that I probably wouldn't be doing that again anytime soon. It was quite an agonizing experience.

****

In the morning, we gathered together before the Holy Hall and the elder thanked me for what I'd done and all the girls wanted to thank me as well. I told them that it was my pleasure and even though I wanted to stay longer, that I felt that I should go home for now. I'd helped them with their problem and knew that they'd now be safe. I also knew that I needed to get back to my home and check in with my family members and friends. I told my new found friends that I'd be back every day to visit with them and that I would always be around if they needed me. They all cheered as I made my way out to the edge of the hollow and once there the Elder turned me back into my rightful size and I slowly walked back home.

On the way home, I pondered what would happen now, where this would all lead, but I already looked forward to seeing them again. I learned in the weeks that followed that all of the females were now expecting a baby, even Sara Lee. Thinking through the possibilities, I created a spell and cast it on the fairies to ensure that their child took after them and had wings. I knew that it would be unfortunate if any of the children took on the human side and didn't have wings.

Several months have passed and after many visits to the Hollow and Sara and I have fallen deeply in love with each other. The elder has given his approval and Sara has asked me to join them there and live at the Hollow, but fate would step in and endanger us all. However, that's another story.

The End

The Cursed (An Erotic Adventure)

Geraldine awoke, looking forward to another day of experimentation. She was a witch, and a very good one. However, she was different from most other witches. She very rarely dabbled in the dark arts, and was more interested in the power of the mind. Over the years, she'd discovered that the brain could to do much more than just amass information.

The discovery that the brain could do special things came about by accident, when she was trying to get rid of a headache through magical means. She'd invented a new spell that when cast upon oneself was supposed to alleviate a headache. Instead, she'd discovered that she could move objects, just by thinking about it. This led to other things, one of which was the power to read minds. The latest discovery was that of levitation, and she was so excited about it all.

She was only thirty-one, which was young for any witch. However, she was already more powerful than any witch she knew. On this day, she wanted to experience her limitations. However, she needed a subject or two to experiment with. The cat was all well and good, but she needed feedback and the cat couldn't provide that. By chance, she sensed that she had visitors, and they were now surrounding her cottage. She didn't know why, but felt that it was serendipitous.

She walked over to the window and spotted a couple of soldiers from the nearby kingdom. She recognized the insignia on their armor. They had crossbows and swords drawn as if hunting for something.

"I wonder what they want with me?" she said aloud as she walked towards the door.

When she opened it and stepped out, she was given orders.

"Lie down on the ground and no one will get hurt, witch," shouted someone she couldn't see.

"I'm not getting down onto the ground, young man, and who do you think you're talking to," she replied.

"We are the King's guards and are under orders to bring you in," said the voice.

Geraldine searched the bushes with her mind and soon located the individual who was talking to her. She heard him yelp as her mind made contact with his, making him rise into the air and drift forward from where he was hiding. As he floated towards her, another overzealous guard let loose a crossbow bolt. It stopped a foot away from Geraldine and then dropped to the ground.

The first guard was now a few feet away, just floating above the path with a terrified look on his face. Geraldine dropped him and watched him sprawl on the ground.

"Now then, perhaps you can tell me what this is all about, in a more civilized manner," she said.

The soldier sat up, trying not to make eye contact.

"There is a curse on the Prince, and the King needs help from a witch to remove it," he said quickly.

"So, let me get this straight; you need my help but are willing to capture and manhandle me in order to obtain it. Does that about sum it up?" she replied.

"I'm sorry; it's just that we were scared and didn't quite know how to approach a witch. We've all heard the stories of what a witch will do to you if you cross them," replied the soldier.

Geraldine could actually sympathize with him there, as she knew a few witches that would indeed hurt them first and talk later. She decided to give them a second chance.

"Okay. Look, if I promise not to hurt you, will you do me the courtesy of the same?" she said.

The soldier stood up and faced her for the first time.

"Oh my, you're a witch?" he said in a surprised tone.

"Why does that surprise you?" she replied.

"I expected to find an old hag, and not an attractive young woman," he said.

Geraldine looked at him more closely. He was a tall, good-looking man, and she placed him in the mid-twenties age group.

"You think I'm attractive?" she replied.

"Oh yes, very attractive. Are you using a spell?" he replied.

"No, what you see is what you get. So tell me, what is this curse you were talking about?"

"It happened a few weeks ago. The Prince was in his room when a witch paid a visit. We don't know where she came from, or why she placed a curse onto the Prince, but once she did she was gone."

"What does this curse entail?"

"Every day after dark, the Prince is turned into a princess until the morning light, where he is then turned back into a prince. As you can imagine, the Prince dare not go anywhere after dark, and only the most loyal of the King's men know about it."

"Um, a transformation spell isn't difficult to remove. I should be able to counter it easily enough. However, I want something in return," said Geraldine.

"What would that be?" replied the soldier.

"I need some assistance with one of my experiments. If you stay with me for one night, I'll return with you to the King's castle in the morning. Have we got a deal?" said Geraldine.

"Um, how do I know that I can trust you?"

"You don't; that's my offer, take it or leave it. I will say this though, if I wanted to hurt you – I could. I simply need your assistance and promise that you won't come to any harm."

The soldier stood up straight, and informed his men that he would be staying for the night. In addition, he told them that they should go back and inform the King to expect the witch in the morning. The soldiers didn't know what to make of it all, but were very happy to be able to leave so quickly. Once they were gone, Geraldine showed the soldier into her cottage.

"Okay, first things first, what's your name," she said.

"Tom, milady," he replied.

"Well Tom, I'll be using my magic on you, and I need to ask you how it feels. I've developed this magic over the last few years, mainly to benefit myself. However, I could see this type of magic benefiting others as well," said Geraldine, noticing how alarmed he looked. "Don't worry. The magic I intend to use won't harm you."

Tom wasn't exactly convinced, but he relaxed a little.

"Okay, let's get started. I want you to tell me if you can hear me," said Geraldine.

I'm talking to you with my mind, are you hearing me? She thought.

"Wow, yes I heard you in my head, but didn't see your lips move," he replied.

"That's good, but I need you to answer me with your mind. I need to know if I can hear the reply," said Geraldine.

"Oh right, sorry."

Can you hear me? He thought.

"Yes, it works. I can now talk to people using telepathy. Okay, the next thing I want you to do is think of an object. Anything will do, and I'll see if I can tell you what that object is."

Tom looked around the room and saw the bucket over near the sink.

"You were thinking of the bucket," she said quickly.

"Yes, I was. That's amazing," he replied.

"It is, isn't it?" said a beaming Geraldine.

"Um, it's getting a bit warm in here, do you mind if I remove my armor?" said Tom.

"No, please do. In fact, let me see if I can do it for you," replied Geraldine, eager to try another experiment.

She concentrated and stared at the buckles that held the armor together, and suddenly they popped open, and the breast plate was free to remove. Next, she looked down at the shin guards and unfastened them with her mind. That was another successful experiment achieved.

"How do you do that? It's quite astounding," said an impressed Tom.

"I'm pleased that you think so. Now then, I'd like to test my levitation spell on you. Could you tell me what you feel when I do?" said Geraldine.

Tom stood in just a tunic and undergarments.

"I will," he replied.

Suddenly, he felt himself rising up about six inches from the floor.

"It feels strange, but apart from the tingling in my feet, I don't actually feel anything," said Tom.

Geraldine was about to let him back down, when she saw the bulge between his legs. She wondered if there was any way she could...

No, what are you thinking? She thought as she admired the bulge. *Still, what harm could it do?*

She concentrated on his crotch and tried to peek beneath the tunic, and for a moment the material did seem to fade, but she couldn't do it. She then let him down and thanked him for his assistance.

"You seemed to be struggling there for a moment. I was reminded of what my mother used to tell me. 'When it seems that you can't do something, take a break and try again later.' She was nearly always right," said Tom.

"It sounds like you had a wise mother. Please, make yourself at home, and I'll make us a meal," replied Geraldine.

They had a fair-sized meal, and Tom slowly began to relax. When the dishes had been washed and put away, Tom asked if she'd care to try again.

If only he knew what I was trying in the first place, I don't think he'd be quite as accommodating.

"Okay, I'll give it another go," she said.

Once again he rose into the air, only this time she showed off a little by moving him around the room. Then she brought him up to few feet away from her and concentrated once again. She could still see the bulge and felt more confident. She stared at the material, and suddenly it began to phase out as if a ten-inch window had been placed into it. She could see the bulge behind his undergarments and concentrated on them. They too began to fade, until finally she could see all the way through. She stood completely still because she couldn't believe what she was seeing. His limp cock was hanging down like a vine from a tree. He was huge and wasn't even hard.

"Is something wrong, milady?" said Tom as he hung in the air completely unaware of what she was looking at.

"Um no, I was just wondering what I should try next," replied Geraldine.

"Well, I'm game for anything at this point; I'm enjoying this."

I wonder if I dare,

She could still see his member, and the sight was making her think naughty things. In fact, she was starting to feel hot and bothered from looking at it. Then she decided. She touched it with her mind and gently pulled the foreskin back.

"Oh, wow, what are you doing to me?" said Tom as he began to blush.

Geraldine could see his foreskin moving back revealing the bulbous end, and then realized that his cock was growing. She watched every inch as it stood up, until finally it was fully erect. The very sight of it was making her wet. She tried to see if she could stroke it with her mind, and suddenly the skin began to move as if a hand were covering it. Back and forth it went.

"Oh god, milady, that feels incredible," whimpered Tom.

She was enjoying the sight of the bulbous end of his cock disappearing behind his foreskin, and then reappearing once more with each stroke that occurred. Yet, although it was the most erotic thing she'd ever experienced, it wasn't enough. She'd not made love to a man for over ten years, and the sight of this man's cock was getting her overly excited. Suddenly, she could take no more. She used her powers to undress him, and once he was naked, his cock sprang to attention.

She left him suspended in the air and walked over to him. Then she raised him up so that his cock was nearer, before she reached forward and grabbed it with her right hand. She stroked its length and licked her lips, before leaning over and taking it into her mouth.

"Oh yes...oh god...please don't stop," said Tom.

She adored the feeling of his huge cock on her tongue, and allowed a few inches to pass her lips. She sucked the end of his member with relish and thrust her other hand down below her skirt. She felt soaked as her finger stroked her clit, and she just had to thrust her finger inside. By now, she was sucking more than half of his cock into her mouth, and enjoying the moans of pleasure coming from him. Then, in a moment of sheer lust, she stopped what she was doing and levitated up to join him. She swung her legs around each side of him and lowered herself onto his cock.

As soon as it started to stretch her, she let out a scream of pleasure. She dropped down onto it, and then used her powers of levitation to rise and fall onto his thick hardness. Her body moved rhythmically up and down, and the more she felt, the more she wanted to feel. She picked up speed, almost needing to feel it going in as deeply as it possibly could, and then suddenly she began to scream. Her orgasm had crept up on her and taken her by surprise. It seemed to begin at her feet and worked its way up to her pussy, and struck with such a force she could barely contain herself.

As if that weren't enough, she could also feel Tom's hot seed exploding inside her. She held him there as they floated above the floor until her orgasm had come to an end. She then disengaged and allowed them both to float down to the floor. They both dressed quickly, and for a moment it was awkward.

"Um…

"Yes…um…oh…I'm sorry, you were going to say something," said Tom.

"Yes, I don't know what came over me, Tom; I do hope you don't think I go around doing that kind of thing every day," she said.

"Heavens no, I think perhaps you were caught up in the moment. It happens, but I must just say that it was a very pleasant encounter," replied Tom.

Geraldine blushed from the compliment, and sat down to take a breather.

****

Later that night, Geraldine was arranging a bed for her guest. She'd gotten to know Tom during the course of the day and found him to be a very likeable young man. He had nobility in his blood as his father was a baron until he lost his lands. The King had looked kindly on his son and made him the captain of the guards. When he got into the makeshift bed, which was situated on the floor directly across the room from Geraldine's, he fell asleep almost immediately. Geraldine, on the other hand, couldn't quite find the sleep she needed. She was finding it hard to forget the incident that occurred earlier and how much she'd enjoyed it. She looked over at Tom in the candle-lit room and peered through the covers that lay across his body.

She could clearly see his limp cock resting against his upper thigh, and touched it with her mind. It pulsated, and she could hear Tom groaning in his sleep. She guessed that he probably thought he was dreaming. She stroked the length of his member with the power she was now becoming more familiar with, and watched it grow in her mind's eye. The bulbous end of his cock popped out from the skin that was covering it and carried on growing.

She felt her body reacting to the sight, and decided to look at her own private parts. Her pussy was moist, and when she moved the lips to either side with her mind, she let out a deep sigh of satisfaction. She could now picture both Tom's erect cock and her own pussy as she slowly moved her clit around with her mind. Then she superimposed the two, and it looked as if the cock were coming out of her pussy. She moved her clit around with her mind more vigorously, and before she knew it, she could feel an orgasm approaching. She could hear Tom groaning in his sleep, and decided to stop touching him with her mind. Then she relaxed with her eyes closed, allowing her orgasm to settle. When it was over, she smiled to herself.

That is one hell of a gift, she thought as she turned to sleep for the night.

****

By midmorning, they were approaching the castle together as promised, and Tom was telling her all about the wonderful dream he had the night before. Geraldine didn't respond; she just smiled to herself. Once inside the castle, Tom introduced Geraldine to both the King and the Prince.

"Can you help my son? I will give you whatever you wish if you can," said the King.

"All I'd require is for you to leave me alone in the future. I believe that I can help your son. From what Tom has told me, it sounds like a simple transformation spell, and if it is, I know how to remove it. However, I'll need to be alone with your son at the moment that he turns, in order to ascertain what kind of spell it is. If I tried to remove it now, and I was wrong about the spell's purpose, I could harm him and we don't want that," replied Geraldine.

"I understand. I'll give you a room for the duration of your stay with us, and send my son along shortly before the transformation is to take place," said the King.

"Very well. I would now like to freshen up a little from the dusty road."

The King ordered his guards to show Geraldine to her room and for the maids to draw a bath. She followed the guards and ended up enjoying a nice warm bath. The day soon passed by, and before she knew it, the Prince was knocking on her door and entering, upon hearing the words come in.

"Well Prince, it would seem that you've made an enemy. Do you know why this has happened to you?" said Geraldine.

"No, until today I've never even met a witch," replied the Prince.

"It would seem that some witches don't need an excuse to cause mischief, although that sort of thing gives other witches a bad name. If I can remove this malady from you, I will, but should there be any complications, I need to know that you won't blame me for any of this?"

"I appreciate your help, and have told my father not to harm you in any way, should the worst happen."

Geraldine then asked him to strip his clothing, and he did so without any fuss. She handed him a blanket to cover his modesty while they waited. Then she heard him groan and push the covers off. Geraldine could see the changes taking place. His cock was shrinking back and was soon replaced with a pussy as his breasts and face began to grow and change. Within seconds, the Prince was now a female and someone Geraldine recognized.

"Sheena, what the hell are you doing?" said Geraldine upon recognition.

Sheena opened her eyes.

"I could ask the same of you, Geraldine," replied Sheena.

"I was asked by the King to remove what I believed to be a transformation spell. I now see that it was more than that," said Geraldine.

"Oh yes, so much more. I've found a way to transfer my very essence into another person. At least during the night, I can enjoy my youth again. That's not all; take a look at this," said an excited Sheena.

She spread her legs, and Geraldine could see a large cock coming from her pussy.

"I can even share his body parts, as long as I'm in control."

Geraldine watched it grow, and had to admit to herself that this was powerful magic. However, she had promised to help the Prince, and no matter how much she admired the magic that had gone into achieving such a feat; she had to keep her word.

"I'm sorry, Sheena. I have to remove you from the Prince."

Sheena allowed the cock to re-enter her and then stood up.

"There's nothing you can do about it. In order for you to stop this, you'd have to know where my real body is," said an angry Sheena.

Geraldine quickly read her mind.

"I already know where it is. Your real body is in a cabin surrounded by a swamp and two big dogs are guarding it," replied Geraldine.

"How could you possibly know that? Besides, whatever happened to the non-interference pact we made as younger witches?" said Sheena.

"That pact didn't include the taking over of someone else's body. It only covered the experimentation of spells. Once you tried this spell of yours and discovered that it worked, you should have vacated the body. Why didn't you?"

"I'm having way too much fun to stop now," replied Sheena.

"That's what I thought. I'm sorry, but I'm going to have to stop you. This will give other witches a bad name," said Geraldine as she walked towards the door.

Suddenly, she felt a spell strike her from behind and was frozen in place. Unbeknown to Sheena though, Geraldine was still able to stop her as her brain functions hadn't been affected. However, Geraldine wanted to see how far Sheena would go. Geraldine watched her coming around to the front.

"I cannot allow you to interfere, but before I do something about it, I think I'll have some fun," said Sheena.

Sheena began to remove Geraldine's clothes and once she was naked, she stood back to admire the package. Geraldine could read her thoughts.

I've always been envious of this body. I can't wait to see how it feels.

Geraldine couldn't help wondering what she was going to do, and held off to find out. Sheena stood up so close that their bodies were touching one another. Then Geraldine could feel the tip of a hard cock sliding along her pussy lips.

"Can you feel that?" said Sheena.

Geraldine couldn't reply, but she could feel it.

"I'm going to fuck you with this cock, and then I'm going to get rid of you," said Sheena.

The cock was poking Geraldine's clit and making her wet, and then suddenly it pushed between her pussy lips and Geraldine could feel a few inches of it penetrating her.

"Doesn't that feel good? Oh Geraldine, you're so tight," said Sheena as she pushed in all the way.

Geraldine closed her eyes, enjoying the moment more than she'd care to admit. She then read Sheena's mind.

Oh my god she's so tight, but it feels amazing. Perhaps I should keep her around as my sex partner.

Geraldine was almost ashamed to admit that the cock inside her was hitting all the right places, and when she started to cum, she could feel her pussy gripping the cock that was penetrating it. Sheena had to push in harder, and her thoughts were becoming wild.

Fuck that feels good. Your cunt is the perfect test bed for my little spell. Oh shit I'm going to cum.

Geraldine was at the height of her orgasm, and then she felt the seed of the Prince exploding inside her. Sheena kept it inside and looked Geraldine in the eyes close up.

"I hope you enjoyed that," she said as she pulled the cock out.

Geraldine watched the cock shrinking and going back inside Sheena's body. She then read her mind once again.

"What to do with you? As much as I'd like to keep you around, you'll probably get in my way, and we can't have that, can we?" said Sheena.

Geraldine knew what Sheena's next move was going to be, and decided to put an end to all this. As Sheena raised her hand to cast a spell, Geraldine deflected it with her mind and took hold of Sheena. She then made it impossible for Sheena to move, before sending a thought over to her.

In a moment, I'm going to let you go. I expect you to unfreeze me.

She let Sheena go and read her mind at the same time. Once again, Geraldine had to deflect the next spell and froze her again, only this time she picked her up using levitation and turned her upside down.

That last spell would have killed me, so I'm not playing anymore. If the next spell you use isn't an unfreeze one, I'm going to kill you. Do you understand? Thought Geraldine.

How is she doing all this? Was the thought Geraldine could hear in her head. *I'd better do as she said; I'm not taking the chance.*

Geraldine unfroze her, and this time sensed the correct spell coming her way. She was now able to move again.

"What you're doing Sheena, is wrong and I'm going to stop you. Now sit down," said Geraldine.

Sheena could feel something pulling her towards the bed and suddenly sat down upon it.

"This is very strange magic, how are you doing it?" she said unable to move.

"That's a secret and not for the likes of you," replied Geraldine.

She then took some cord from the curtains and tied Sheena up on the bed securely. After that, she fetched the guards and told them to watch over her and to do nothing else. The guards watched the window opening and then saw Geraldine floating out of the room. She was on her way, and managed to cover a lot of ground very quickly in this form of transport. Pretty soon she was flying over the swamp and came down to rest near to the cabin. The two dogs saw her and gave chase, but she threw them to one side without hurting them and entered the cabin.

There on a chair sat Sheena, the aged version. She seemed to be in some sort of trance. Geraldine tried to read her mind, but it was blank. All she could do now was to wait until the light of day. When it eventually came around, she saw Sheena opening her eyes to become aware of her surroundings.

"Remove the spell afflicting the Prince, otherwise I will kill you. I know that will do the job just as easily," said Geraldine.

Sheena tried to stand up, but found that she couldn't.

"Very well, you win. The Guild will hear of this, Geraldine, and they won't take kindly to a witch that interferes," said Sheena as she mumbled what Geraldine knew to be the counter spell.

"I couldn't care less what the Guild think. They're outdated and obsolete as far as I'm concerned. No one deserves to have their life ruined for the pleasure of others. I'm going to leave you now. Let's hope we never meet again," replied Geraldine.

With that, Geraldine returned to the castle. She waited for nightfall with the Prince, and when he didn't turn into a woman, she declared him free of the curse. The King couldn't thank her enough, and gave orders that no one was to bother her or go near her cottage. That was all Geraldine wanted, and she was satisfied. She walked out of the castle to find Tom waiting for her.

"I'd like to thank you for everything. I wish you well in the future," he said.

She just smiled at him and set off into the air.

****

Three days after the Sheena incident, Geraldine picked up some thoughts coming from outside the cottage. They were very disturbing thoughts.

Okay, we've been ordered to kill her and burn the cottage down as a message to all those witches who think they can interfere with others, was the thought she picked up.

She sensed there were two of them, and they were both armed with swords. After the last two encounters, one with Tom and the other with Sheena, Geraldine was feeling quite horny, and this new incident represented an opportunity to experiment further. She waited for them at the back of the cottage and turned out all the lights.

She heard the door opening and waited until they'd entered. Once they were inside, she lit all the candles at the same time, and the room was bathed in light.

"Hello gentlemen, how can I be of assistance?" she said.

"We're here to kill you witch," said the bigger of the two.

She could sense their confidence, and after reading their minds, she found out why. They had a spell on them that guarded against other spells. They probably thought they were immune to her, and that this would be a walk in the park. However, her abilities went beyond mere spells, and that was something they couldn't know. They moved closer, and suddenly their swords were forcefully yanked from their hands and thrown into the corner of the room. She then addressed them both.

"You're probably not going to believe what happens next," she said.

Suddenly, they found themselves frozen and unable to move. Then their clothes began to come apart and fall to the floor one item at a time until they were both naked. Geraldine read their thoughts.

How is she doing this? We're supposed to be immune to a witch's spells, thought one, *this is so embarrassing*, thought the other.

Then they felt their private parts being touched, yet the witch was across the room. Neither one of them could do anything about it. What was worse was that they were actually getting turned on. Their cocks began to grow, and they watched as Geraldine's clothes began to fall away. They felt themselves lifting up off the floor and gliding over to where the witch stood. The tallest one was then made to lie in a horizontal position mere inches from the floor. As he laid there, his cock, which was still being touched by invisible forces, was fully erect.

Geraldine stood astride him, and made him rise up to greet her. She slowly allowed his cock into her pussy and then pulled him up sharply.

"Ah, that feels incredible," she said as the cock penetrated her as far as it could go.

He then found himself being moved up and down, and had no say in the matter. Geraldine moved the other one behind her and between his friend's legs. She guided him up close until she could feel his hardness at her back door, and slowly pulled him into her.

"Ah god, that feels so full," she screamed.

Their bodies began to fuck her involuntarily as she pulled her nipples around with both hands. Anyone watching would've seen one guy floating below her with his hips moving rapidly up and down, while another was behind moving his to and fro. The combined sounds of the wet cocks and pussy along with her moans of pleasure were echoing around the room. When the one below started to cum, Geraldine made him move faster.

Her nipples felt rock-hard as she pulled and tugged on them. Then her first orgasm approached, and she made them move even faster. They began to move with a blur, and within five minutes, she started to scream as her second orgasm hit. She waited until they both came a second time and then stopped it all. She released them and allowed them to fall to the floor.

"Oh my god, please let us go; we won't ever come back again, you have our word," said the tallest with the other nodding in agreement.

"Get your clothes together and get out of here," said Geraldine.

They gathered their clothes, but didn't even bother to dress. Instead, they took them and ran out the door as quickly as they could. Geraldine had to laugh; she'd really enjoyed that. However, now she was left to wait for the next man to come along, and that might take another month or even six, and she couldn't wait that long. She decided she'd go on a trip and maybe pick a man up along the way; who knows, stranger things have happened.

She packed a few essentials and then set off. With her levitation ability, she wasn't concerned about the distances involved, and decided to head for the largest town in the area. The town in question was called Pebble Falls, named because of the large waterfall.

Geraldine covered quite a distance the first night, but had to stop at an inn as it was threatening to rain. She was given a nice room with an open fire, and treated well by the landlord's son, who just happened to be a very good-looking young man. In fact, he was such a head-turner that she decided to have a little fun with him. She threw a spell on him while he was making her bed, and when he asked if there were anything else he could do, Geraldine thanked him and told him no. She then got herself ready for bed and waited. An hour later, she could hear voices in the hallway. She listened in from where she lay.

"Mark, what are you doing?" said a woman as he walked towards Geraldine's room.

"Damn, she must have seen him leave his bed. She probably thinks that he's sleepwalking," said Geraldine to herself.

She got out of bed, opened the door, and peeked around the corner to see a young woman trying to block his way. Geraldine quickly threw the same spell onto her and quickly got back into bed. The door opened, and the couple walked in. Geraldine had used a hypnotic spell that simply instructed the one to whom it was attached, to follow her every command. The first thing the person would do is to ask what their task was. They both walked up to the bed and asked that very question.

"Both of you take your clothes off," said Geraldine.

They obeyed without question, and when they were naked, they stood there waiting for further instructions.

"Get into my bed and make love to me," said Geraldine.

They both moved together and climbed in next to her, one on either side. The female began by kissing her breasts and sucking her nipples while the male kissed her entire body. When he was between her thighs, he started to kiss her tender red lips, and Geraldine moaned with the pleasure of his tongue swiping her clit. While the female kissed Geraldine's nipples and fondled them, Geraldine moved her clit with her mind, making her squirm as she licked and sucked harder.

The landlord's son was now spreading Geraldine's legs apart, and moving up her body until the tip of his hard cock was touching her womanhood. She was already extremely wet, so when he pushed forward, he had no trouble entering her. Geraldine let out a loud moan of satisfaction as his cock moved in as far as it would go. Her nipples were fully erect and feeling extremely sensitive, and the female responsible for that was almost screaming with pleasure as her clit was moved around by an unseen force.

Geraldine commanded the young man to go faster, which he did. She arched her back as he pounded her, and felt incredibly hot. The female was now in the grips of an orgasm from all the stimulation given to her by Geraldine's mind. She was screaming with pleasure, which turned Geraldine on and made her want to do more. She visualized the woman's pussy and then moved the moist lips around with her mind. The female's screams of pleasure increased as she felt something invisible entering her. The landlord's son was also groaning, and it was evident that he was about to cum. Geraldine gripped his butt cheeks as he did so, and held him tightly as his hot seed shot out deep inside her. Then she stopped them both and told them to make love to each other. They obeyed without question and were soon fucking one another beside Geraldine.

Geraldine enjoyed watching them both as they groaned and moaned with pleasure. She also helped by stimulating the female's clit as the young man pounded her. They seemed to glow as she watched, because of the moonlight coming through the window. It seemed like such an erotic scene. Geraldine waited until they'd both cum once more, and then instructed them to go back to bed. She also informed them that they wouldn't remember any of this night's events.

****

In the morning, Geraldine had a quick breakfast and was off once more. The town was now just twenty miles down the lane and with the ability to cross over the meadows, she saw it coming up in the distance very quickly. She came down to the ground half a mile from the town and walked in. She didn't want to announce her presence as she knew that witches weren't welcome anywhere, even good ones.

Once inside the town, she started to look around. She hadn't been here for well over three years and by the looks of it, things had changed in that time. There were new stores, and the paths were cobbled. She remembered the last time she visited, and it was simply dirt tracks back then. She could smell something nice in the air, and upon following the odor, she came across a bakery. The fresh smell of bread baking was very tempting, so much so that she decided to buy a loaf. As Geraldine was walking away with her purchase, a couple of thugs knocked into her, which sent the bread sprawling to the ground.

"Hey, watch where you're going. Lady," said the taller of the two.

Geraldine picked the bread up, rubbed it off and carried on walking.

"Hey lady, aren't you going to apologize?" said the lout as he and his friend caught up with her.

Geraldine had given them a chance to walk away, but now she was angry. She turned to face them.

"Son, I have very little tolerance for stupid people. If I were you, I'd leave while you still can," she said calmly.

The two louts laughed, and the taller of the two made his biggest mistake yet. He placed his hand onto her shoulder. Suddenly, he shot up into the air, much to his partner's dismay. He was screaming as he went up and hovered fifty feet above the ground. Geraldine turned her attention to the other one.

"If I'm still looking at you in the next sixty seconds, you'll be joining him," she said.

Within five seconds, he could no longer be seen. There was now a crowd gathering and looking up at the lout as he flayed his arms in an effort to move. Then suddenly he began to drop. He screamed as he neared the ground and stopped three inches from it.

"I hope that we never meet again, because the next time will not go well for you," said Geraldine.

He couldn't stop apologizing, and once she felt that he'd groveled enough, she let him go. He hit the ground running and didn't look back. However, Geraldine now saw that people were staring and some were pointing as they talked with one another. She hadn't wanted to draw attention to herself, but couldn't do anything about it now. She walked into the next street looking for an inn. As luck would have it, she'd chosen the correct street as there was a large inn just up the road.

She was glad to get off the street and away from prying eyes. She was just being shown to her room when she overheard a conversation at the main desk.

"I hear a witch just booked in, is it possible for me to see her?" said an agitated elderly gentleman.

"I'll have you know this is a respectable establishment, and you won't find any witches in here," replied the clerk.

Geraldine watched him leave, but as she did, she read his mind.

I've got to find help, if the townsfolk find out what's happening to my boys, they'll be burned at the stake for being demonically possessed, was the thought she heard.

Geraldine could sense the compassion from this man, and knew that he deserved help. She then excused herself and told the innkeeper that she'd be back shortly. She went outside and spotted the old man near the end of the street. She quickly caught up with him and introduced herself.

"Oh thank god, I've been looking for anyone who might be able to help me. However, we can't talk here. Would you mind coming with me to my home?" he said.

"Lead the way," replied Geraldine.

He owned a butcher shop, and when they arrived, the old man introduced Geraldine to his staff members Matt and Jack, and told them to tell her what had happened.

"We went hunting in the forest, the one just over the meadow. We caught a wild boar and were on the way home when a witch stopped us. She cursed us for trespassing and then flew off. We were shaken by it all, but we soon shrugged it off and came back home. At midnight that day, we changed into monsters, or at least that's what Mr. Knots told us. He also told us that we tried to have our evil way with one of the village girls, and that if he hadn't been there, we would have done. All we remember is waking up in the cellar chained against the wall," said Matt.

"It sounds as if she's cast a transformation spell onto you both. These spells are very specific, in that they only work at certain times of the day. I think I'd better stay here until midnight to see what I'm up against. I would suggest, old man, that you stay somewhere else for the night. Come back in the morning and everything will be fine," replied Geraldine.

The old man did as he was told, and Geraldine stayed to talk to the guys a little more.

"Do you remember what you turned into?" she said.

"All we remember before waking up is being in pain, but after that, it all goes blank," replied Jack.

"Well, it's not unusual to have no memory of the change. I'm just curious as to what you change into, but I guess we'll see tonight."

They talked most of the day away, and even cooked a meal as they talked. Just before midnight, Geraldine suggested that they all go down into the cellar and prepare. They agreed, and soon she was chaining them to the wall and sitting back to wait. As she heard the town clock strike twelve, the change began. They both let out a bloodcurdling scream of pain, and she could see their clothes ripping and their limbs growing.

Before it started, they were five and a half feet tall, but by the time it stopped they'd grown another two feet. However, they weren't demons or monsters, they were simply big. Geraldine had seen this before; it was indeed a transformation spell but the witch that cast it had got it wrong. She guessed that they were supposed to be hideous beasts, but instead they were merely large. Their memory was still affected by the spell, so they didn't know who or where they were.

They tried to free themselves with grunts and groans, and when Geraldine tried to talk with them, they couldn't string two words together. She then stood up and undressed, which made them go silent as they watched. They seemed fascinated by her body, and they both looked as if they would do anything to have it. Once she was naked, she unchained them with her mind. The guys stood up and walked over to her. They literally towered over her as she began to remove their clothes with her mind.

When their tunics fell to the floor, Geraldine let out a gasp. Their cocks had grown along with the rest of them and swung between their legs like pendulums. Geraldine reached out with her hands and stroked them both. They looked at one another with a devilish grin across their faces. Geraldine could feel their cocks growing as the skin passed through the palm of her hands.

When she looked down she was stunned by their size, and before she could admire them, the brothers suddenly picked her up off the floor as if she were a feather. Matt was in front and Jack was behind, and they didn't mess around. Geraldine suddenly felt the ends of their cocks pushing against her two holes, and before she could do anything, they were entering together.

"Oh my lord...ahh...that feels incredible," she shouted.

As their cocks penetrated her, Geraldine gripped Matt's shoulders to brace herself. They were stretching her as never before, and the fact that they were doing all the work made it all the more enjoyable. Each time they penetrated her, she let out a sigh of approval. She adored how easily they held her in place and could feel how wet she was getting. Their grunts and groans as they continued were sounds of ecstasy to Geraldine.

Her nipples felt solid they were so hard, and her first orgasm came as they were both as far inside her as they could go. She cried out for them to fuck her harder, even knowing that they probably didn't understand anything she was saying. Her pussy pulsated with aftershocks as their cocks violated her, and she started to wonder when they would cum themselves.

By the time they did, she could feel her second orgasm approaching and felt it hit just as they both exploded inside her. They made an almighty growl of satisfaction as they let loose their hot seed, and a few minutes later they stopped and placed her back onto the floor. They then sat down onto the floor to catch their breath, but Geraldine hadn't finished with them yet. She pushed Matt down onto his back and took his cock in her hands. She stroked him until she could see his cock growing again, and then took the end of it into her mouth.

She could barely get the first three inches in but tried for more anyway. Then she felt Jack gripping her butt cheeks from behind and the end of his hardened cock pushing its way into her pussy. The sheer amount of cock that entered her made her cry out with pleasure, and each time Jack moved forward, she felt herself lifting slightly off the floor. She sucked Matt's cock hungrily and started to climax one more time.

It was another twenty minutes before they both came again and when they did, they showered her with their cream. She lay on the floor recovering, and could feel Matt's seed running out between her thighs and Jack's down her neck and breasts. She mistakenly thought that it was all over, when suddenly Jack picked her up again and sat her on his still-hard cock. He then began to pull her up and down.

However, when Matt tried to do the same again behind her, she froze them both.

After getting loose, she got dressed and removed the spell they were under. She watched them as the transformation spell faded away and they shrank to their normal size. They both collapsed onto the floor after that, and Geraldine used a spell to clothe them. When they awoke the sun was coming up.

"What happened, did you manage to remove the curse?" said Matt.

"Yes, the curse is gone."

Although technically, it was a spell; still, they didn't need to know that. Their boss came in shortly after that and was told the good news. He offered to pay Geraldine for her services, but she refused. What she didn't say was that it had been the single most thrilling night of her life. She wished them well and then left to return to the inn.

By the time she'd reached the inn and was in her own room, she felt exhausted. However, before she fell asleep, she couldn't help thinking that she could travel the country looking for the cursed. Perhaps she could make a name for herself. All she knew for sure was that she was having the time of her life.

****

Geraldine was eating breakfast earlier than most the next day as she wanted to explore the town. It was during that trip that she saw the Princess in her carriage. She was waving to the crowds as she passed by on her way to the castle on the hill above the town. The thing that struck Geraldine was how beautiful she was. Stunning would have been a better word. Her long golden hair hung down behind her like a cascading waterfall and shone in the light of day. Her perfect face seemed to glow with a radiance that Geraldine had never witnessed before.

"Now there goes a lady," she said to herself.

Once the carriage had passed, the crowds all dissipated, and Geraldine went back to window shopping. She was snared several times by the things she saw, and ended up buying more than she'd planned to. Still, it wasn't every day that she could overindulge. It was later that afternoon when she heard the commotion in the street. Upon investigation, she found that guards from the castle were pinning declarations up around town. Geraldine walked over to read one.

"Whosoever can stop the demon from reaching my quarters by midnight on this day, will receive a reward of one million gold coins," signed Princess Annabelle.

"I wonder what that's all about?" said Geraldine out loud.

"You must be a stranger if you don't know about the demon," replied an old woman in the crowd.

"I am a stranger. Could you tell me what's happening here?"

"It happened on the Princess's eighteenth birthday. She had an unwelcome visitor who told her that he would visit every year at the same time. He then proceeds to violate the princess and takes away her ability to love for another year. She has many admirers, but none that can get close. If she is ever to marry, the demon has to be dealt with. However, no one can get into her chambers once the demon arrives, and are helpless to stop it from having its wicked way. Many brave men have died trying to stop this thing, by staying in her quarters when it arrives, but they're never seen again," replied the old woman.

Geraldine looked up at the castle.

"Which is the Princess's room?" she said.

"Her room is in the highest tower. In fact, you can just see it from here," replied the old woman as she pointed it out.

Geraldine thanked her for the information and then set out for the castle. Once she was out of sight of the town, she took to the air. As she approached the castle walls, she could see arrows flying in her direction. She easily blocked them and flew over the wall. She understood why they would fire on her without provocation, and did nothing to stop them. When she reached the window, she knocked on it and waited. The Princess suddenly appeared looking out from the other side.

"I'm here to help," said Geraldine.

The Princess hesitated, but upon looking closely at this strange woman's face, she wavered and opened the window. Geraldine floated inside the room to find three men armed and ready for anything.

"Hold witch, what are your intentions here today?" said one of them.

"My name is Geraldine, and I'm here to stop whatever it is that plagues the Princess. I'm doing it for two reasons. I'm here for the reward, and to allow the princess to love again. No one should be denied love; it's too valuable," replied Geraldine.

The Princess told the men to lower their weapons, and Geraldine convinced her to make them leave. There was no reason for anyone else to die trying to protect her. Once they were alone, Geraldine started to ask questions.

"I need you to be perfectly honest with me, my dear. You see, I need to know what I'm up against," said Geraldine.

"I understand. On my eighteenth birthday, a vile demon appeared in the middle of this room. He told me that I would be his and his alone. In order that I never disobeyed him, he would take away my ability to love another. I have met many men whom I like, but I have never loved. At twenty-five, I was beginning to think I never would," replied the Princess as a tear rolled from her cheek.

"Why do you say demon? In all my years, I've never seen a demon even though I know that my sisters make pacts with them. However, those pacts are made in a spiritual plane and not in person.

As far as I know, demons aren't allowed to enter this realm." said Geraldine.

"Well, I don't know any other way to describe it. It's big and black from head to toe, and it has more than one sexual organ. I know of no other creature that would fit that description," replied Princess Annabelle.

"Um, this will be interesting. Okay Princess, this is what will happen. I'm guessing here, but I believe that it will probably sense your presence, so you have to be here. However, I want you to hide in the closet while I deal with it. In case you're wondering, I'll be using a transformation spell, and I will look exactly like you. The fact that it will sense your presence in the room will probably be enough to fool it. I'll then assess the situation and act accordingly. I can't tell you that I'll succeed, but I can tell you that I will try and free you from this curse," said Geraldine.

"You can do that? Change into the likeness of others, I mean?"

"Oh yes, that is an old favorite of many witches. There is, however, something I need you to do before I use that spell. I need to know exactly how you look, in the flesh as it were."

The Princess understood and immediately removed her clothes. Once she was naked, Geraldine walked around her to see all the various bumps and any defects. She found no defects and was impressed with how beautiful the Princess was. She then told her to get dressed, and they talked together for the rest of the day.

When the time drew near, Geraldine stood naked in front of the Princess and used a spell on herself. The Princess watched the transformation and was astounded by the magic being used. When it was finished, they stood staring at one another. It was like looking into a mirror.

"Quickly child, hide in the closet and don't come out no matter what you hear, is that understood?" said Geraldine.

"Yes, I understand, and thank you Geraldine for trying to help me; I won't soon forget it," replied the Princess.

Geraldine believed how sincere she was and realized how much she liked this Princess. Then, when the time was near, Geraldine was fully-clothed once more and waiting. It wasn't a long wait. Suddenly, she could see the shape of a pentagram on the floor in the middle of the room. She then witnessed smoke seemingly coming from the floorboards inside the circle.

All very impressive so far, she thought.

The smoke didn't seem to be able to cross the lines of the circle, and carried on up until it looked like a windowed tube that held the smoke back. Then it began to dissipate, and once it had thinned out enough, Geraldine could see a figure taking shape. It was hard to ascertain what it looked like as it was dark in the room and whatever it was, was black from head to toe. Its head then moved and it opened its eyes. In that moment, Geraldine read its mind, and knew exactly what she was up against. She almost instantly found out several things.

It was a warlock, a male witch. He'd made a pact with a demon, to be able to use its form and that of its mode of travel. She also found out that Princess Annabelle wasn't his only victim. He visited eleven others throughout the land and seduced them all. It stared at her and then stepped out of the circle. It seemed extraordinarily large from the shoulders down, and very menacing. In fact, Geraldine might have been quite intimidated had she not had the ability to see through the genuinely frightening disguise.

"I see you've stopped wasting the lives of others to stop me, my dear. That is wise," he said walking up close to Geraldine.

Geraldine didn't respond; she made herself appear frightened and watched everything he did.

"You also haven't changed since the last time I saw you. You're still as beautiful as ever," he said as he reached up and started to remove her clothing.

Geraldine acted nervous and timid as she didn't want to give anything away just yet. His hands were huge, but she couldn't see anything else as he wore a large cape. Once he'd removed her clothing he walked around her, taking in the sight of her beautiful body. Then, once he was behind her, he spread out his cape and covered her body. She could feel him pressed against her skin and wondered what was going to happen next.

Next, she felt something sliding along the back of her upper thigh. She didn't know what it was, but felt excited as it seemed to have a life of its own. Then she felt it touching her womanhood and probing for the entrance. When it found what it was looking for, she felt the bulbous end pushing and spreading her pussy lips apart. It then moved inside her, and she let out an involuntary moan of pleasure. Next, it moved around in circles as if it were making room before moving further inside her.

Geraldine sighed heavily with the pleasure she was feeling, and from how stretched she felt from whatever it was that was violating her. She swallowed hard and felt it suddenly moving faster. It was making her stand on her toes each time it thrust forward, and she was getting extremely wet from it all. Then she was shocked to feel another one creeping up the back of her legs. She didn't know what they were, but she expected this new one to probe for the back door. She was wrong. Instead, it joined the first one and pushed its way in beside it.

"Ahh...oh my god," she called out.

Once the second was inside her, she felt them taking turns to move in and out. As one moved in, the other moved out and it was driving her crazy. Her very first orgasm was messy as she gushed all over the appendages that were making her feel so incredibly hot. The faster they moved the more pleasure she felt, and then she felt yet another one creeping up the front and touching her breasts.

What are these things?

She tried to read his mind, but was too distracted from all the stimulation she was feeling. The third appendage moved through the middle of her breasts and up towards her head. When it reached the front of her face, it probed for her mouth. Geraldine was enjoying this so much that she actually wanted to feel this thing in her mouth, so she opened it and allowed the appendage inside.

To her surprise, it felt exactly like a cock only much bigger. She felt it sliding along her tongue, seeking the back of her throat. When it reached the back, it slid out again and moved in the same way as the ones in her pussy. Then it went further, and Geraldine knew that magic was involved; she guessed that the magic was coming from the cape that surrounded her, but she didn't know for sure. The appendage was going down her throat, and she knew that under normal circumstances, she'd never be able to accommodate such a thing. She felt her neck muscles bulging as it repeatedly moved deep inside her throat.

Her second orgasm came back to back with her third, and she was in ecstasy. She'd never experienced anything approaching this kind of stimulation, and the more it went on, the more she wanted. In the throes of her third orgasm, she felt its appendages start to pulsate violently, and suddenly its seed was gushing from both her pussy and her mouth. Her inner thighs were soon soaking wet, and she could feel the semen running down between her breasts. However, he didn't stop. He carried on fucking her as if nothing had happened.

Geraldine felt messy and sticky, but the feelings of his cocks as they continued the onslaught were undeniably fantastic. She moved her hips in time with his thrusts, in an attempt to feel greater sensations if that were even possible. Then she felt one of the appendages pulling out and probing her back door. It was covered in manseed, and was able to penetrate her easily. She felt incredibly full as it moved inside and made a muffled scream of pleasure as it carried on as before.

Twenty minutes later, all three appendages pulled out, and she could feel the seed hitting her from all directions. The amount of seed coming from each appendage was immense, and by the time he'd finished coming, Geraldine was covered in the stuff. If he hadn't been holding her at that point, she felt that she would've collapsed onto the floor. She felt completely exhausted. The warlock wasted no time after that; he laid her down on the bed and then stepped back into the pentagram. Once he was gone, the Princess came out from her hiding place.

"Oh my god, I saw everything. Are you alright?" she said as she covered her still-naked body.

"I will be in a minute," replied Geraldine.

"I thought you were going to get rid of the demon?"

"First of all, it isn't a demon. It's a warlock in disguise, and secondly, I said I could free you, which I've done. I'll take your place every year from this moment on. You are now free to love and be loved. I do hope you choose wisely, my dear," replied Geraldine.

"You actually enjoyed that, didn't you?" said the Princess.

"It was the most incredible feeling I've ever experienced, so yes, I would have to say I did enjoy it. I also thought that if I took a warlock on and lost, you'd be right back where you started from and no one would gain anything."

The Princess was full of gratitude for what Geraldine had done, and gave her the reward as promised. However, there was still one thing she couldn't do, and Geraldine warned her about it.

"If you fall in love with someone, you can't let it be known. If the warlock finds out, he'll try to interfere, and that's something you don't need," said Geraldine.

"I understand, and I will keep any love I find a secret."

With that, Geraldine left and had some serious plans to make. She wanted to locate every other Princess who was being abused and take their places. She felt it was the most profitable way of getting rich quickly, not to mention the side benefits of being taken by the warlock once every month. She smiled with that thought and continued her adventures.

The End

Bound to Hell (An Erotic Adventure)

Dale sat in his chair fidgeting. He was trying really hard to listen to the lecture, but he just couldn't get into it. His worst fears were coming true after being in college for the past year and a half. He'd chosen Economics as his course and was starting to believe that he'd chosen badly. When he chose it at the age of eighteen, he felt that it was something he could change the world with. He could see himself trying to persuade people where to put their money, and forecast future economic events. He was wrong.

He was now finding the learning to be too boring, but he was stuck with it. He didn't want to let his parents down after they'd put so much money into his education. At nineteen and a half, he was learning one valuable lesson. There is nothing easy in life. However, what he didn't know, was that his life was about to change – dramatically.

The lecture was almost over when the incident happened. Dale was listening intently when suddenly a scantily-clad female came into the lecture room. Dale saw two things almost immediately. First, she was wearing next to nothing, but more importantly, no one was watching her as she passed them by. Even the professor carried on talking as if nothing were happening. She was heading straight towards Dale and looking directly at him.

As she got nearer, Dale could see the items of clothing she wore more clearly, and couldn't believe what he was seeing. Her skimpy panties were so tight they were showing the outline of her pussy. The top she wore barely covered her nipples and was straining to keep her breasts in check. When she reached him, she simply said hi.

Dale tried not to make eye contact, and looked around the room to find that no one was paying any attention to her, not even the professor. When Dale eventually said hi back, he received a few strange looks from the people around him. Just then the lecture ended, and everyone got up to leave. Dale asked the mysterious woman to excuse him and started to leave the lecture room himself. However, before he managed to reach the door, she grabbed his arm and pulled him back. He suddenly felt a wrenching feeling in his chest, and clutched at it as if to cover the pain. Then once they were alone, she forcefully sat him down.

"Lady, who are you? What do you want with me and why aren't you wearing any clothes?"

As he sat there waiting for answers, he looked her up and down again. Being this close, he could now see that her panties were riding up between her pussy lips as if they were being sucked in. The outline of her pussy was so obvious it was as if she weren't wearing anything. He also realized that the sight was causing an erection.

"Oh, is that for me?" she said reaching down and stroking his hardness over his pants.

Dale jumped up as if he'd been stung and backed away.

"Lady, you can't do that type of thing here, I'll get expelled," he shouted, still backing away.

"Oh, you don't have to worry about that anymore. The moment I touched you was the moment the life you knew ended," she replied.

"What are you talking about?" he said trying to edge around her.

"Look, go into the corridor and try to speak to someone – anyone will do. When you're satisfied that no one can see you, come back here," she replied.

Dale managed to get past her and rushed through the door. He then ran down the corridor and stopped at the end to look back. He heard voices, and turned around to see a good friend approaching.

"Hey Jack, you'll never believe what just happened to me," he said as his friend got nearer.

Dale turned to make sure that she hadn't followed him, but when he turned back again, Jack walked straight through him.

"Whoa, what the fuck!" said Dale as he backed away sharply and fell against the side wall.

He then looked around, after remembering what she had said. He got up and talked to the first person who came along, and they completely ignored him. His only course of action now was to go back to the lecture room and find out what the hell was going on. When he opened the door, she was still there, waiting patiently.

"You see, no one can see you or interact with you," she said.

"Why, what have you done to me?" asked Dale.

"It's actually what you've done to yourself. You see, you killed the Reaper, and the rules state that whoever kills a reaper has to take their place," she said.

"Whoa Lady... I didn't—

"Please, stop calling me Lady. My name is Candy," she interrupted.

"Okay, Candy it is, but I didn't kill anyone," replied Dale.

"Did you, or did you not go up to the roof of the cafeteria a month ago and lean against one of the gargoyle statues? Did you hear the creak as you put your weight on it and immediately step back from it?" said Candy.

Dale remembered that incident vividly.

"Yes, I remember that; so what?"

"Well, it took a month, but eventually it worked its way free and landed on my master, who is now dead. Therefore, you killed him," replied Candy.

"If I killed anyone from doing all of that, it wasn't deliberate," insisted Dale.

"Oh, I know that, but that doesn't change the fact that you are responsible for his death."

"How on God's earth am I going to face my mother if she can't even see me?" said Dale.

"Um, I hate to break this to you, but you no longer exist. Your mother never had you, at least in her mind, and no one whom you knew before today knows you from Adam. In other words, you get to start from the very beginning. In addition, you now have powers. In a way, you're sort of like a superhero," replied Candy.

"So, my family doesn't know me. My friends don't know me, and no one can see me. Does that about sum it up?"

"Yes, I think he's got it," responded Candy sarcastically.

"How is any of this fair; I had a good life before any of this and a bright future," said Dale.

"In point of fact, you drop out of college at the age of twenty, and you die at the age of thirty-two from a hit-and-run incident. This is a step up from all of that."

"How could you possibly know any of that?"

"I had to look you up to ascertain who was responsible for my master's death, and while I was at it, I looked into your future."

"You can do that?"

"Oh yes, these things are necessary in order to accomplish the job at hand," replied Candy.

"And what exactly is this job? You mentioned the Reaper, am I to collect souls?"

"No, you're not that kind of reaper. You kill monsters, at least what humans would define as monsters."

"What are you talking about, there's no such thing as monsters," replied Dale knowingly.

"I'll have you know there's a monster in this very college, which was where we were headed until a certain stone statue fell on my master's head," said Candy.

"You keep saying your master; does that mean I'm your master now?"

"Yes, but there are a few things you need to know about me. I am a Succubus, a Spawn of Hell. I can be anyone you want me to be, and I'm your bodyguard," replied Candy.

"My bodyguard; so you were the last reaper's bodyguard as well?"

"Yes I was."

"Well, you suck," said Dale.

"Yes, and very well I'm told," replied Candy.

"No, I mean—"

"I know what you meant, Dale...that was humor. Perhaps you don't yet grasp the concept of humor; I mean you are still young."

"When you said you could be anyone I want, what did you mean by that?" said Dale, ignoring her remark.

Candy didn't reply; instead, she suddenly turned into Dale's next-door neighbor Ms. Jones, and she was naked. Dale had had a crush on her for as long as he could remember.

"Oh my god, how did you do that?"

"Like I said, I'm a Succubus. I have to be able to change into whomever you desire. That is my role in life. We are the seductresses of all those who would promise their souls to the Devil. I may not be in the market for seduction at the moment, but it is part of my nature. God also recognized the fact that mortals have certain needs, and I am here to fulfill those needs."

Dale hadn't stopped looking at her body. He'd always tried to picture what his neighbor looked like without clothes on, and now he knew. It was everything he had imagined. Candy then turned back again in a blink of an eye.

"You also mentioned that I'd be going after monsters, what kind of monsters?"

"As I said before, we were on the way to deal with the latest one at this college when the death occurred. All we knew was that we were up against a doppelganger. And before you ask, a doppelganger is a monster that is a copy of someone who is living. They take over the life of the one they are copying. The very first thing a doppelganger does upon being brought to life is to kill the original so that it can take over that life. That is why you never see them or rather you think you never see them. They are the very epitome of evil."

"You said that you were Hell Spawn, but doesn't that mean you serve the Devil?" said Dale.

"Satan is my true master, but when God decrees that a person such as I serve the greater good. Satan has no say in it," replied Candy, "You see it's in Satan's best interest for these monsters to be eradicated, because whenever a monster kills a mortal, that mortal automatically goes to Heaven."

"Why is that?" said Dale.

"Because their deaths were deemed unnatural, and if they were left alone to develop naturally, they might turn bad; in which case Satan has a right to their souls."

"I can see the logic in that. But tell me, why didn't God take my memories away? It would've made this transition far less difficult," said Dale.

"Two words...life experiences. If he took all of your memories, you wouldn't even know how to use a phone or any number of things that would come in handy during your new life."

"Here's the thing, how am I supposed to kill monsters? I don't even think I could kill," said Dale.

"You don't have to know how to do it you just need to hold your weapon. As soon as you're holding that, it will take over."

"Why, is it alive?"

"It's not exactly alive, but it does know why it was created, and it bestows that knowledge onto anyone who wields it," said Candy.

"What kind of weapon is it?"

Candy held her hands out, and suddenly a sheathed samurai sword appeared in them. Dale took hold of its cover and picked it up. Then he gripped the handle, and suddenly he knew everything there was to know about fighting monsters. He quickly re-sheathed it and felt like himself again.

"Wow, that was traumatic," he said pushing it back into Candy's hands.

"You need to keep a hold of this. Take hold of it again and throw it over your shoulder, as if you were sheathing it behind you," said Candy.

Dale took hold of it again and did what he was told. As he placed it over his shoulder, it suddenly disappeared.

"Whenever you want it, imagine it's in your hand when you reach up to your shoulder and it will be there. You also cannot lose it. If you drop it, it will automatically return to the invisible sheath over your shoulder."

Dale tried it and sure enough, it appeared back in his hand.

"That's pretty cool," he said as he put it back again.

"If there are no more questions, it's time we took care of the monster in this college. Are you ready?"

"I still have many questions, but they can wait. Let's do this," replied Dale.

They left the room together and headed for the teachers' faculty room; once outside Candy turned to Dale.

"The only ones who can see us are monsters. That is how we're able to locate them. Once we enter this room, if the doppelganger is in there, he or she will be the only ones looking at us. Is that clear?"

"Yes, perfectly," replied Dale as he reached for the door handle.

He opened the door and they walked in. No one looked in their direction. However, three of them had their backs to the door. Dale walked up to one of them.

"Professor Jones," he said, but got no response.

He then turned to the second one, nearer the window.

"Professor Smith," he said.

"Yes Dale, what can I do for you?" she said.

Dale reached up for the sword that he knew would be there, and as soon as it was in his hand, he knew what to do. Professor Smith saw the sword and had a pained look on her face, as if in recognition of what was about to happen. She then saw a flash of the blade as it passed through her head, and suddenly her body turned into a green oozing slime and fell to the floor. There was a scream from another professor who had witnessed her colleague's collapse, and everyone else looked around. All they could see was the mass of slime on the floor and didn't equate it to a once living person. Dale and Candy left the room as they had entered it – unobserved.

They both walked off the campus together, and Dale took one last look before walking through the archway that was the entrance.

"Where do we live now? I mean, do we even have to sleep?" said Dale.

"Oh yes, we still have to sleep and eat. As for where we live, we can live wherever you want to. Mortals can't see us unless we want them too, so we can use the best hotels. That's what my last master and I did," replied Candy.

That, it turned out, was what they did that night. Dale took her to a hotel that he'd slept in once before. It was a beautiful place, not to mention a five-star hotel. Candy then showed him a trick at the front desk. If you don't want to be disturbed, take a room that is last on the list. The chances are they won't let that room for the night you want to stay, so you won't get disturbed by anyone checking into it. Soon they found themselves in one such room and made themselves comfortable.

"If you don't mind, I'd like to take a shower. I need to unwind after today," said Candy.

"No, I don't mind. I need to rest as I feel utterly exhausted. Is that normal?"

"Yes, it is quite normal. The energy you felt leaving your body when I touched you saps your strength for a while. A good night's sleep is all you need to fully recover though," replied Candy.

She then went into the bathroom, and Dale lie on the bed. Before he knew it, he was asleep. It didn't last long. Candy came out of the shower and was full of energy. Dale could hear her jumping on her bed, and turned to see what the hell she was playing at. The sight he saw when he turned made him stare. She acted like a little child as she jumped on the mattress, but she looked nothing like a child as her large breasts bounced up and down.

She was completely naked, and Dale couldn't help but admire her body. When she saw him staring, she got off the bed and walked over to him.

"Would you like some fun?" she said.

"As much as I appreciate your beauty, I'm very tired," replied Dale.

"What if I do this," she said and then promptly turned into someone Dale recognized.

He sat up, staring intently. She'd turned into a naked Brittany Spears.

"When I read your mind earlier, I saw several women that you have the hots for," she said as she held her breasts in a suggestive manner.

It was true; Dale had always liked Brittany, but what hot-blooded male wouldn't. Then he saw her turning into Pamela Anderson.

"This one is strong in your memory; I found her in several corners of your mind."

Dale sat up and could feel his cock growing. He had or did have several posters of Pamela on his bedroom wall. He'd always imagined her naked and in his bedroom. Then Candy turned into Janet Jackson.

"Okay, stop it. You've proven that you know all of my likes and needs, but I don't think it's right somehow," said Dale.

Candy turned back to herself and sat on the edge of his bed.

"Why? I don't think there's any harm in a good fantasy," replied Candy.

"If I were to touch you in those forms, it would feel as if I were invading their privacy, even though I know it's not really them. Besides, if I took you in one of their forms, the fantasy would be crushed."

Candy didn't respond to that. Instead, she reached over and stroked the erection she could see pushing up the covers.

"Well, they certainly got your attention," she said as her hand traced the length of his cock.

Then she turned into his former next-door neighbor Ms. Jones, and carried on stroking him. Dale suddenly remembered watching his neighbor bending over in her garden and how he imagined coming up behind her and taking her in that position. His cock suddenly sprang to attention.

"Oh, you're quite a big boy, aren't you," said Candy before pulling the covers back.

Dale's erection sprang to attention as the sheets that protected it were uncovered, and he watched the woman of his fantasies reach for his cock. When she grasped it, he took a deep breath and closed his eyes as her hand stroked him. He felt guilty, even though he knew it wasn't really Ms. Jones. However, he couldn't deny that it was the hottest thing he'd ever experienced. He opened his eyes to see her leaning forward and then felt her lips surrounding the end of his cock.

"Oh shit...that feels so good," he said.

He knew who was doing it, but the fact that she looked like his former neighbor was driving him crazy. He watched as Candy allowed more of his meat into her mouth and threw his head back to enjoy the sensations. He could still see his neighbor bending over in the garden in his mind's eye and flashing her panties. Then he felt the end of his cock hitting the back of Candy's throat, and it was all too much. He called out that he was going to cum, but Candy ignored him.

When he did explode inside her mouth, she carried on sucking him as if nothing had happened. It wasn't until he'd completely stopped ejaculating that Candy allowed it to slip from her mouth. She then climbed onto the bed, still looking like Ms. Jones, and sat astride his still hard cock. Her breasts were perfect, and the long hair that cascaded over her shoulders looked incredibly smooth and silken.

Candy squatted down facing him, and he felt the tightness of her pussy as she lowered herself onto his cock. She moved slowly but deliberately, allowing it all in before using her knees to slide off it again. Her breasts bounced and jiggled around as her movements increased in speed, and Dale couldn't resist reaching up and cupping them both. He squeezed them hard and heard her tell him to squeeze them harder. He obeyed, and then pulled on her pink nipples as she began to moan from the pleasure of his cock buried deep inside her.

She began to moan louder, and he could suddenly feel her pussy getting tighter as her orgasm approached. Just as she screamed that she was going to climax, he came deep inside her. She rocked leisurely back and forth rubbing her clit along his slowly deflating cock, enjoying the last moments of her climax before slumping down onto his chest. They stayed like that for a few minutes, and then Candy rolled off onto her back next to him.

"You are an incredibly sexual person; are you made that way?" said Dale.

"The succubae were made to be sexual. We are the very essence of what you would call a slut. To us, sex is a tool, something to use when we need to get our own way," replied Candy.

Dale appreciated her honesty, but the thoughts of his family were still on his mind. He would miss his parents, no matter how much his life had now changed.

****

The next morning, Dale awoke to find his surroundings different from those he was used to. Then he remembered the day before, and shot up in bed to look around.

"No, it wasn't a dream," said Candy as she sat on her own bed staring at him.

Dale rubbed his eyes and then looked at her again. Her perfect body was something worth waking up to, but Dale tried to keep his cool. He looked again. It was hard not to look.

"Um, Candy, is there something you could wear that's a little less distracting?" he said eventually.

"Oh, you mean something like this," she replied.

Suddenly, she was wearing a tiny see-through nightie. Her breasts, along with her hardened nipples, were pushing the front out, and the hem barely reached her hips. She stood up and spun around for him to see. She wore no panties, which left nothing to the imagination. He started to get hard, but was determined to stop her from manipulating him.

"I can see more now than I did a minute ago. Is there nothing you can wear that allows a modicum of modesty?" he said, trying his best not to let her tease him.

"Um, let me think. Oh, how about this," she replied.

He looked again and saw her dressed in a tight leotard. Her breasts were straining the material surrounding them, and the crotch part of the outfit was riding up the slit of her pussy.

"Okay, you're doing that deliberately, aren't you?" he said.

"Well, of course I am. I'm a succubus. I have no desire to dress appropriately. I'm comfortable with whom and what I am. You need to accept that and we can then move on," she replied.

Then she turned into the famous pop star Beyonce and was completely naked.

"Oh my, this one makes you blush. Why's that?" said Candy as she walked over to his bed.

"Because Beyonce is special to me; she's someone whom I admire and not a sex object," replied Dale sternly.

Candy turned back to her natural form and then sat on Dale's bed.

"From now on, I'll only change if you want me to. I'm just trying to make you see that being my partner can be a lot of fun," she said.

"I realize that, but I think I prefer reality as opposed to fantasy. That's just the way I am."

"You're different from those I've been involved with in the past. You're more mature than most, and you have an innocence about you that I find refreshing," said Candy "Anyway, it's time for business."

She then produced two small cubes, which she placed onto the table between the two beds. Next, she laid a metal bar over the top of them and held it with the palm of her hand. Suddenly, an image began to materialize from a smoke-like substance appearing between both cubes. It began to form; first, it was a man then it changed into a dog, and finally, a horse.

"Ah, I haven't seen one of them for a while," she said as she picked the cubes up again.

"What haven't you seen for a while?" said Dale.

"That was our next target. It's a shape-shifter. I haven't come across one of those for well over a year."

Dale got dressed, and they both left together. The maid saw the door opening from the hallway, but saw no one coming out. She looked inside, but the room was vacant. She shook her head and carried on with her job.

Candy held another object in her hand when they reached the street, and as they approached the main road, she turned to Dale.

"It's that way," she said pointing towards town.

She walked slightly in front of Dale, and he couldn't help staring at her tight and well-formed butt as she walked along.

Oh my god, she's perfect, he thought.

"I can almost feel your eyes burning into my butt, young man," she said, teasing him.

Dale felt a flush in his cheeks and wondered why he was like he was. He adored and even lusted after women, but he admired them as well. He admired their form, and he admired the way that they could make him react to it. Perhaps it was just his age, and with time, he would learn to accept embarrassing moments like these. He resigned himself to trying harder, and not allowing Candy's slutty behavior to faze him.

Soon, they were approaching a huge shopping mall, and Candy's hand-held gadget was telling them that their objective could be found within.

"Okay, we know our target is in here, but finding him or her will be difficult. How would you like to proceed?" said Candy.

"Well, I could enter each store and watch for anyone looking my way. Sooner or later we would enter the right one," suggested Dale.

"The trouble with that approach is that our target could be on a break or out back retrieving some stock, and we'd miss them without knowing it," replied Candy.

"Can't your gadget pinpoint their location?"

"No, it's merely for general directions in which the target is located; it can't tell me which person is using a disguise," replied Candy.

"In that case, I think our best bet is to wait for the mall to close and use the locator when they go home. At least that way, we'll know where the individual lives," said Dale.

Candy just nodded in agreement.

"That leaves us several hours to kill. What would you like to do in the meantime?" she said.

Dale wanted to go home and visit his parents, but he shook that idea off. Then he realized he was hungry.

"How do we eat in public?" he said.

"We can become tangible and visible. Eating in public places is the one time we do. Why do you ask, are you hungry?"

"Yes, I could eat some food right about now," responded Dale.

Candy led the way to a small diner and just as they reached it, her clothing changed into an acceptable short dress with high heels. She then opened the door and they both entered.

"Good morning," said the server behind the counter, who was looking directly at Dale.

"Good morning," he replied.

They sat down in one of the many booths, and each picked up a menu.

"I didn't even feel the transition from invisible to corporeal," whispered Dale.

"No, you won't feel it. It's something that's natural. However, it's also the one time that you're vulnerable, which is why my last master is no longer with us. He preferred to feel the air on his skin, but look where that got him," replied Candy.

They had a good breakfast and Candy paid for it, leaving a generous tip as they left.

"Where do you keep the things you keep using, like money and the gadgets you use?" said Dale when they were no longer corporeal.

"Money is just an illusion to those we have to pay, whereas the gadgets I use are always with me, just like your sword," replied Candy.

They talked a lot more in town, and Dale started to feel comfortable around Candy towards the end of everyone's work shift. As soon as they saw that the stores were closing, Candy used her locator gadget once more, and this time it was pointing out of town.

"He or she must have left for the day, so let's follow and see where they lead us," said Candy.

"Incidentally Candy, why is a shape-shifter considered a monster?"

"In order for a shape-shifter to take on another form, they have to kill the original and absorb them into their being. So, every time they use a different person or animal, that person or animal is no more," replied Candy.

"Wow, to think I've been surrounded by this type of thing all of my life and had no idea," said Dale.

"Personally, I don't think humans would want to know that they exist. They believe they're at the top of the food chain, and if that notion were suddenly dispelled, well, let's just say that I don't think they could handle it."

They walked until they eventually came to the suburbs, and soon located the home where the shape-shifter resided. It was a large house with a beautiful garden and well-kept lawn.

"These monsters really try to fit in, don't they?" said Dale.

"That's why they're so successful in fooling you all," replied Candy.

They knocked on the door but didn't get an answer, so they went around to the back. There was a little old lady pulling up some weeds in the back garden.

"Hello, can I help you?" she said.

Dale momentarily forgot that he wasn't visible and nearly answered her question. Then he remembered that if she could see him, she had to be his target. He reached up and withdrew his blade.

She saw it and stood up quickly, having dropped all pretense of being fragile.

"I always knew that this day would come, but I'm not going without a fight," she said as she changed into a lion.

Dale stepped back, before realizing that in his current form, the lion couldn't harm him. He didn't think she knew that because she suddenly sprang up and was bearing down on him. Dale swung his sword, and as it passed through the head of the lion, she let out a squeal of anguish before hitting the ground in two halves. She then turned into her original form, which Dale didn't recognize, and evaporated. Dale placed the sword at his back and turned to Candy.

"That's twice it's been a female. Is there any reason for that?" said Dale.

"No, that's just the luck of the draw. The next three could all be male for all we know," replied Candy.

They left to find another hotel, and as luck would have it, there was one a mile down the road. Dale quickly looked at the list of available rooms behind the clerk's desk and located a room at the back of the list. Once inside, they became solid and lay on the beds to relax.

"Tell me Candy, will we have a target every day?"

"No, there'll be times that we'll have to move on. However, sooner or later we'll have to return. Monsters are always on the move, at least in the most part. Very few actually set root to a single place because they know that we exist. In fact, the ones that live the longest are those that are on the move constantly," replied Candy.

"Um, I don't quite know how to put this, but I'm in the mood for some fun tonight," said Dale, much to Candy's surprise.

"Oh, what would you like me to do?" responded Candy.

Dale thought about it for a moment, and although he knew what he wanted her to do, he was still finding it difficult to admit. Candy could see his hesitation and touched his head.

"Oh, you little devil you. You enjoy role playing," she said knowingly with a huge grin.

Suddenly, she was wearing a low-cut French maid's outfit with a frilly underlay. Her legs were covered with black seamless stockings with a red garter belt around her upper thigh, but the lowest part of her uniform barely covered her butt. She leaned over him, showing a good portion of her cleavage as she did so, and started to stroke the growing hardness beneath his pants.

"Is this to your liking?" she whispered.

His cock was already fully erect so she didn't need the question answered, as she followed the shape of it with the palm of her hand. Her breasts heaved as she breathed in and out and moved nearer. Dale was transfixed he was so turned on. His cock was responding to her touch, but was starting to feel uncomfortable beneath his pants. She suddenly relieved him when she pulled the zipper down and reached inside to take hold of his solid shaft.

"You have a nice cock, Dale; it makes for a pleasant change from the last two masters I had," said Candy as her hand traveled the entire length of his pulsating member.

"Turn around, I want to taste you," replied Dale.

Candy could tell that this was exciting him and didn't refuse his request. By the time she'd turned around, her stockings were no longer there, and Dale could see her sweet shaven pussy approaching his face. He pushed the frills from her maid's dress up and over her back and then started to lick her slit. She pushed back a bit further, making him move back until his cock was directly below her head. She covered it and allowed all of it inside her mouth as she felt his tongue repeatedly swipe her protruding clit.

Dale adored the feeling of the end of his cock brushing the back of her throat as he licked her furiously. He enjoyed how she squirmed each time he flicked her clit with the tip of his tongue, and how her mouth seemed to tighten around the end of his cock when she was drawing it out. Above all though, the way she was dressed excited the hell out of him. In fact, it excited him so much that he started to cum all too quickly.

Candy caressed his balls as she felt his seed surging up to explode inside her mouth, and then commenced in sucking him dry. From the moment he started to cum, he pushed his tongue inside her pussy and kept darting in and out. He loved the bittersweet taste of her nectar, and as his seed filled her mouth, she began to experience her own orgasm. Candy didn't stop sucking him until she thought he'd stay hard, and then she got off the bed. She sat on the edge as she stroked him and asked what he wanted her to do next.

"I'll let you decide this time," replied Dale.

Suddenly, Candy was dressed in a school uniform. She was wearing a short plaid skirt, a white blouse and cotton socks. Her hair was braided into two pony tails, and her breasts were threatening to break the buttons that were holding them back. She pulled her skirt up to flash him, which is when he realized that she was wearing skimpy, white cotton panties.

"Do you want to play with me?" she said as she held one leg up and swayed back and forth.

Dale got off the bed and turned her around, before bending her over the bed. He lifted her skirt and gripped her panties with both hands, before ripping a huge hole in them. He pushed her forward and lined himself up with her pussy before pushing his cock in. She screamed with pleasure, which only made him push harder. She'd really turned him on, and now all he wanted to do was fuck her hard. As he gripped her butt cheeks, he decided to slap her as well. The sound reverberated around the room, and she begged for more. He slapped her harder repeatedly until she screamed that she was going to cum.

When she did climax, he could feel her pussy tightening around his cock, making it harder for him to push in. He kept pushing, and then suddenly he started to cum himself and moaned aloud that he was doing so. Candy ground her butt against him, wanting to feel his seed as it spewed into her. When he'd finished, he held his cock inside her as deep as it would go, and stayed there for a minute before disengaging. They both fell to the bed after that to catch their breath, and when Dale looked her way once more, he discovered that she was now dressed as normal.

"Did you enjoy that?" said Candy.

"You know I did; after all, you read my mind," replied Dale.

"It might interest you to know that your fantasies are pretty much the norm for guys. I'm glad about that though, I don't particularly like men who are too kinky."

"Tell me Candy, how long have you been doing this?" said Dale.

"A little over two hundred years now, but who's counting," replied Candy.

"So, would it be fair to say that you're immortal?"

"We both are as long as you're careful," replied Candy.

"Seriously, you mean as long as I don't make the kind of mistake my predecessor made, I could live forever?"

"Yes, that's your reward for doing the job. I'm sorry, I thought you knew that."

"Oh my god, but then there's the down side; I'll have to do this for the rest of eternity," said Dale.

"Not true; there will come a time when all the monsters have been eradicated. On that day, you will be free to do whatever you wish. I, on the other hand, will have to return to Hell, so I'd be happy if we never run out of monsters to kill."

All of that left Dale with a lot to think about, but as he lay there thinking, he soon fell asleep. He awoke to a sound coming from the bathroom and got out of bed. He opened the door to find Candy lying on the bathroom floor groaning. She looked as if she were in pain.

"Candy, what's wrong?" shouted Dale rushing to her side.

"Someone is using voodoo on an effigy of me. They somehow managed to get some of my hair, or something else that belongs to me. I've felt this before, many years ago, and it turned out to be a witch. The locator found her for me but aaah..."

She suddenly doubled up again and couldn't speak anymore. Dale held her, and then asked her if he could use the gadget for looking at their next target. When the pain died down a little, Candy brought it out and handed it over. Dale had seen how she'd used it once before and did the same thing. The smoke-like substance began to form a shape, and sure enough, the picture of an old hag appeared between the cubes. "I need the locator so that I can take her out." Candy reached behind, and suddenly the locator appeared in her hand. Dale took hold of it, and it immediately pulled him towards the door.

"Stay here, Candy. I'll track her down as quickly as I can and take her out," said Dale.

Candy tried to call out, but the pain stopped her; besides, Dale was already out the door and running down the corridor. Once outside, Dale discovered something he didn't know. He was running and realizing that he was moving extremely fast. He figured it must be that there was no mass or resistance from the air to slow him down. Pretty soon he was homing in on the location, which turned out to be a large fenced-off mansion. He walked through the gate, appreciating just one of the abilities he now possessed.

When he reached the front door, he walked through and was aware almost immediately that the people he saw inside were all watching him. He didn't know how they could see him, but they weren't his target so, for now, he ignored them. He put the locator away and began to search the building. It was when he passed through into an upstairs bedroom that he discovered what he was looking for. Directly in front of him and standing in front of the window was the old hag he'd seen in the monster imager.

"I'm here to end you," he said as he reached up for his sword.

"We've been expecting you, young man," she replied calmly.

Dale suspected there was more to this than met the eye, but he didn't know what it was. Just then, he could hear chanting coming from various parts of the room. He stepped forward, ready to take out the witch but suddenly felt strange. He stopped walking, looked around, and when he didn't see anything, he took another step. Then he felt a hand on his shoulder and turned to find a young man.

How is he able to touch me? Thought Dale?

Just as he was thinking that, the same man pulled him backwards and slammed him into the door. Dale was dazed but conscious, and tried to regain his footing.

"You may be wondering why your powers are deserting you, young man. I think before we kill you, you deserve to know whom you are up against," said the old hag from across the room.

Dale managed to stand up, only to find two men blocking his path. He could still hear the chanting and knew that he was now solid and unable to use his gifts. The sword had vanished from his hand as he hit the door. He guessed that it had probably returned to its scabbard, but dare not reach up for it. Besides, he wanted to learn a little about whom he was up against.

"We've known about your kind for some time now. However, what we didn't know was when our turn would show up on your list of things to kill. I came up with a spell that would inform me when I was to be next. I knew that wasn't enough though, I needed allies. I knew that the only ally I could ever hope to get help from was another one of your targets. After all, they would appear on your list sooner or later. I then devised a spell that would make you corporeal and at the same time vulnerable, which is what the chant you hear is doing. I see you looking at the men before you. I'm guessing you're trying to work out what kind of monsters they are," said the old hag.

Dale was curious as to what they were, but he wasn't about to admit it.

"Well, let me tell you. You're in the presence of vampires."

Dale looked shocked; he wasn't even aware that vampires were real. Candy had never mentioned them, and he assumed that the reason for that was because they were fictional characters, or so he believed.

"You look surprised, I'm guessing that you're new to all of this," she said.

Dale could see a doll in her hand as she lifted it up in front of her.

"Of course, stopping you was only one part of the plan. We had to stop your bodyguard as well. In fact, it was essential that we stopped her first. You may or may not know this, but the succubae are a most formidable enemy. They are even stronger than vampires, which is the main reason the vampires were willing to help me. Now then, it is time to die," she said with a smile.

The vampires on either side turned to face him. He quickly reached up for his sword, but his hand was blocked from reaching it with a speed that surprised him. Then one of the vampires bit his neck, and he could feel the blood being drawn out at an alarming rate. He was going to die and he knew it, but even though he knew that fact, he still wanted to live. His mind raced as to what he should do, and then an idea occurred to him. He'd always heard that to become a vampire you had to be both bitten and to have tasted the blood of the vampire biting you. With that in mind, and being so close to the vampire that was sucking out his blood, he opened his mouth and bit the vampire's arm as hard as he could. He just managed to taste the blood as the vampire pulled away, and he fell to the floor in a heap.

He was still alive, but then the room seemed to be spinning, and he blacked out. When he opened his eyes again, he found that he was in a wooden box. He had no idea how long he'd been there, but he had to get free. He pushed the top of the box but there was no give whatsoever. Then he remembered his abilities and turned intangible. He sat up and discovered that his head was just clearing the ground he'd been buried in. After standing and climbing out of the coffin, he looked around. He was in a forest, with no clue as to where it was.

He reached up, and his sword was still there. He guessed that no one could steal that. Then he remembered the locator, and sure enough he still had it. When it was activated, it was telling him that his target was due east. He started to run and found that he could now run even faster than before. It didn't take him long before reaching the edge of the forest, and discovered the mansion he'd been attacked in was just a mile ahead.

His thoughts as he ran were of Candy and how she must still be in pain. He had to stop the witch at all costs. How was he still alive, and why, were the main thoughts that entered his mind, but such questions could wait. Soon he was approaching the front of the mansion again, only this time it would be different. As he passed through the door, he saw two vampires ahead of him. He lifted his arm and reached for the sword. Once in hand, he ran forward and with an arcing swing, he cut through them both. Their tops seemed to be detaching from the rest of them at first, and then they suddenly turned to dust.

He ran up the stairs and did the same to everyone he knew could see him. Until now, he'd gotten lucky as they weren't prepared for him, but as he entered the same room as before, there were four vampires blocking his path from the hag who stood behind them. The chanting started up again, only this time he didn't wait to be told what it was. He moved with a purpose and sliced the air with speed and meaning. The vampires might be able to move fast, but they'd have to be quick to avoid the blade that could barely be seen as it passed through the air.

His first target wasn't quick enough, and the dust coming from his corpse filled the room around him. They attacked him together, and he was somehow able to dodge each of their attacks. He kept swinging and caught another one, and then he did something unexpected. He ignored the two remaining vampires and ran straight to the hag. Before she could even move, she felt the blade at her throat.

"Goodbye," was all he said as his sword cut through her neck and severed her head.

The vampires had stopped behind him and then backed up. They had failed and saw no reason to die for a lost cause. In a moment, they were gone. Dale allowed them to leave as they weren't his target, at least not on this day. He reached down and took a hold of the doll that was still in the witch's hand. He pulled out two pins that were sticking in its chest, and he could see a long hair wrapped around it. He gently untied it, before dropping the doll onto the floor. He had no way of knowing if that was all he had to do, but decided to wait outside. Within twenty minutes, Candy was coming down the driveway.

"I'm sorry it took me so long, I was trapped for a while," he said as she got nearer.

When she reached him, she placed her hand around his neck and squeezed hard.

"I'm sorry too, Dale; I wish I could've been here. I genuinely like you and would've enjoyed working alongside you in the coming years," she said as a tear formed in each corner of her eyes.

"Wait, please," he managed to say.

Uncharacteristically, Candy loosened her grip enough to allow him to speak.

"Why are you doing this?" he said.

"Of all my abilities, I have one that allows me to see through certain things and find the truth. I knew as soon as I saw you that you'd been turned into a vampire," replied Candy.

"So, it worked. I was in deep trouble, Candy. The blood was being drained from me, and the only thing I could think of doing was to bite the vampire, thereby making myself one so that I could finish what I started. When I came to, I found that they'd buried me out in the forest. I quickly came back here to take the witch out, but I didn't know for sure that I'd been turned," said Dale as he sat down heavily on the ground.

Candy was conflicted; she knew that she had to take him out, but she also knew that he'd saved her. She didn't know what to do.

"Tell me, Candy; is there such a thing as a good monster? I mean, I don't feel evil, and I certainly don't want to kill anybody," said Dale.

"That may be true now, but there will come a time when you'll want to feed on the blood of a human," replied Candy.

"Couldn't you procure the blood I'll need from time to time so that I never have to go that far?"

"I could, but there is no precedent for a monster becoming a monster slayer."

"Well, how about this; if my image ever appears between the two cubes, you take me out. If not, we carry on as before," suggested Dale.

Candy thought about it for a minute and then came to a decision.

"Up until now, you haven't done anything evil, and provided I supply you with the blood I know that you'll need, I see no reason why that should ever change. However, I might receive a calling on this matter, and I'll have to follow any decision that's made. The powers that be probably already know what's happened to you, but I doubt they'll come to a decision as to what to do about it anytime soon. Until then, we will carry on as before," said Candy.

Dale stood up and thanked her before they both left to return to the hotel.

****

Dale sat in the hotel room, trying to get his head around the fact that he was now a vampire. He looked up at Candy, who was pacing the room deep in thought.

"Tell me, Candy; why did you decide not to kill me?"

Candy stopped pacing and turned to him.

"There are two reasons. The first is because of me. On Earth, I'm considered a monster, so how can I judge you. However, it was the second reason that stopped me. You can still hold the sword and use the ability to become intangible, which tells me that you're still good. There are just two people who can touch that sword, and they are both in this room. If you'd become evil, you wouldn't be able to hold it as it wouldn't recognize you as a slayer."

"I didn't think of it that way. So, are we going to carry on as before?"

"Until I'm told otherwise, we will carry on as before. However, this does change a few things. The first is that you no longer have to sleep or eat, except for the blood that you'll need on a weekly basis. In addition, I'm not sure about the sunlight. Will it affect you when you use the intangible ability or will it burn you?"

"I forgot about the sun, and I hate the fact that I won't need sleep. I enjoyed sleeping, not to mention the food," replied Dale feeling depressed.

Candy sat down beside him.

"In all the excitement, I forgot to thank you for saving me. I do appreciate it and know how hard it must have been for you," she said.

"I tried my best, but the fact is they were not only expecting me – they were prepared. They took you out of the picture first with the voodoo doll, knowing that I'd try to stop them. They had a chant that made me vulnerable by disabling my ability to become intangible. I don't think we've seen the last of them either. On the plus side, I'm now able to do things that I couldn't do before. I'm much stronger than a mere human and a lot faster," replied Dale.

"How do you feel though, are you feeling the need to feed yet?"

"That's the strange thing about it all. I don't feel any different than I did before it happened. Is that normal?"

"I don't know. I wish I had the answers for you. I think the best thing we can do is to carry on and do the job at hand. With that in mind," said Candy, taking out the two cubes.

Dale watched her place them close together and hold her hand over the bar. A figure began to show itself. It had a male face, with two horns coming out at the top of its head.

"That's unfortunate– we're up against a demon," said Candy.

"I'm assuming they're dangerous?" replied Dale.

"It depends on what kind of demon we're up against. You see, there are several kinds of demon. The lesser demons are the weakest, but the higher demons have abilities that make them formidable enemies. I'm a demon myself, one of the most powerful in Hell, but there are some demons who are stronger and faster than me."

They left the hotel and followed the locator, which led them out of town. Soon, they were entering the industrial sector, and the locator was taking them to an abandoned warehouse. Once they entered the locator turned off, indicating that the demon was in that building.

"How do you want to handle this one, Candy?" said Dale.

"Be on your guard and stick with me. If I know demons, it will try to separate us," replied Candy.

"Then you don't know demons very well, my dear," said a voice that seemed to be coming from the rafters.

Candy looked up and around but couldn't see anyone.

"You know why we're here. If you come out now, we will make it as painless as possible," she called out.

"That's very considerate of you, but I have a counter offer. If you leave now, I won't kill you painfully," said what they assumed was the demon.

"The only death here tonight will be yours, and I'll be sending you back to Hell," replied Candy.

"You know you're only here through sheer luck of the draw. You're no different from me. In fact, in many ways you're inferior," said the demon.

Just then a loud sound made them both reach for their ears to block it out. When it didn't stop Candy tried to locate its origin, but before she could, a mass of something large fell to the floor from the rafters twenty feet away. Dale noticed something immediately.

"Candy, we're both solid. That's the second time in two days the power to become intangible has failed me. It's becoming a liability," said Dale.

Candy was trying to concentrate on the figure before them, and couldn't quite discern what they were up against. The lighting was poor at best.

"Keep on your toes, Dale; he's about to attack," said Candy.

As if on cue, a huge tentacle suddenly shot through the air towards them, taking Dale off his feet and pinning him to the back wall. Dale looked down to feel the thick hide that surrounded the tentacle and then reached up for his sword. Taking it out, he raised his hand and sliced straight through the slimy limb. He heard a cry in the background, but before he could celebrate his release, the severed limb re-formed and pinned him again. This time it drove harder and pierced Dale's stomach. Dale coughed up blood and tried to raise his sword arm again, but before he could, he lost consciousness.

"We can now talk freely," said the demon as it moved forward towards Candy.

When it was a few feet away, Candy realized what it was.

"You can't be free; you'd have to be summoned with the aid of a sacrifice," said Candy.

"In point of fact, several," replied the demon.

"It was the vampires, wasn't it?" said Candy knowingly.

"Yes, my dear; they seem to think that you're a threat. Personally, I'd put you squarely down as an annoyance, but that's just me. I think before I kill you, I'll have a bit of fun," replied the demon.

Before Candy could reply, several tentacles shot out from its body and gripped both her legs and her arms. The demon then moved nearer. Candy knew it as the inseminator, a demon that was made to impregnate any captives with Hell spawn. His only function was to bring about the rebirth of Satan upon Earth. However, the recipient had to be a willing host.

"Try not to struggle, my dear; I'm sure you'll enjoy what I'm about to do to you," said the demon.

Another tentacle came out of its chest and ripped her clothing away, before the ones restraining her pulled her nearer to him. Until now, all of the tentacles had emerged from his chest, but the next one came from his groin. It slowly writhed in the air, creeping ever closer until it was touching her inner thigh. Then it moved up until it was caressing her pussy lips. The tip probed the opening and moved slowly back and forth over her clit. Candy was a succubus, and if the succubae have one flaw, it's their insatiable appetite for sex. Although she would never admit it, the urges of her creation were telling her to enjoy the moment.

She felt the end of his tentacle pushing forward, stretching her opening wide as it slid inside her. Her mind wanted to rip it apart, but her body wanted it to take her hard and fast. Then she felt herself being lifted up into the air by the tentacles around her legs and arms. Once she was a few feet off the ground, the tentacle inside her began to pick up speed.

"Ah, fuck yes. Harder, you piece of shit, fuck me harder," she cried out.

Her legs were then pulled apart wider and the tentacle between her legs moved in further. Her nipples hardened from all the pounding, and her juices flowed freely as the onslaught continued. Then with her eyes closed she could feel another tentacle moving up the back of her leg. She opened her eyes to look down and watched the second one drawing nearer to its prize. It squirted something as it approached her ass and then spread her cheeks before slipping inside her.

Candy threw her head back to enjoy this new sensation, and felt guilty for not being able to help Dale. She was hoping that he'd come to the rescue, but she had no way of knowing if he were even capable of doing so. Then the two tentacles inside her moved in time with one another, and she began to experience her first orgasm.

****

Dale was now waking up again, and looked down to see the tentacle still pinning him to the wall. He knew that he could get free, but he had to heal before he could attack otherwise he'd just die trying. He looked around as he heard Candy screaming out with pleasure. He was thankful that the demon was otherwise distracted. Then he spotted a window at the far side of the warehouse. He took hold of his sword again, took a deep breath and sliced through the tentacle with one strike. He heard the scream coming from the demon, but ignored it and hit the floor running.

The tentacle healed within seconds and turned to chase him. It was as if it had a life of its own, but long before it reached him Dale knew that he was going to make the window. He dived through it, sending shards of glass flying in all directions. When he hit the ground outside, he carried on running until he was sure that he was safe. He then ripped his shirt off to look at the wound. He had a large hole straight through his stomach. He willed it to heal, but nothing happened, and then he heard a voice behind him.

"What are you doing here, young man?" it said.

He turned to find a security guard walking towards him. He suddenly had an idea, but he was loath to try it. However, his partner was in trouble, and this was an emergency. He suddenly darted to the security guard and bit into his neck, taking a mouthful of blood as he did so. The guard fell down once Dale felt he had enough and began to crawl away whimpering. Dale spat the blood from his mouth into his hand, and then smothered it around the wound on his stomach. Sure enough, the wound started to heal faster.

****

"Even your friend has left you behind, my dear; you're all mine now," said the demon as he pushed his tentacles in a little deeper.

Candy let out a groan of satisfaction. She'd now climaxed three times and was heading for a fourth.

"Stop the talking and fuck me harder," she screamed.

"You truly are a succubus, aren't you? You're such a slut, yet perfect in every way. It's going to be a shame that I have to kill you," replied the demon.

Just then, the tentacle that was holding Candy's left leg was severed. The demon let out a scream of anguish and looked around. He couldn't see anyone, and just as he remembered to use the sound that would stop the use of Dale's power, the right tentacle was severed. He let the sound go, and Dale stood before him.

"You fucking insect, I'll tear you limb from limb," screamed the demon.

It then let go of Candy, allowing her to drop to the floor, and turned its attention onto Dale. Its tentacles began to heal, and several others came out at speed towards Dale's position. Dale had decided to use his speed instead of just rushing in, and managed to evade every tentacle that came his way. At first, he would make out that he was on the run, and then he'd turn and attack. By doing that randomly, he managed to inflict several wounds on the demon's appendages.

Candy was a mere memory to the demon, which was its biggest mistake. Once she was composed, she waited until it had its back to her and moved with a purpose. She jumped onto its oversized head and threw her arms around its thick neck. She squeezed as hard as she could and that got the demon's attention. A succubus is not to be ignored. Suddenly, the tentacles were coming back and trying to shake her off. That made Dale's decision to attack head on all the easier. He ran as fast as he could, and just as he was within five feet, he shouted for Candy to let go. She did and slid to the floor. Dale then launched himself off the floor and passed his blade straight through the demon's neck and out the other side. Candy looked up to see the head sliding off and the rest of the body slumping to the floor.

"Are you okay?" said Dale as he helped her to get up from the floor.

"I will be. I'm sorry I wasn't much help with this one, Dale," she said feeling guilty.

"Don't be, I still have a lot to learn. I'll tell you one thing though. If it hadn't been for the fact that I was now a vampire, we'd both have lost this one," replied Dale.

They walked out of the warehouse to the sound of police sirens in the distance. Dale figured the security guard had phoned them. They both used their gift of intangibility as the cars pulled up, and walked straight by them.

****

Back at the hotel and after a quick shower, they sat on the bed together to talk.

"I'm not sure of our future together, but I do know one thing – it's a pleasure to have you as my partner."

"Thanks Candy, that means a lot to me. Incidentally, have you ever made love to a vampire?" replied Dale.

"As a matter of fact I have, but it was over seventy years ago."

Dale threw her back onto the bed and then spread her legs, before kissing his way up her inner thigh and biting the tender skin near her pussy. He licked the blood from the end of one of his fangs and started to lick her moist pussy lips. Candy let out a squeal and spread her legs further.

This is going to be a long night, she thought.

The End

Soul Mates

Arianna sat in the garden, her face full of concentration. She was staring intently at the flower that had just lost another petal. As it fell, she prayed to God to grant her the power to heal. The petal touched the ground, and nothing else happened. She heard a voice coming from behind and turned to see Gabriel.

"Are you ready, Arianna?" he said.

"Yes, I have to admit though, I'm afraid," she replied.

"Fear is not always a bad thing, Arianna; it will keep you on your toes," said Gabriel.

She stood up and followed him into the grand hall. This was where she came to pray. It always seemed so majestic, with all the huge statues depicting angels both alive and dead. She wondered what the coming days would reveal as they approached the celestial chamber.

"I can almost feel your apprehension, Arianna. Just remember that you have God's love inside you. There was a reason that God chose you – it hasn't revealed itself yet, but it will. I know I needn't tell you to have faith in that belief, but try to look on the positive side. If your gifts haven't shown yet, it's because God has a plan for you. When you get down there, search for those that need help. They can be found in abundance," said Gabriel.

Gabriel opened the door to the chamber, and Arianna stepped inside. She could see the pedestal in the center of the room all lit up and waiting.

"When you did this Gabriel, how long did it take for you to find the light?" she said, as they approached the pedestal.

"A year, but it was a year that I will never forget. I learned things during that time which God had intended for me to learn. What happened to me back then is what defines me now. I wouldn't change it for the world. You will undoubtedly go through a similar experience. Whether it takes you a year or two days, it will be something that will remain with you forever," replied Gabriel.

Arianna took hope from that and after taking a deep breath, she stepped onto the pedestal.

"God be with you," said Gabriel as the light surrounded Arianna.

Arianna tingled all over, and as Gabriel's image began to fade, she smiled and then closed her eyes. Seconds later, she opened them again as she could feel a light breeze on her face and discovered she was now standing upon Earth. She looked around and felt a sense of awe from the sight of the mountains in the distance, as well as the meadows that spread out in front of her.

'Which way to go...' She thought as she looked around.

She spotted a road in the distance and decided to head towards that. A road meant civilization, and she was here, after all, to help those in need. As she walked, she saw a deer and smiled at it. The deer approached her, sniffing the air as it did so. It came up close and then nudged the back of her hand. Arianna stroked its head and back, before walking on. The birds sang in the trees, and some came nearer to take a closer look. She couldn't help watching them as they glided down to land on branches that stood in her path.

Her long white gown seemed out of place here, as well as restricting. It made walking through this wooded area seem like a chore. She reached down and held the dress above the knees, and then ripped a hole in it. Once it was started, she pulled the fabric around her legs, tearing it as best she could in a straight line. She discarded the excess and looked down. It wasn't perfect, but she did feel more comfortable now as she walked on.

Soon, she was walking on the road that she'd spotted earlier and marveled at the various modes of transport that passed by. Some would sound loud horns, and others could be heard whistling as they passed. She had no idea what these customs meant, but she waved to them all as they passed. Then a stray dog appeared from the bushes and started to walk beside her.

"Hello little one, it sure is loud here, isn't it?" she said.

The dog looked up at her and gave a single bark. She carried on walking and then, in the distance, she could see one of the many vehicles that had passed her on the road, pulled over to the side with its front opened up. Smoke seemed to be escaping from the interior, and as she got nearer, she saw that there had been three men inside the vehicle. One of them spotted her as she approached.

"Hello, what have we here then?" he said, making the other two look in the same direction.

"Hello there, it's a lovely day," said Arianna as she got near enough for them to hear.

"It sure is, and it's getting better by the minute," said the first man, "so, what are you doing out here?"

"I'm just walking towards my destiny," she said innocently.

"Is that right," he laughed, "perhaps we are part of that destiny."

"I don't think so, do you need saving?" replied Arianna.

"Oh yes, I've needed saving for quite some time now," he replied sarcastically as he stared at her cleavage.

His friends laughed at that, which only helped to confuse Arianna. The dog started to bark at him until he received a look of contempt, and then it hid behind Arianna.

"Are you coming from a wedding or something? That dress looks so out of place here," he said as he walked up to her.

"My attire is all I'm allowed to bring with me into this world," she responded as she watched him circle her.

He was inspecting her from head to toe, trying to gauge her appearance and understand why someone so attractive would be walking in the middle of nowhere. He placed his hand onto her shoulder and then turned her around to face him.

"Honey, you are not in Kansas. You are, however, in the presence of someone who can help you in ways you couldn't possibly imagine," he said, still staring at her cleavage with lust in his eyes.

Arianna pulled away from him, having sensed something not quite right. She was too naïve to understand what that something was, but she was sure it was coming from this stranger.

"I think I will look for help elsewhere as you don't seem to need my assistance," she said as she tried to walk away.

"Whoa sister, you don't have to rush off straight away. My friends and I could give you a lift once the pickup arrives," he said blocking her path once again.

Arianna started to feel uncomfortable now and wondered what she should do. His friends were now coming up behind him, and they didn't seem any friendlier than he was. She tried to excuse herself, but they wouldn't let her go, and then the man who had blocked her originally touched her inappropriately.

"Stop that, I am not for you," she said as she tried again to escape.

Suddenly, a voice could be heard from the side of the woods.

"Leave her alone."

The men looked around to see a farmhand climbing over a fence and coming towards them.

"Beat it pal, this is none of your concern," said the bully.

"It looks to me as if you're stopping this woman from going on her way, and it ends right now," said the farmhand.

Unfortunately, he got a little too close and the bully whipped around on him, smacking him in the face with his fist. The farmhand went down, and Arianna called out for them to stop. They ignored her, and then the other two started to kick the farmhand while he was on the ground.

Arianna screamed as she had never witnessed violence before, and didn't like what she was seeing. They turned to face her as she screamed and suddenly stopped what they were doing. They looked scared, and for a moment, Arianna thought that they were looking at her. However, they had seen something behind her, something they couldn't explain. Arianna turned around and saw a dark spinning cloud a few feet away. It got bigger and then stopped spinning as she watched, then suddenly a beautiful woman walked through to stand a few feet away from Arianna.

****

Brandy stood over the bed, where her assigned target was located. He was fast asleep, and being a baby, completely helpless. She raised her fist, ready to strike. However, she wavered and realized that she couldn't do it. For the first time in her life, she couldn't fulfill her master's wish. She knew the assignment was going to be difficult, as taking the firstborn from those who disobeyed Satan was standard fare. She bowed her head and realized that her life was about to end.

No one ever disobeyed an order from the master and expected to tell about it. She'd had a good run though. She was over three hundred years old and could remember the day she was created as if it were yesterday. She'd been Satan's favorite for a while back then, and her life was full of amazing events. She'd seduced so many men and women that Satan named her the Princess of Seduction. She turned to face the wall and then created a portal. As it started to open, she looked back on the baby and smiled. There might be better ways to come to the end of one's life, but none came to mind as she looked upon the child's face and smiled.

Brandy turned back to the wall and then stepped through. She came out inside Satan's quarters.

"Ah, my faithful Brandy, is it done, child?" said Satan.

"Master, it is time. I've had a good run, and I've always enjoyed serving you. However, on this occasion, I simply couldn't do it. I thank you for my life and hope that a more worthy succubus replaces me," said Brandy.

Satan turned to look at her kneeling on the floor.

"Ah, you disappoint me Brandy. I thought I could count on your loyalty," he said and then clapped his hands.

Two succubae walked into the room, and Brandy was friends with both of them.

"Take her away, until I can decide what to do with her," said Satan, as he placed a bracelet around her wrist.

Brandy stood up next to her friends, and they walked her out. They headed to the dungeons, and none of them spoke. They exchanged glances and eye contact that couldn't be maintained, before they locked her up and walked away. Brandy sat on the stone floor with her head buried in her knees, wishing that things could've been different. Within five minutes, Sabrina came back. Sabrina was as close a friend in hell as one could get, being a succubus.

"I cannot see you in here and do nothing about it," said Sabrina.

She then looked at the far wall, and a portal began to form.

"No, I will not allow my disgrace to bear down on you. You are my friend and someone I care deeply for," said Brandy.

"He will not know who helped you Brandy; he might guess it was me, but he won't know. Satan is a man of habits, and he won't do anything to me without proof that I was directly responsible. The chances are he will send me along with others to locate and bring you back. I will of course obey his commands, but at least you have a chance to escape."

Brandy looked up at the portal, now fully formed and then back at Sabrina. She shook her head and stood up.

"Thank you Sabrina, I will try to escape. I hope I get to see you again; you are a true friend," said Brandy as she stepped through the portal.

****

Brandy stepped through next to a road, and witnessed three men backing away, before turning to run. She took in the scene before her and saw the woman dressed in white. She then saw an injured man trying to get to his feet.

"I see you managed to subdue one of them, my dear," said Brandy.

Arianna looked at where she was pointing.

"Oh no, he tried to help me, but those ruffians hurt him," replied Arianna.

The farmhand looked up as best he could as the dog was licking his face, and then a sort of shocked expression appeared across his face as he pointed towards Arianna. Brandy was standing next to Arianna now and looked at where the man was pointing. Arianna was literally glowing, which made Brandy step away from her. As she moved away, the glow faded. She gave Arianna a puzzled look and then stepped closer again. The glow returned.

"What are you?" said Brandy.

Arianna didn't hear that; instead, she ran over to help the man to stand up.

"Are you alright, kind sir? I hated it when they were hurting you. Those ruffians should be punished for what they did," said Arianna.

Brandy came over next and grabbed his other arm, at which point he clutched his side.

"I think they cracked a rib or two," he said painfully, "I'm Jake by the way, and who are you two?"

"My name is Arianna; I'm on a mission to save a soul. Gabriel told me that there would be trials and that I should look out for them. I believe I've just experienced one."

Brandy gave her another look of disbelief but kept her tongue. Then she noticed that Arianna's arm was glowing as it was close to her own.

"Okay, what in God's name is that?" she said.

Arianna looked at her own arm and suddenly let out a scream of joy, while letting go of Jake. This made Brandy jump, and she let go of Jake's other arm. Jake went down like a sack of potatoes and landed in a painful heap.

"The one I'm here to save is close by!" shouted Arianna.

The sun was going down over the trees so twilight was upon them when Brandy stepped up close to Arianna again and watched her light up like a Christmas tree.

"Whoever it is, they must be close," said Arianna.

Brandy looked down at her feet and mumbled, "This might possibly be the dumbest woman on the face of this planet."

Arianna was looking around, when Brandy tapped her on the shoulder. Arianna turned to face her and watched as Brandy placed her own arm up close to hers. The glow was more than evident. The penny finally dropped and Arianna stood staring at Brandy.

"Hi, I'm Brandy."

"Oh, it's you. I'm here to save you, although I don't know what from," said Arianna.

Then they both heard the dog barking and Jake's groaning, and turned to find him trying to stand again. They immediately took an arm each and asked him where they should go.

"There's a large barn over that hill; if you could take me there I can rest and possibly get help," said Jake.

They all started to walk, and by the time they'd reached the top of the hill, it was getting dark. Brandy told Jake to hang on to her shoulder and then told Arianna to come around to her side. Arianna did that and then Brandy placed her arm around Arianna. Suddenly, the path was lit up as Arianna started to glow.

"Arianna, are you an angel?" said Jake.

"No...at least not yet, but I will be when I've saved Brandy," replied Arianna.

"And what are you, Brandy? I mean, it isn't every day you see someone pop out of midair," said Jake.

"I'm a succubus, although, with this bracelet on, I can't prove it," replied Brandy.

"A succubus…isn't that a spawn of hell…no insult intended?" said Jake.

"None taken, but to answer your question, yes I am a spawn of hell."

"How can this be; you're clearly the one I'm supposed to save, but there is no way I could cleanse a succubus, let alone save their soul," said Arianna, "they are by very definition a spawn of Satan and don't even have a soul."

"Ours is not to question why, but to do or die. I forget who said that," replied Brandy.

"You did…although I don't know what it means," said Arianna naïvely.

Brandy shook her head and bit her tongue, as she couldn't believe she was in the presence of an angel. Angels are to be feared, where she came from. They arrived at the barn shortly after that and helped Jake to lie down at the back where there was a pile of hay.

"Take your top off Jake, I might not be a fully-fledged angel just yet, but I do have some healing powers," said Arianna.

Jake removed his shirt painfully and lay back on the hay. He then felt Arianna's hand touching the side that hurt and could see a glow coming for her hand. It felt warm to the touch, and they could all see the bruise visibly beginning to fade away until there was nothing there. Jake sat up and couldn't feel any more pain.

"Do you mean to tell me, you could have healed him back there, and we wouldn't have had to carry him?" said Brandy loudly.

"Um…oh yes, I suppose I could have," replied Arianna, before turning to Jake and mouthing the words 'I'm sorry'.

"It's okay, no harm done. So, what are you two going to do now?"

"We might as well make use of this barn for the night and figure that out tomorrow," said Brandy as she tried to get the bracelet off.

Arianna saw what she was doing and leaned over to touch it. The clasp suddenly sprang open, and the bracelet fell off.

"How did you do that?" said Brandy.

"I can unlock anything. Gabriel said it would help me a lot down here," replied Arianna.

Brandy lay next to Jake, who was in the middle, and then rolled over, before turning back and saying thank you reluctantly. They all awoke the next morning to a great deal of rain, and Brandy wasn't feeling good. In fact, she was shivering, and she knew why.

"You have a temperature," said Arianna, "I've been touching your forehead for the past hour, and it's not doing you any good."

"That's because I'm not sick and what's happening to me is only going to get worse," replied Brandy.

"What is happening to you, if you don't mind me asking?" said Jake coming in from outside the barn carrying fruit.

"As a succubus I have to seduce people from around the world. I seduce someone every day. Sometimes, I seduce more than one. That keeps the fever away, because Satan needed a way to control us and do the job we were designed to do. If I don't seduce someone, this happens. However, I haven't needed help in over a hundred years, until today."

"Let me get this straight, if you seduced me or Arianna here, you'd be fine afterwards?" said Jake.

"Yes, that about sums it up," replied Brandy.

"That's it. Perhaps I'm supposed to help you here. I was told I had to save someone. Well, doing this would save you," said Arianna.

"I seriously doubt that you were sent here to be seduced Arianna," replied Brandy.

"I have to try, otherwise I will never know."

Brandy looked at how serious Arianna was and then turned to Jake.

"Jake, I'm here because I escaped from hell. They will be looking for me, and if you are here when they find me, your life will be in mortal danger. I suggest that you leave here and keep what you have learned to yourself. Trust me when I say that they will not show any mercy," she said.

Jake stood up, having heard enough.

"I will leave, but I leave reluctantly. I think I'd better take the dog with me. I wish you both well and hope that you find some closure to all of this," he said.

Arianna hugged him and thanked him for coming to her aid. She then made a fuss of the dog. Jake just smiled and shook Brandy's hand in goodbye and then left. As he left, he wondered who would believe this story anyway, even if he had the courage to confess to it happening.

Once he'd gone, Brandy turned to Arianna.

"Are you sure about this Arianna, normally I wouldn't hesitate to take advantage but knowing that you are destined to save me in some way, gives me pause."

"Yes, I'm sure...but I must tell you, I am quite innocent in the ways of seduction," replied Arianna.

Brandy allowed her lust to envelope Arianna. The lust made those around her feel as if they were the only ones that mattered. It made Brandy, in this case, look so sexually appealing that Arianna looked upon her as if she'd only just seen her.

"What are these feelings?" cried Arianna.

"Let yourself go with them and trust me; I would never harm you," replied Brandy.

Arianna could feel strange things happening between her legs, things she'd never experienced before. She felt warm inside, and a need to get closer to Brandy. She didn't fight the need, and as she touched Brandy's arm, her skin glowed. Brandy reached over and pulled the straps down on either side of Arianna's dress, before pulling the top itself down. Arianna's perfect breasts stood out, and her nipples already looked hard and erect.

Brandy noticed that whichever part of Arianna's body she touched, it glowed. She laid her hands upon Arianna's breasts making Arianna take a deep breath. Brandy pushed her back onto the hay and then slid the dress off the rest of the way. To say that Arianna's body looked angelic, would, in this case, be extremely accurate. There wasn't a single flaw on her entire body. Brandy started slowly as she realized that Arianna was probably a virgin.

She spread her legs in the hay and then started to lick and kiss her inner thighs. Arianna couldn't believe the sweet sensations she was experiencing and looked down to watch Brandy as she moved up her body. The moment Arianna felt Brandy's tongue touching her private parts she let out a squeal of both shock and awe.

"Oh, why is that so sensitive?" she cried.

Brandy ignored her and carried on. She was enjoying the sweet taste of the forbidden fruit and pushed her tongue past Arianna's angelic slit.

"Mmm...oh God on high, what is this feeling that courses through my body?" said Arianna.

Brandy gripped her thighs and spread them open more, to get nearer to the target. She then kept rolling her tongue over the now erect clit, listening to the sounds of delight coming from Arianna. She then pressed a finger against the warm blushing skin and pushed it inside.

"Ah...ah I don't understand," murmured Arianna with a single tear rolling down her cheek.

Brandy didn't know to what she was referring, and then watched in awe and wonder as Arianna's body started to rise from the hay. She stood up as it rose and kept sucking Arianna's opening until she realized that Arianna was experiencing her very first orgasm. The glow around Arianna's body intensified and just at the pinnacle of excitement, Brandy stopped what she was doing and spread Arianna's legs wider apart. She then looked down between her own legs and a bulge appeared above her pussy, which turned out to be a cock growing inside her.

Suddenly, it popped out and carried on growing. When it was finished growing, she pressed it up against Arianna's opening and pushed it forward. Arianna screamed as the sudden pressure was hurting her and then they both heard a popping sound, and Brandy's cock moved deeper.

"Holy mother, protect me from these overwhelming feelings!" cried Arianna.

Brandy moved her cock in slowly, and once she was sure that it was safe, she began to move faster. Arianna's reaction was that of sheer bliss and utter disbelief. She thought she'd known the joys of life, but doubted that anything could ever approach what she was feeling at this very moment. She was wrong, because Brandy now gripped both her legs as she still hovered above the hay and started to pull her onto the cock faster.

Arianna's eyes glazed over as if she were entering another stage of her euphoric journey, and her body reacted with sudden jerks of motion. Brandy had never seen this before and then felt the tightness of Arianna's womanhood around her cock. Arianna was already experiencing another orgasm. The tightness excited Brandy and suddenly she realized that she too was about to climax. They both came together, and each made a moan of exquisite pleasure as they did so. Then, at the very pinnacle of the orgasm, Arianna began to sink back to the hay and lay there with a soft glow and an aura that surrounded her.

Brandy stood up, looking down on her, and a feeling of warmth passed through her body. She also felt well again, now that she'd seduced someone. She sat down next to Arianna, marveling at the sight before her. Arianna looked as if she were asleep, but suddenly opened her eyes. She looked up at Brandy, smiled and then sat up having realized that they'd done it, she had saved Brandy. However, there was no change in her persona. She was still an angel on a mission, and all she knew for sure was that Brandy had something to do with that mission.

"That was incredible, Brandy. I have never known such intense feelings," she said.

"Come on, we'd better get out of here. If we stay in one place too long, they will find me," said Brandy.

They both got up and walked out to find that the rain had stopped. Brandy didn't know which way to go, so she allowed Arianna to lead the way.

****

Arianna was fascinated by the crystal figurines, which were shaped like angels. She was still with Brandy, but was told she couldn't stand too close as the glowing tended to give her away. They had come across a town, and Brandy had told her to wait and look around while she procured a few essential items that they'd need on their journey. The next store was a women's clothes boutique. She went inside and caught sight of a beautiful red dress in the corner. As she was staring at it, an assistant asked her if she'd like to try it on. She clearly didn't know with whom she was talking.

Arianna decided there and then that she would like to try it on, now that she'd been asked. She suddenly removed her own clothes before the assistant realized what she was doing. Standing in the store completely naked, she grabbed the dress and placed it over her head. The assistant quickly helped her cover up and thanked god that no one had seen her. She then moved her over so that she could see the effect in a freestanding mirror.

"You look beautiful," said the assistant in all honesty.

"Thank you, it is a wonderful dress, but I'm not used to such vivid colors," replied Arianna.

She was about to remove the dress, but the assistant was ready for her this time and directed her to a changing cubicle. As she was changing, Brandy came back with a few supplies and thanked the heavens that Arianna hadn't drawn attention to herself.

"Brandy, can you do that thing to me again?" asked Arianna.

"What thing are you referring to?"

"The seduction thing that you did in the barn," replied Arianna.

"Not here I can't it would draw too much attention, and that's one thing we don't need," said Brandy, making sure there were a few feet of space between them both.

When they left the stores, Arianna followed like a lost sheep and looked forward to being alone with Brandy once more. However, being alone was not something that was going to happen anytime soon, as Brandy suddenly stopped dead in her tracks, making Arianna walk into her. When she spotted her skin start to glow, she quickly backed off, having remembered that it wasn't a good thing in public.

"Stay behind me Arianna, they've found me already," said Brandy.

Arianna looked down the street and saw two very attractive women approaching from either side of the road.

"Do you see that hill above the town?" said Brandy. Arianna nodded. "I'll meet you there, now go and don't look back."

Arianna passed her and kept walking, but as she did, she saw a portal appearing to the side and realized that Brandy wasn't going to fight her way out, she was going to run instead. Arianna proceeded to the top of the hill, and when she got there, Brandy was waiting.

"Did they follow?" said Arianna.

"No, they cannot know where a portal will open, so they will assume I'm a long way from their position. We need to find shelter for the night, and I spotted a cottage just over there," replied Brandy as she pointed in the direction she'd seen the lights.

When they reached it, there was a lot of activity outside. Three men were unpacking a van and taking their belongings into the cottage. One of them, by the name of Eric, saw them first.

"Hello there, can I help you?" he said trying not to stare at such beauties.

"We are looking for a place to stay for the night; I kind of hoped that the cottage I saw from the distance was vacant," said Brandy.

"Well, it might not be vacant, but we do have room for anyone who would want to sleep on the floor in the sitting room. I'm sure my friends wouldn't mind the company," he said.

Eric's friends suddenly reappeared. They were told what the girls were asking for, and they both agreed that there was room for one night at least. The girls helped them take the last of the luggage into the cottage, where they learned their names. Eric, who was the first one they met, introduced Steve and Mark. It turned out they were on a hiking trip and that the cottage was one of three places they would call their base for a while. They didn't intend to start until the morning, having traveled for over five hours just to get there.

The girls helped them to unpack once inside, and Mark, who had been designated the cook, asked if they'd like to share in a meal. The girls said yes, and he ended up cooking a stew. They all sat down at the large table in the kitchen to eat, and a couple of bottles of wine were poured. The conversation soon led to questions about where the girls were heading, but Brandy deflected most of them with vague and incomplete answers.

The drink, which was new to Arianna, was going to her head, and by the time it was getting dark, she was saying things that Brandy felt shouldn't be said. The only thing that Brandy could think of doing was to turn her lust on. She knew that nothing else would matter to the men if they were distracted in such a way. When she turned it on, Arianna recognized the sensations and blurted out that she was glad her friend was using her gift again.

Of course, the men didn't know what she meant by that and were now seeing the girls in a completely new light.

"Oh Guys, I'm feeling so hot; can one of you help me out of this dress?" asked Brandy.

"I'll do it!" they all said simultaneously as they scampered forward to be the first to unzip it.

Eric was the quickest and took great pleasure in pulling the zipper down. When it was all the way down to the bottom, Brandy let go of it at the front, and it pooled at her feet leaving her completely naked.

"Impressive...hic...body...hic... isn't it?" said Arianna as she tried to stand and promptly fell back down again.

The men all agreed, especially when Brandy turned around to face them all. Her long hair came to rest on her shoulders, and the firelight in the sitting room cast a shadow of her beautiful full-breasted figure on the wall. She had no hair between her legs, and for the longest moment, the men just stood agape at the sight in front of them. Brandy moved her hands over her breasts and pulled on her nipples.

"I think I'm in need of a man's touch," she said as she allowed one hand to move between her legs.

The men didn't need any further prompting; they all started to get undressed. Arianna tried to stand again as she was feeling the lust every bit as much as the men were. However, it seemed that angels and alcohol did not mix. She sat back and had to be content in watching the men as they discarded their clothes. As the first one finishing undressing, Arianna caught sight of his manhood and turned her head to the side in order to gauge his size.

"That's nice," she said and then went to sleep.

Brandy took hold of Mark and drew him in close as she reached down and grabbed his hardened cock.

"I hope you know how to use this?" she said as she stroked its length.

The other two soon caught up and suddenly their hands were all over her. Mark was behind her, and Eric was in front. Brandy didn't mess around; she immediately jumped up onto Eric and wrapped her arms around his neck, before skillfully placing her pussy over his cock. As soon as he felt it, he pushed up, and she felt it impaling her.

"Lay down onto your back," whispered Brandy in Eric's ear.

Eric did as he was told and when he was down, she began to move her butt up and down, making his cock slip in and out. Mark now had an opening and took it. He got into position from behind and entered her rosebud opening. She felt tight, but he easily managed to push all the way inside her. Brandy moved her hips in time with their thrusts and then looked up to see Steve stroking his cock to the action.

Brandy summoned him over with a finger, and when he was near enough, she took his cock past her lips. Steve watched her take it all, and slowly he began to fuck her mouth. Arianna woke up at that moment and saw the action going on and felt how wet she was from all the lust that filled the air.

"Not fair, I wanted that too," she murmured, before closing her eyes again.

Eric was getting too excited, and he started to cum far too soon. Brandy carried on fucking him though, and soon he was hard again. Mark was deep inside her and couldn't believe how much she could take. As for Steve, he'd never witnessed anything like this. She was engulfing his member as if it were a tiny adolescent cock, when, in fact, it was quite large. He could feel it hitting the back of her throat almost violently, yet she was taking it as if it were nothing. He started to cum moments later, and was again surprised to see her swallowing it all.

Mark came next, and he was as deep inside her as he could get. He could feel her grinding her butt onto it as he released his load and the feeling was indescribable. Eric started to cum for the second time moments later, and she fucked him for all she was worth. By the time they all pulled out and away, she still wasn't satisfied, and as she stood up, she made it painfully clear. She kicked Steve onto his back, as he seemed to be the only one who still had an erection. She then lowered herself onto it and began to ride him. The other men were in awe at the way she was using her legs to rise and fall repeatedly onto his cock.

Five minutes later, she started to scream out that she was coming, and Steve made an extra effort to thrust up into her during her orgasm. When it was all over, they collapsed onto the floor and relaxed. Brandy looked up at Arianna to see that she was fast asleep.

By morning, the guys were waking them up with a promise of breakfast. They had plans to leave after eating, so they needed to clean up before they left. Brandy told them that they needed to move on as well, and that it had been a pleasure to meet them all.

As the girls were leaving the cottage, Arianna turned to Brandy.

"Can you do that thing to me again sometime today?" she says.

Brandy promised and then smiled to herself, before thinking, *'this woman takes being innocent to an entirely new level.'*

****

At midday, they stopped to rest, mainly because Arianna needed to. Brandy could not help staring at Arianna as they talked. She wondered how many angels went through what she was, and whether or not she had actually seen one before.

"Tell me something Arianna, are you born an angel or are you created, like the succubus?"

"I was born and trained to become an angel, and only when God deems you worthy, are you allowed to venture onto earth. When I've saved a soul, I will get my wings and am then able to return to heaven if I want to," replied Arianna.

"Are there many angels on earth?"

"Yes, there are many such as me. Sometimes it can take a long time to find your-self, but angels don't mind as they get to interact with God's favorites for a while."

"God's favorites...do you mean man?"

"Yes, they were created in his image and need to be watched over as they grow," replied Arianna.

"I don't understand it. I mean, I see so much bad in this world. Why has He never given up on them?"

"Yes, but you are drawn to the bad and fail to see the good, which is far more prevalent."

Brandy was left in thought after that; she was thinking that perhaps she'd only ever looked for the bad and found it easy to locate. After all, the bad were her business. In addition, she'd not always succeeded in retrieving a soul from someone she deemed bad. She had witnessed good in the world. She just hadn't looked for it.

They walked on, with Arianna holding Brandy's arm and still glowing when she was too close. Then they came up against a river that couldn't be crossed and decided to follow it. Five miles later, they came across a lodge. This one was empty, and Brandy guessed it was a hunting lodge. She found a key under the mat at the front door, and they entered. There was water here and electricity, but no food. Brandy decided to use her gift and opened a portal, telling Arianna not to go anywhere.

Thirty minutes later, she returned and was loaded with all kinds of goodies. She'd brought some chocolate back with her and wondered if Arianna had ever tasted it.

"Here Arianna, try this," said Brandy, throwing her a bar.

Arianna opened it and broke a piece off before sitting back to eat it. When it started to melt in her mouth, she sat up.

"Oh my goodness, what is this?" she said.

"It's called chocolate, and it's something all humans love," replied Brandy.

"Mmm...I can understand why, do you want a piece?"

"No, that's just for you; I'm going to make us some soup."

Brandy watched Arianna devour the chocolate as she prepared the soup. She was as a child lost in a world that was far too big for her. Yet, Brandy couldn't help liking her. It was as if they were meant to be together. Perhaps they were; perhaps it had always been fated.

Soon, the soup was ready, and it was beginning to get dark outside. Brandy made up a fire and quickly set it ablaze. It lit up the lodge nicely and made it look quite cozy inside. They both enjoyed the soup, and when it was over, they talked some more.

"Do you ever get to rest like this, doing your work?" said Arianna.

"No, not really I'm normally going to the next job after finishing the one before it. The succubae never rest, at least not like we are now," replied Brandy.

"It must be a boring job, but at least you get to do that thing with other people."

"I sometimes find even that a chore from time to time, even though it's something I need to do."

"How about when you don't need it, but desire it?" said Arianna.

"That's different; it seems more like a pleasure and less like a job then."

Arianna yawned and sat back in her chair before drifting off. Brandy looked at her perfect shape, her gorgeous long legs, her breasts and sweet butt. Then she remembered her promise and turned her lust on. It went to work straight away as Arianna was reacting to it in her sleep. Brandy crept forward on her knees and pulled the bottom of Arianna's dress up to reveal her pussy. She wasn't wearing any panties. *She must have forgotten to put them back on when she tried that dress on*, thought Brandy.

Brandy moved her hand along Arianna's leg, making her moan in her sleep. When she reached her pussy, she placed a finger between the lips and stroked it gently.

"Mmm...oh Brandy, do that thing to me again," murmured Arianna in her sleep.

Brandy smiled, more from the fact that Arianna's body was glowing again, than from what she said. Brandy spread Arianna's legs and moved in to lick her tender skin. Arianna woke up as she felt the tongue moving across her bud.

"Oh, that feels nice," she said holding the back of Brandy's head gently.

Brandy pleasured her for a few minutes and then stood up and removed her clothes. Arianna watched as the bulge appeared before the cock popped out and grew in front of her.

"That is so cool," said Arianna innocently.

Brandy grabbed her legs and pulled her to the edge of the seat. She then lined herself up and rubbed her cock against the moist tender flesh. Arianna lay back and closed her eyes as the feelings of pleasure passed over her body. She then opened them again when she felt the head of the cock entering her. She looked up into Brandy's eyes, almost begging her to do it. Brandy smiled back and then pushed forward. Arianna was so tight, and she could feel the sides of her pussy gripping her cock as she entered.

Brandy moved slowly, wanting to savor the sweet feelings of lust that were building inside her own body. Arianna was moaning aloud, wanting to feel this entire and wonderful thing inside her. When Brandy did pick up speed, Arianna gripped the sides of the chair she sat in. Her entire body was glowing and lighting up the area around the chair. At the very height of it all, Arianna began to climax, and a sensation of pure bliss once again overtook her body.

Then, when she felt Brandy coming inside her, she held onto her butt to pull her in as close as she could. The pair of them stayed together like that for minutes until finally Brandy disengaged. Arianna opened her eyes to see the cock shrinking back down and moving up into Brandy's body.

"You know, that never gets old," she said smiling.

Brandy laughed and sat down next to her, naked. Their bodies felt warm together, and they would have stayed like that if it hadn't been for the sudden intrusion.

Suddenly, portals started opening up around the room. Brandy didn't have time to open her own, so instead she produced her wings and tail. Arianna watched as the wings sprang from Brandy's shoulders, and the tail grew from the base of her spine. They were both defensive as well as offensive weapons. She stood her ground and waited. The first one shot through the portal, and Brandy's tail whipped around and glanced off the succubus's head, knocking her out.

Two others appeared behind her, and both dived into the air, with their own wings and tail showing. Brandy managed to deflect one, knocking her into the side of the lodge wall, but the tail of the other one glanced off her shoulder. Brandy got down low, holding her shoulder, and swiveled around on the balls of her feet to keep her attacker in sight. As her attacker reoriented on the target, Brandy moved like lightning and kicked her in the stomach. Any normal human kick would have been a glancing blow at best, but this one knocked the wind out of her attacker.

Brandy turned to face three others, and one of them was Sabrina. Brandy stopped and stood up straight. Sabrina held her steel hardened tail up, pointing towards Brandy and just a foot away.

"Please Brandy, I need to take you in," said Sabrina.

Brandy looked down at Arianna, who was looking like a frightened child. Then she looked back at her old friend, before suddenly moving forward in a blur. Sabrina cried out, but it was too late. Brandy had impaled herself onto the end of Sabrina's tail.

"No, my friend," cried Sabrina, as the tears rolled down her cheeks, "I didn't want this."

"I know you didn't, my friend," replied a mortally wounded Brandy, "I wanted this. I've tasted freedom, and it was too good to let go. Please do me a favor; leave me here when I die and come back later," whispered Brandy with her last breath.

Sabrina pulled her tail away, and Brandy fell to the floor. "Yes, my friend," she said as she turned and instructed the others to follow.

Once they'd gone, Arianna could see what had been blocked before. Brandy's body lay on the floor. She ran to her side crying her name and placed her hands onto her lifeless body. Her hands glowed as she willed her back from the dead, but nothing was happening. She tried repeatedly, but she couldn't heal her. She then looked up to the ceiling and cried from the top of her lungs.

"NO...I WILL NOT LET YOU GO."

She looked down with a look of determination written across her face and placed her hands onto Brandy's chest. The glow from her hands now became a light, and it spread up her arms and enveloped her entire body. Suddenly, the light intensified, and lit up the room to such an extent that anyone watching would have had to turn away from the sheer brilliance. Brandy's body started to rise from the floor, and then suddenly wings began to sprout from Arianna's shoulders. They grew until they were six feet across and fully opened.

Arianna shone like a beacon, and when she looked down, she witnessed the wound on Brandy's chest closing up until it was fully healed. Then Brandy opened her eyes and took in the scene around her and the serene look of joy on Arianna's face.

"You know; you may be slightly tainted, but you are most definitely an angel," she said.

Arianna's light began to fade, and she began to cry.

"I thought I'd lost you," she sobbed, in between laughs of joy.

Her wings were still fully extended, and she looked impressive.

"Well, Arianna you certainly didn't waste any time did you?" said a voice Arianna recognized as the archangel, Gabriel.

She turned to see him standing in the corner of the room, and ran to embrace him as her wings folded up at the back.

"Are you ready to come back?" he said, "you know that you're a fully-fledged angel now don't you?"

"I know, but I'm not quite ready yet; I'd like to stay for a while," she replied.

Gabriel looked up and saw Brandy; he smiled and then looked back to Arianna.

"Okay, child of God, let me know when you want to return," he said, before fading away.

Arianna turned back to Brandy and hugged her as well.

"I'm so happy," she said.

Just then, another portal opened up, only this time Arianna spread her wings and stood between Brandy and whomever it was coming through. It turned out to be Sabrina, returning as Brandy had requested.

"You will not have her!" shouted Arianna, looking quite formidable with her white wings outstretched in such a fashion.

"It's okay, Arianna, Sabrina is my friend," said Brandy as she lay her hand onto Arianna's shoulder.

Arianna stepped aside.

"How is this possible," said Sabrina, "I never thought to talk with you again, let alone embrace you," she added as they hugged one another.

"I have a new friend, and she's, shall we say, a little special," replied Brandy.

They laughed together, and Brandy introduced Sabrina to Arianna. Arianna was very happy, but couldn't help wondering where they would go from here.

****

"Isn't that stealing?" said Arianna.

"No, he had the money and he gave me it of his own free will," replied Brandy.

"But you had to seduce him first, so he was coerced, which means you took advantage of him."

"Ah, now there I do agree, I did take advantage of him. The fact is we need money here. We can't survive without it. So, in order for us to live from one day to the next, one of us needs to find money," said Brandy.

"I thought that we could earn it, like all the people you see here doing," replied Arianna, pointing to the people in the town they had encountered in their travels.

"The trouble with earning it the way they do is that we would have to stop for days to pick up our earnings. Satan would probably catch up with me by then."

"Oh yes, I forgot about that. Couldn't we do favors for people in exchange for money?"

"Then it wouldn't be a favor would it. Look at it this way I didn't steal his wallet did I?"

"No, you didn't do that."

"I also told him he would get something he wanted if he gave me the money, isn't that true?" added Brandy.

"Yes, you did give him something he wanted."

"Therefore, I earned the money he gave me. I gave him something and he gave me something in return. Isn't that true?"

"Well, when you put it like that I suppose it is true. He was very pleased with what he received."

"There you go, now, we have money for food and he's happy that he was able to satisfy his lust. It's a win...win for everybody," finished Brandy, as she turned with a smirk on her face.

"Talking about food, are we going to eat soon, my stomach is making funny noises?" said Arianna.

Brandy smiled and led the way to a diner. Once inside, she told Arianna to order whatever she wanted. She ended up with bacon, eggs and a couple of slices of toast. Arianna watched her eat and wondered at her innocence. They just finished breakfast when the accident outside the window happened. A young child had darted out into the street and the driver of the car had no chance to stop in time. Brandy was too busy watching from the window of the diner to notice Arianna leaving. She only found out when she spotted her entering the road.

"Oh shit, what she is doing now," she said leaving money next to her empty plate and rushing out.

Arianna walked over to the still child and pushed her way through the crowd that had gathered. When she reached the child, who wasn't moving, she laid her hands onto him. Her hands started to glow and then her body followed suit. The crowd stepped back, not knowing what was going on. Then the child moved and turned around to face Arianna.

"Are you an angel?" he said.

"Yes, but keep it to yourself," she whispered back.

When she stood up, she held her hand out and helped him get to his feet. All the people were now looking at her and had forgotten the child. Brandy then came onto the scene and grabbed Arianna's arm, before moving off in the direction of the town's edge.

"You have got to stop drawing attention to yourself. It's going to get us into trouble," said Brandy.

"Would you have me do nothing?" replied Arianna.

Brandy looked back at the child, whose mother was scolding him.

"No, you did the right thing, let's just get out of here and find a place to stay for the night," said Brandy.

They walked for hours after that, until they came to a small campsite. Brandy saw a sign on the gate that read, "RV's for rent, forty bucks per night."

"This will do for the night, I'll go in and get the key," said Brandy.

"What's an RV?" replied Arianna.

"You'll see, just wait here."

Brandy was only gone for five minutes, and then she returned with the key and a piece of paper. She looked at the paper and then told Arianna to follow her. The paper was a map of the campsite and where their RV could be located. When they found it, it looked in reasonable order and Brandy opened the door for Arianna to climb onboard.

"This looks nice," she said as Brandy put the light on.

"It'll do for the night at least. Humans seem to want to travel a lot and these things are popular, apparently."

Brandy made some sandwiches next and a hot drink and they sat down together to talk.

"Tell me something Arianna, why do you want to stay with me, now that you have your wings?" said Brandy.

"You still need me and besides you're my friend," replied Arianna.

"Yes, I am that. You do know that you will have to go back though, don't you?"

"I will, but not until I know that you are safe. I want to ask you something now."

Oh yes, and what would that be?"

"Can you show me how to do the thing you were doing in the alley, with that man earlier today," said Arianna.

"We've already done the thing, as you put it," replied Brandy.

"No, not that thing the other one, you know, when you were down on your knees. He seemed to like it a lot and so did you."

"Oh, that thing...you know it isn't as easy as I make it look," replied Brandy.

"I want to see what it feels like and I want to please you."

Brandy didn't say anything else, suddenly the front of her dress moved upward as she sat in the chair. Arianna saw it rising and immediately got onto her knees knowing what it was and crawled over to Brandy. She then lifted the front of the dress up to reveal Brandy's cock sticking out.

"Oh, I love this thing...now then what was it you did. You took hold of it like this and then slipped your mouth around the end, like this."

Brandy closed her eyes for a second as she felt Arianna's lips surrounding her cock. When she opened them again, Arianna was trying too hard to get it all in and failing miserably.

"You have to concentrate on the end first and only allow what you are comfortable with into your mouth. Doing what I do takes a lot of practice and I've been doing it for hundreds of years," said Brandy.

Arianna slowed down and concentrated on the end, before allowing any more in. She stroked it and realized that she was getting excited from doing it. Brandy allowed her to try for a while and then gave her what she knew she wanted. She stood up, bringing Arianna to her feet and then picked her up and placed her onto the still hardened cock.

"Oh my, I love that feeling," said Arianna as the cock penetrated her.

Brandy gripped her butt cheeks and began to lift and drop her, as Arianna clung to her neck. Within minutes, the glow returned and suddenly Arianna's wings tore through the back of her dress and spread out. The gentle flapping of her wings made her seem lighter, but as they both started to climax, Brandy spotted a couple of brilliant white feathers falling to the floor. She held her in that position, until she was sure her orgasm was over. Brandy kissed her then, as she placed her onto the chair and soon Arianna was asleep. Brandy sat watching her and then was startled by a voice behind her.

"You know, you will have to let her go eventually, don't you?" said Gabriel, as he stepped from the shadows.

"I know, I honestly don't think she's ready to leave just yet," replied Brandy.

"She is one of the most innocent of God's creatures and I don't think she realizes that you are the complete opposite of what she stands for, she just sees someone in trouble and will help, no matter what the cost. If you don't let her go soon, she's the one who will be in trouble," said Gabriel as he picked up a fallen feather.

"I will tell her that it's time to move on, but she can be very stubborn, you know."

"I know... she has the kind of determination that I once possessed. Her light will fade soon, if she doesn't come home, so take care of her Brandy, she's very special," added Gabriel as he stepped into the shadows and was gone.

Brandy turned back to Arianna and watched her sleep. Then remembered the dress ripping as Arianna's wings came out.

"I really should've removed that dress before taking her like that," she said as she closed her own eyes.

****

In the morning, the sun was shining and everything was right with the world, at least in Arianna's eyes. Brandy tried to think of a way to broach the subject of Arianna going home, but couldn't seem to find the words. She handed the key to the RV over to the clerk in the main office and they were off once again. On the way down the road, a van pulled over in front of them and a young man popped his head out of the window.

"Do you girls want a lift, it's a long way to the next town?" he said.

Brandy said yes and then pulled the doors open on the side and climbed in. It was very comfortable inside, as the owner had decorated the interior with soft padded foam and covered it all with red colored leather. He obviously travelled a lot and probably slept in the back. They talked while he drove and found out that he'd recently finished college and was on his way to the coast for a well-deserved break. His name was Hank and he enjoyed music.

Arianna sat and listened to the music he was playing and enjoyed how it seemed to fill the van around them. An hour later, Hank pulled over at a rest stop so that they could all freshen up. When he returned, he found the girls waiting and offered them both a drink from his cooler. They sat and talked for a while and then he pulled out of the rest stop and they were off again.

"Have you girls got a place to stay tonight?" said Hank a few miles down the road.

"Not yet, we didn't know where we'd be this morning so we haven't arranged anything yet," replied Brandy.

"Well, you're welcome to sleep in the van tonight, there's plenty of room and I'd enjoy the company," he said.

"That would be nice, thank you."

"Not a problem, my mom always told me to look out for people in need and help wherever possible," said Hank.

"Your mom sounds like a nice person," said Arianna.

"She was, but she's gone now. She was hit by a drunk driver a year ago and died instantly. Ever since then I have sworn off alcohol in the van, as it always reminds me of her," he replied.

"I'm sorry to hear that. Is your father still alive?" said Brandy.

"Yes, he's still around and I still live with him. I really need to get my own place soon, but with college and other things, I just haven't gotten around to it yet. I'm hoping to find work down at the coast, but I'm not counting on it."

They sat watching the scenery go by for the next few miles and then they came to another rest area and Hank decided to stay there for the night. When nighttime came, Hank was trying to teach them some card games and couldn't understand how neither one of them was familiar with cards. They both seemed completely lost when it came to the various suits and what they meant. For the first hour, he had to explain the rules on a couple of games.

"It's a shame you don't know how to play poker, we could have some fun with that one," said Hank, "I know a game called strip poker and, well, you'd probably enjoy it."

"I've heard of that, isn't that the game where you bet your clothing for every hand you play?" said Brandy.

"Yes, that's the one, but I wouldn't want to take advantage of you both if you've never played it before."

"Well, why don't you teach us, I'm sure we can quickly pick it up," suggested Brandy.

Hank did just that, and within thirty minutes, they had picked up the premise of the game and Hank dealt to start the real game.

"I just thought you're only wearing a dress and shoes. Whereas, I'm wearing a shirt, pants, socks and underwear. I have too much of an advantage, so I'm going to take off my shoes and socks, to even it out a little," said Hank.

Then they started to play and he lost the first game. He removed his shirt and then dealt the cards again. This time Brandy lost and she pulled her top down, much to Hanks approval. Then he lost again and had to remove his pants. He sat there trying his best not to look at Brandy's breasts, but it was very hard. Then Arianna lost the next game and pulled her top down. Hank couldn't believe how perfect these two were and without even thinking about it, he suddenly realized that he was getting hard. The trouble was they could see his predicament as he tried to ignore it.

"I think he's getting excited," said Arianna much to Hanks embarrassment.

Brandy looked down at his ever-expanding briefs and smiled.

"He certainly is, isn't he," she said.

Hank dealt the next hand, lost it and had to stand in order to remove his briefs and for the first time in his life, he felt embarrassed as he had an erection that couldn't be hidden. He pulled his briefs off and his cock sprang out for all to see.

"Nice, can we do the thing with it?" said Arianna as she stared at it.

"I would have to say yes, we can do the thing with it," replied Brandy with a smile.

Suddenly Arianna reached over and grabbed his cock. He stood up from the suddenness of her movement and promptly banged his head on the vans roof. He sat down and Arianna moved over to him still holding his cock in her hand and started to suck the end. He laid back to enjoy the sensations coming from the end of his cock and looked up to see Brandy moving up closer. She indicated to Arianna that she wanted to have a go as well and Arianna passed it over.

Hank had always dreamed of this happening to him and now it was coming true. He watched as his cock virtually disappeared inside Brandy's mouth and couldn't believe she was able to take it all. She then passed it back to Arianna, who immediately tried to do the same thing and started to gag.

"I wish I could do that," she said as she brought it back out.

"Me too," said Hank with a laugh.

Brandy took over again and soon the sheer professional way she was sucking his cock made him realize that he was going to cum. He shouted it out as he felt the surge and Brandy pulled away as it shot out of the end.

"Ooh, that's a lot, isn't it?" said Arianna as she watched it arc into the air and land on the vans floor.

He came again, only this time Brandy placed her mouth over it and sucked him dry. He arched his back as the last drops escaped and then relaxed flat on his back on the vans floor. Arianna didn't give him any chance to recoup though; instead, she immediately sat astride his still hard cock and sat down on it.

"Oh that feels so good," she said as it sank into her.

She began to copy what she'd seen Brandy doing and moved her butt up and down, the effect made his cock move in and out. She started to go faster and Hank was enjoying how tight she felt. Then he felt a mouth covering and licking his ball sack and realized that Brandy was joining in. He adored looking up and seeing Arianna's breasts moving up and down the way only breasts can do. Then Arianna started to climax and he was turned on by how passionate she behaved as the throes of her orgasm took over. As her orgasm came to a head, he felt his seed about to make another appearance and suddenly shot his load deep inside her.

He then felt Brandy pulling his cock free and sucking it dry once again. The end of his cock tingled with delight and as he finally stopped coming, Brandy let it go and sat up. Arianna was slumped on his chest, having experienced yet another moment of sheer bliss. Minutes later, she rolled off and lay next to him.

"I enjoyed that, thank you for letting me do it," she said.

"It was my pleasure," he responded.

Brandy smiled to herself and then heard a knock on the vans door. She quickly placed her dress over her head and pulled it down, before answering it. The other's scrambled to cover them-selves up. When Brandy opened the door, she found Sabrina waiting for her.

"The master is here and wishes to see you Brandy," she said.

Brandy stepped out of the van and followed her, and Arianna looked out the window to see what was going on. When she saw Sabrina she immediately re-dressed and followed them, telling Hank she'd be back shortly as she left. They walked behind the rest area and into a field where a dozen Succubae stood in a circle. In the center was a large pentagram made from ash, with torches sticking out of each corner. The girls started to chant when Brandy arrived and within seconds, smoke began to billow, from the center and flames shot out of the ground. Then a figure could be seen forming and suddenly Satan was standing before her.

He started to talk, when they were suddenly interrupted by Arianna. She forced her way through the ring of girls and as she walked towards Satan, her wings unfolded and she stood before him an imposing figure.

"You will not harm my friend!" she screamed.

"I have no intention of harming her," said Satan, "I think there's been a misunderstanding here, it is true that I locked Brandy up to punish her for disobeying my orders, but killing her was never on the menu."

"Then why did you keep sending your minions to attack her?" replied Arianna.

"I sent my girls to retrieve her, not to harm her, but she wouldn't come back," said Satan, "I was mortified when I saw her life force fade away, but elated when I witnessed it return. If anyone should die, it was the coward who knew that defying me would cost him his first born."

Brandy didn't realize any of this, she just assumed that he wouldn't allow her to disobey his order and that he would end her life. Arianna's glow had dimmed by now as she watched Brandy step forward.

"I didn't know, I thought my life was forfeit when I returned unsuccessful from my mission."

"Brandy, you have given me three hundred years of loyal service, I could never repay you for that by taking your life. I want you to come back and stand by my side once again, I need my best with me in the coming months," replied Satan.

"Can you give me a minute; I need to tell my friend what's going to happen." said Brandy.

Satan just nodded and stepped back. Then Brandy turned to Arianna. Arianna's wings folded back up as Brandy approached.

"It is time my friend, it's time for me to go home as well as you," said Brandy.

"Do you have to go just yet, I wanted to see so much, while in your company," said Arianna as the tears started to roll down her face.

"I will miss you. You have shown me a friendship I could never have imagined and I will never forget that. We are both needed elsewhere now and it would be selfish of us to ignore that call. Besides, you will make other friends and I will see you again, of that I'm sure," replied Brandy.

Arianna almost jumped into her arms and hugged her tightly.

"I love you," she whispered.

"I love you too," replied Brandy.

They stood holding one another for a while and then Brandy let go and told her to behave herself and save all those that deserve saving. Arianna watched her walk into the circle and saw Brandy wave just before they all vanished and returned to hell.

Arianna dropped to her knees and sobbed, but then she felt a hand on her shoulder and looked up to find Gabriel.

"I'm glad you made a good friend, it's an important time in your life," he said.

Arianna stopped crying and stood up.

"I think I'm ready to go home now Gabriel," she said.

Gabriel held her close and suddenly they were gone.

The End

Erotic Paranormal Activity

I'll always remember seeing the house for the first time. It was a cold Tuesday morning, and a thin mist was just beginning to fade away. As I turned the corner on the leaf-filled road, I spotted the roof above the trees in front of me. The driveway was littered with branches, probably from a recent storm, and the air was cold. I closed my car door window and drove up to the front of the house. I was met by the owners, who were busy packing things into their truck.

"Good morning," I said as I got out of the car.

"You must be Angela?" replied the man.

"Yes, I'm here to get the keys. I assume my agent got in touch with you?"

"Yes he did and to be honest, it was the best news we could have received. My wife can't get out of this house fast enough. Oh, I'm sorry, I'm Cliff, and this is my wife Jenny," he said.

"I'm pleased to meet you both. So tell me, is it true that this house is supposed to be haunted?" I replied.

"Believe me when I say, there is no supposed about it, this house is most definitely haunted," said Jenny.

"As far as we can ascertain, the ghost that inhabits this house is friendly. At least, he hasn't hurt either one of us, but my wife says he's a little too friendly."

I turned to Jenny when he said that, without saying anything, and looked at her questioningly.

"I told my skeptical husband what I'm about to tell you, whether you choose to believe it or not is entirely up to you. However, what I'm about to tell you, really did happen. It wasn't just my imagination, as my husband seems to think. I got ready for bed two nights ago while Cliff was working in the study on his computer. I lay there for a while before drifting off to sleep. Suddenly, I thought I was having an erotic dream. I was being touched all over, in a very sensual way, and at the precise moment when my supposed dream was about to take me over the edge, I woke up. For a brief moment, I could feel a weight on top of me, but there was no one there. Then the covers were thrown off the bed. Whatever the weight was suddenly lifted, and something got off the bed. I watched the bedroom door open and close. It took me a while to compose myself, and then I screamed for Cliff. Of course, when he arrived there was nothing there, and there was no way for me to prove that what I was saying was the truth," explained Jenny.

"I may be having trouble believing Jenny's story, but if she says something strange happened, then I believe her. She's not the type to let her imagination get the better of her. I would seriously reconsider staying here, Angela, especially as you're on your own," added Cliff.

"I'm writing a book about hauntings at the moment, and this will be the third time I've stayed in a supposed haunted house. I've heard strange noises during my journey and witnessed some bizarre things, but I've yet to see a ghost. I'm trying to be open-minded about the whole thing, but I can't help wondering if most of the stories I hear aren't being created by an overactive imagination on the part of the witnesses. Don't get me wrong, I believe that something happened here, but whether it has anything to do with a ghost is something I aim to find out," I replied.

"Well, you'll have the house all to yourself now, so here's the key," said Cliff handing me said key. "My advice, for what it's worth, is to get out as soon as you witness or experience anything untoward."

I told them that I would and then watched them drive off. I then took my case from the trunk and entered the house for the first time. I was pleasantly surprised to see the very large staircase that dominated the hallway just inside the door. I opened my case on a small table inside the sitting room, which was situated in front of a large, open, logged fireplace. Above the mantel, was a portrait of a young man riding a black-as-night stallion? I guessed that the painting had been there for some time as I could see that the paint on the wall around it had faded with time, but the color underneath the painting was still vibrant.

As I took my laptop out, I had a sense of excitement. I could almost feel the years that had filled this house and wondered what the story behind it would be. As my computer came to life, I quickly checked to see if my internet connection was good. I found that it was just as my agent had said; I could get a good, clean signal from here, thanks to my 3G network.

I quickly hooked up to the database I'd stored online and looked up the house I was now occupying. Apart from the owners that had just left, the house had been lived in on six separate occasions. The original owners were builders of note, at least back then. Upon reading further, I discovered that the son of the original owner was killed when his horse kicked him in the head while he was mucking out the stables.

I also read that the stables were removed in later years to make way for a garage. One interesting side note was that of the father, who had lived to the age of ninety-nine. He'd been married five times, but only ever had one child. Each of his wives had died from various illnesses, which made me feel sad for him. He seemed to have lived a life full of loss, which must have been hard to come to terms with.

I also noted that the house had been reportedly haunted from the day his son had died. It was probably fair to assume that if the house were indeed haunted, it had to be the son who was haunting it. I stopped looking at that moment as I heard a sound coming from upstairs. I quickly closed the lid of my laptop and went out into the hallway. I looked up the grand staircase and then slowly walked up.

The sound seemed to be coming from the main bedroom, so I quickly opened the door and entered. I found that the curtain was blowing inward because of the open window and was hitting the wardrobe next to it. I closed the window and decided to check out the rest of the floor. The bathroom had been modernized and had a gorgeous shower with a marble floor. There was a spare bedroom with a single bed, and a few other rooms, which were all empty. I guessed the previous owners never intended to use them, so why fill them with anything.

There was what I suspected to be, an attic door, but it was locked, and I didn't have the key for it. I then went back downstairs and entered the kitchen, which again had been modernized. The cooker was gas fed, and there was a large fridge-freezer standing by the back door. There were all the comforts of home here, and I actually looked forward to staying for a few days. I'd only rented the place for a week, which I thought was more than enough time to research the place and come to some sort of decision.

Next, I unpacked my clothes and decided to make myself some soup, which I had brought with me. I then carried on doing some more research, and before I knew it, night was drawing in. I'd traveled for over two hundred miles that day, so I was getting tired. I finished reading the page I was on and then turned all the lights off before going up to bed. Upon getting ready for bed, I discovered I'd forgotten my night case, which was in the trunk of my car. I couldn't be bothered going back down, so I decided to sleep in just my panties for one night.

I must have been asleep within five minutes and felt cozy as I cuddled the pillow. Then I began to dream. It started with me sitting up in bed, and a young man walking into the bedroom and asking me to follow him. I didn't know who he was, but I felt compelled to see what he wanted to show me. He led me down the stairs and into the kitchen and upon opening the pantry door, he walked into it and pulled on a hook that was in the center of the back wall. Suddenly, a secret door revealed itself and the young man pushed on it. The door slowly opened and revealed a narrow staircase going down. I followed him and could hear murmurs of pleasure coming from below.

When we reached the foot of the stairs, I found myself in a room full of naked men and women. There were also many different contraptions lining the walls, such as a table with chains to bind wrists and ankles. There were whips on hooks, and handcuffs, masks and leather clothing. In the middle of the room, there was a large bed, and at that very moment, there were two men together, fucking a young woman on it. In one corner of the room, I could see another young woman sucking the cock of an older man.

With all the sounds of excitement echoing throughout that room, I found myself being turned on by what I was seeing. Then suddenly, the young man who had shown me all of this, stood in front of me. He was naked and muscular, and when he reached up to caress my breasts, I didn't stop him. It was as he squeezed my nipples that I woke up. I immediately sat up in bed and then quickly got dressed.

I rushed down the stairs and into the kitchen. I opened the pantry door and sure enough, there was a hook on the back wall. I reached in and pulled on it and to my amazement, a secret door opened up. There was a light switch on the side of the wall, which I flicked. It illuminated the stairs and the room below. When I reached the bottom of the stairs, it was just like my dream, except that I was alone. The various contraptions were still there, and I couldn't help wondering how long all the debauchery in this house had been going on.

Who were those people I'd seen in my dream, and why was I shown it all in the first place? I was standing next to a wall where there were shackles dangling as I was pondering these questions, when suddenly something grabbed me from behind, spun me around and pinned my hands to the wall. The shackles were closed around my wrists, and I was helpless. I looked around frantically, but there was no one there. I then pulled on the shackles, only to find that they held me securely, and I was trapped.

I could feel a cold breeze on my right shoulder and pulled on the shackles harder, but to no avail. Then I felt something touching my blouse and looked down to witness my blouse buttons unfastening on their own. I kicked out but felt no resistance, and another button was undone. I could swear that I could feel breathing over my cleavage as a third button was loosened. The feeling of helplessness was both annoying and frustrating.

When the final button was unfastened, my blouse was pulled open, revealing the bra that was straining to hold my large breasts. My skirt suddenly blew upwards as if being lifted, which made me cry out, more from surprise than fright. Then I heard the zipper being pulled down on the side and felt my skirt fall around my ankles. For a moment, nothing more happened, and as I tried desperately to think of a way out of all this, I felt my bra loosening and then falling to the floor next to my skirt.

Then, I would swear that I could feel hands touching my bare breasts and upon looking down, I could see and feel the depressions as invisible hands with equally invisible fingers moved my breasts around. My nipples hardened as they too were touched and pulled about. *Who is this*? I thought.

The waistband on my panties began to move next, so I crossed my legs in an effort to stop whoever it was from removing them. This had no effect as my legs were suddenly opened with force, and I felt my panties sliding down my legs. I pulled on my shackles again, and again I was frustrated. Then I tried a different approach. If I couldn't stop what was happening physically, how about with reason.

"I mean you no harm, whoever you are. Is there no way to communicate with one another?" I said aloud.

I listened intently, but all I heard was silence. Then I felt hands all over my body, which made me jump. Up until that moment, I thought I was dealing with just one entity, but now I could feel at least three distinct hands touching different parts of my naked body. My breasts were moving around, and my nipples were hardening. Then I felt something gently sliding over my womanhood. I took a deep breath and couldn't help wondering how far this would go.

The next thing that happened made me call out for help, even though I knew no one could possibly hear me. I started to leave the floor and float in midair. As I floated up my legs were pulled outward, and I continued going up until I was lying in a horizontal position. My shackles were keeping me near the wall, and I was looking all around to find some sort of escape route. Of course, nothing sprang to mind; I felt like a fly in a spider's web.

Then hands began to move, pull, and pinch my breasts, and my legs were spread apart. I could feel two fingers rubbing my clit, and suddenly one of them pushed its way into my pussy. Looking down, I could see and feel my nipples being pulled around and finger depressions massaging my breasts. I consciously pushed my hips up to meet the thrust of the finger that had been inserted into me, and then felt ashamed for enjoying what was happening.

I kept thinking that any moment now I would wake up and find that this was all a dream. I couldn't imagine anything more happening, but I was wrong. I could suddenly feel something hard pressing against my mouth, or more specifically my lower lip. You have to understand at this point that my body was reacting to all of this outside stimuli, and my mind was racing. I was actually enjoying the sensations I was feeling, so, I opened my mouth.

The unmistakable feel of a hard cock brushed my lower lip, and my mouth was stretched open. I had my lips around some entity's erection, and God help me—I loved it. Like many women out there, I'd fantasized about being taken by more than one person. I just never thought that what was occurring to me now was even possible, let alone happening to me. I could feel a good five inches of cock entering my mouth, and I sucked it as I would during normal sex. I could feel myself getting wetter, and when I moved my hips up faster to meet the thrusts of the finger, I felt it withdraw.

Then I felt a cock replacing it, and found it stretching my opening wider. By now, the cock in my mouth was moving faster, and I was gripping it with my lips. I could feel the ridge of it each time it touched them, yet I still couldn't hear any sounds besides my own. I was beginning to moan aloud as the stimulus my body was reacting to, made me feel excited and needy. My breasts were still being massaged, and my nipples were still being pulled around. It was almost becoming a sensory overload.

The cock inside my pussy was now going deeper inside me, and I knew that it was big without even seeing it. It was stretching me wider than I'd ever experienced, and the entry was exciting me. I could feel my juices trickling down onto the crack of my ass. Then I felt a mouth sucking on my right nipple, and everything started to become a blur. I was already close to coming, and I was still enjoying the cock inside my mouth, when I felt yet another one pushing my asshole.

'*Oh god, not there,*' I thought as it entered me.

My own juices must have eased its way through, as I couldn't feel any pain. After a few thrusts, I felt incredibly full and started to climax. I came so hard it made me feel faint. Nothing changed though. They carried on as if nothing had happened. The cock in my mouth was trying to go deeper and making me work harder to keep it going. The cocks in each hole below were moving faster and in time with one another. As one went in, the other came out. My nipples felt almost sore from all the tugging, yet it all felt amazing.

I was now so wet I could hear a dripping on the floor and then even more hands began to touch my body. Then I started to see a glow around me, and certain shapes were taking form. Suddenly, I could see at least five distinct figures hovering over me and knew that another had to be beneath me. I wondered if their own excitement was making them visible. Perhaps it was a sign that they were all close to the end. I could only guess, but as the cock in my mouth pulled out I could see small drops of vapor, which I guessed was semen.

It covered my face, although I couldn't feel it touching me. Then, when I looked down, the cock inside my pussy pulled out, and again, I could see a small cloud of vapor shooting out and landing on my stomach. The figures were more defined as they released their loads, and I could just about tell their sizes and the fact that they were all men. What I couldn't see was their faces, as their heads were merely shapes, as I looked closer. I witnessed a few more vapor clouds coming from the sides and my breasts were then left alone.

I then felt my body sinking back down to the floor, and when I was supporting my own weight, the shackles came undone. As I freed myself, I witnessed the glowing figures dissipating until they were gone and no longer visible. I wished I could communicate with them, but instead I grabbed my clothes and ran up the stairs, before closing the secret door behind me. I immediately went straight to my laptop and turned it on. I wanted to get everything down while it was fresh in my mind.

By the time I'd written the first paragraph, I started to have doubts on what to write. Then I let go of the keyboard and sat back.

If I write what actually happened, who is going to believe me? I thought.

I was having trouble believing it myself, yet, it was me, it happened to. In the end, I decided that I would describe the shackles. How I was forced into them, and the secret door in the pantry. I knew that a couple of these things were provable. I left out the sex completely because I knew that no one would believe me. When I'd finished writing, I had over ten thousand words added to my book. I turned off my laptop and then went back to bed.

I had high hopes that something else would happen in the days that followed, but for the next three, I was completely alone. On the fourth night, I went to bed in my buttoned-up nightdress and tried to sleep. I set up my video camera, which could record up to an hour's playback and placed it on the shelf at the end of my bed. I then placed the remote control on the table next to my bed. I was just starting to drift off when I heard the bedroom door creaking open. I kept my eyes closed and strained to hear more, but at the same time, I reached over and pressed the play button on the remote. I knew that with the moon being full and bathing the bedroom with light, and the fact that I had a night-light on, that anything that happened would be captured on my video camera. Then I felt the bedcovers moving down the bed. They moved until they fell off the end and I was uncovered and lying on my back.

For at least three minutes, I lay there, with nothing more happening until finally; I felt a button on my nightdress unfastening. It was followed closely by another and then another. Then my nightdress was spread open, and all that covered me were my panties. I never wore anything else under my nightdress. When I felt my panties moving down my legs, I took in a lungful of air, not realizing that I'd been holding my breath. Once my panties were off, I felt a pair of hands touching my breasts and squeezing them.

I slowly opened my eyes and could see the sort of impressions fingers would make if they were squeezing my breasts, so I knew they were hands. My nipples were erect within seconds, and then I felt those same hands moving down my body. They passed over my stomach and didn't stop until they reached my womanhood. Then, two fingers pulled my pussy lips apart, and something else was added to the mix. It took me a moment to realize that it was a tongue. It started to lick my clit, making it peak out from behind its hood. I don't know about other women, but I adore my clit being licked. It always sent me over the edge, which was why I always made a point of telling any boyfriend about it.

Whomever this tongue belonged to, knew exactly how to use it on a woman. The tongue kept flicking my clit and then sliding over it before the mouth would cover it and suck. It kept repeating this action until I started to writhe on the bed. I started to pull my own breasts around and pinch my nipples as the sweet sensations built up between my legs.

"Oh my god, please don't stop," I said.

It then changed tactics, as suddenly it was entering my pussy and licking me inside. At the same time, I could feel a finger as well, and that was it. I started to cum, big time. When I started to climax, the entity didn't once stop licking me, and for a moment, it was too much. I screamed that I was coming, and the sweet, overpowering sensations coursed through my body. Then it stopped and I collapsed onto the bed, not realizing that I'd been arching my back and thrusting my hips upwards.

I lay there trying to catch my breath, when suddenly my legs were spread apart, and I could feel a cock entering me. When the end sank into me, I closed my eyes. I was so wet that it had no trouble penetrating me, but what I didn't foresee was how big he was. I thought the one in the secret room was big, but this person was huge. That's when I felt other hands touching me, only they were gripping my breasts as if they were below me, which was strange as I was on a bed.

I quickly realized that a bed or anything else, for that matter, couldn't stop a ghost. Then my attention was drawn back to the cock that was entering me. I'd never been so stretched before, and the amount of flesh I could feel fucking me was incredibly exciting. I then rose into the air and felt my legs being spread even wider. My breasts were still being fondled, and now the fucking was getting intense.

The huge cock inside me was pounding my soaking wet pussy, and I screamed out for more each time it entered me. My nipples felt like bullets they were so hard, and my clit was once again feeling oversensitive. The next five minutes will forever be burned into my brain. I started to cum, and it wouldn't stop. I'd heard about multi-orgasms before, but I'd never experienced one. In fact, I always thought it was a myth and that no one could cum more than once or twice. I was wrong. When it started, I couldn't believe how draining it felt, but no sooner did I think that it was over, when another took its place.

All of this happened four times, and by the time the entity pulled out of me, I felt utterly exhausted and fell back onto the bed. I opened my eyes just in time to see the ghost materializing and what a sight. I can only guess that the moonlight played a part in what I was seeing. First, a huge cloud of vapor appeared where its cock was and then another, which floated in the air for a while before dropping down onto the bed. Then the ghost itself came into focus, even more so than the time in the secret room. It was so clear that I could instantly tell it was the young man in the portrait above the mantel in the sitting room.

He looked down on me and smiled, and I could see him mouthing the words 'thank you,' as he started to fade away. When it was all over, I was so excited. I got off the bed and immediately grabbed the video recorder. I then got my mini player out of the wardrobe and put the video disk in. I pressed play and sat on the bed to watch what I'd captured. I was right, the moonlight and the night-light were just enough. I could see myself clearly on the bed and moments later, I could see the bedcovers being pulled off by unseen hands.

When it reached the point when I had risen into the air, I got excited. I could see my pussy being stretched open, and you could tell that something was thrusting in and out of me. You could even see my breasts being manhandled, but the most compelling part was when the ghost materialized after ejaculating. I'd actually captured it on film and there could be no doubt. The only trouble I could foresee was the fact that to prove it, I would have to show the film to other people, and frankly, some porno movies weren't this hot. I could always blur my face out, but then they'd say I tampered with the film. Still, I had all the time in the world to think about that. For now, I simply had to write all of this down and continue with my research.

I still had many questions that needed answering, like who are all the other ghosts in this house. Why are they all able to interact with me on a physical level, and could it be possible to talk with them somehow. I had over two more weeks left to find out the answers to some of these questions, and I wasn't about to waste any of it.

****

Having stayed in a haunted house for five days, I can confirm that ghosts do exist. I now have video evidence of that fact and am in the process of writing a book about my exploration into the world of the paranormal. There are still quite a few questions that need answering, not least of which is how they are able to interact with me on a physical level.

This is day six and I've yet to see any activity during the daylight hours. The night before was the most exciting time of my life. It also produced questions that have stumped me. For some reason I was able to see the ghosts during their excited stage, more clearly in the light of the moon than at any other time. After doing some research I found out two things about the moon, although neither one of them really helps me. First, it was the second full moon of the month, which is known as a 'Blue Moon,' and secondly, the moonlight is diffuse. This meant that the light isn't as severe or as intense as that of the sun or a light bulb.

This all got me thinking that perhaps ghosts could only be seen when the lighting is poor or at best dim. I went out earlier today to buy some new gadgets. I needed a couple more video cameras and some specialized sound equipment. I'd set these things up in various places and was all ready for another night. I felt extremely tired when it came time for bed and I hoped that in the morning I would have captured maybe a few sounds or filmed something in the corridors. Everything was set up to trip if sounds or movements were detected; I just had to turn it on.

I think I fell asleep within a minute of hitting the pillow and that's when the second dream came along. In this dream, I was awoken by the same person who woke me the last time and told to follow him. I did and he led me into the secret room again, only this time there seemed to be some kind of ritual going on. I could see a pentagram on the floor in the center of the room, with candles placed at all the various points within the pattern.

People were surrounding it, both men and women and they were chanting something. I then witnessed something materializing from the middle of the pentagram and knew as soon as I saw it, that it was a demon. It talked to all of the people in the room about the bargain, and then all but told me everything I needed to know.

"Remember, as long as you are within these walls, you will enjoy sexual pleasures for the rest of eternity. All that we ask, is that you do not break our pact and that you give us one sacrifice every year for the next ten years," it said.

At that point, a sacrifice was brought forth and to my horror, I discovered that it was a child. I watched as they placed her on a small alter, before the head of the coven took hold of a knife and held it above her. Thankfully, as he brought the knife down, I awoke. I sat upright in bed and shook my head. *'How could they do such a thing,'* I thought.

I did have one question answered though. The demon had promised they could enjoy sexual favors for all of eternity provided they were within these walls. I assumed that that meant even after death. I'd also care to wager that all the people who have interacted with me have died in this house, which would explain why their ghosts run free within these walls. Now, if I could just communicate with one of them, it would complete my mission.

I didn't go back to sleep, instead I got up and went down stairs in my nightdress. I needed to get all of this down onto my laptop and I was too excited to go back to sleep. I'd already gotten thirty thousand words for my book and I knew that this new information would add another five thousand at least. I was just getting started when I felt something touch my shoulder, but upon turning, I found nothing there. Then I felt my nightgown being pulled around and a couple of the buttons unfastening. It was the second night of a full moon and I wanted to try something, so, knowing what was about to happen I turned off the light on my desk. Suddenly, I could see a figure in front of me. At least bits of him, parts of him were fading in and out as if he couldn't control what parts of him were seen and what parts were invisible. It reminded me of a mist, that when blown would dissipate.

"Oh, you're here again. Can we communicate in some way?" I said aloud, only to find the response was another unfastened button.

I stood up and looked down to watch, as the last button was undone. Then I saw my nightdress being parted and pulled off my shoulders to fall to the floor. My nipples were already hard, as I knew what was coming. Then other figures entered the room directly through the walls. I could make out five figures in total. I knew for sure that two of them were women, as their womanly shapes gave them away.

I was then surrounded and could feel and see them reaching forward to touch me. Their fingertips seemed to become solid when they touched me, but no other parts of their bodies did. One of the females cupped both my breasts and I could feel the palms of her hands pushing my nipples around. Then I saw the face of the person in that portrait above the mantel and he smiled at me. I watched him slipping his fingers into the band around my panties and then pull them down, to fall at my feet.

Suddenly, five more ghostly shapes came through the wall and hands were placed all over my back. I was then lifted into the air, about four feet off the floor and placed in a horizontal position. The person in the picture spread my legs apart and then moved his head between my legs. I could feel the tip of his tongue stroking my clit and a finger entering me. Even more hands began to stroke me all over as I felt my erect clit being moved around. I closed my eyes and started to moan aloud and then felt a cock pushing my lips apart.

Opening my eyes, I saw a wisp of a cock as it entered my mouth. I could only feel the ridge on my tongue, but the sensation of it running over my tongue made me even wetter. Then something pressed against my ass cheeks from below and suddenly it was inside me as my clit was licked harder. I then saw the person who had been licking me, float up and hover above me. Once in position, he entered my soaked pussy and stretched me open once again. As he did this, I could still feel my clit being moved around. Talk about sensory overload, I was squirming in midair, enjoying all of the sensations I was feeling.

That's when I remembered that I'd forgotten to turn the video camera on, which I'd set up earlier. The cock inside my mouth was going in further, as I could feel the end brushing the back of my throat. I was so wet by now that I knew I was going to climax soon. My pussy felt on fire and my nipples felt incredibly tender as they were being pulled around and at one point sucked.

When I came for the first time that day I screamed, it was so intense. Until coming to this house, I'd never known such intense orgasms. Then the cock in my mouth pulled out and I could see the vapor shooting out over my face. I couldn't feel anything touching me as it covered my face I just knew he'd cum, as his whole body became more solid and brighter. When the two that were fucking me came, I could see their seed in the form of vapor shooting upwards, before dissipating in the air.

I was then lowered back to the floor and suddenly I was supporting my own weight. After regaining my composure, I watched as they all started to leave. It felt ethereal, as they all moved like mist towards the wall.

"Wait, is there any way we could communicate with one another?" I said.

The person in the picture turned to face me and I could see him shaking his head.

"So, you can hear me. You just can't talk to me," I said.

He nodded and then turned to leave again. I watched him pass through the wall and that was it, they'd all gone again. As I turned on my laptop, it suddenly dawned on me how we could communicate with one another.

"Oh my god, I've been so stupid," I said as I rushed to the door.

Upon opening it, I shouted for them to stop. Fortunately, the person I needed was still in the hallway.

"I have a way to talk with you, could you come back inside the room?"

He looked at me at least I think he did, as I saw the head part of his diffuse body turn towards me. I then re-entered the sitting room and watched him follow me. I walked over to my laptop and brought up my word processor. Then I typed in my first question.

"Are you trapped in this house?" I typed.

He looked at the words on the screen and then tapped the keys with one finger.

"BOUND," he typed.

"You're bound to the house? Is there a way to set you free?"

"NEW PACT," he typed.

"Ah, you mean a new pact to cancel out the first?"

"YES."

I typed the words 'thank you,' and watched him leave again. As long as the original pact was intact, they would live in this limbo for all eternity. I sat down on my chair and remembered the last dream I'd had. *'Why am I even thinking about helping these people, they sacrificed a child and at least nine other people to gain what they wanted,'* I thought.

I started to type out all the new things that I'd learned and after finishing it, I'd come to a decision. I was going to leave, but not until I'd gotten a few more shots of all the ghosts in this house. I wanted to help them, but from what I dreamed, they really didn't deserve my help. I packed my case and then slept.

In the morning, I double checked all of my equipment and remembered to turn it on. I then decided to do some editing of my book, a task that I always disliked, as it was so time-consuming. I intended to have it edited professionally once I'd finished it, but for now, it needed to be checked for errors.

I'd made up my mind that I wasn't going to help these people. I remembered the old saying, "you reap what you sow," and it was as true today as it was back then. I also decided that that night was going to be my last. It was the last night of the full moon and I didn't care to wait for the next one. It took me hours to tidy up my work and by then I'd lost about three thousand words, mostly unnecessary sidelines and brief descriptions. I had something to eat and decided to read in bed until I felt tired.

I was reading a romance novel, although, it has to be said it wasn't a very good one. I heard a sound out in the corridor and looked over to see flashes under the crack of the door. My cameras had been activated, which meant that they were on the move again. I quickly turned out the light and the room was bathed in moonlight. I was very fortunate, as it was a cloudless night. Then, as if they'd all lined up outside my room, they all passed through the wall and into my room.

I could make out certain features of each of them, but some were clearer than others were. I instantly recognized the young man in the picture above the mantel, which made me think that perhaps he was the leader of all of them. As they all approached my bed, something happened that I wasn't expecting. The demon I'd seen in my dream opened the door and entered the room. I took notice of this, for one particular reason, he was solid.

I noticed several things, straight away. He was completely naked and his huge cock dangled between his legs for all to see. The only thing that gave him away as a demon was the two small horns on the top of his head. He would've looked like any other man if it hadn't been for the horns. I also didn't expect him to look so handsome, or built like a body builder.

The ghosts stood aside as he approached my bed, which made me think that perhaps I'd been wrong and that he was the leader here. When he almost stood over me, he suddenly grabbed his cock and started to slide it through his hand. I think he wanted me to watch as it grew. I couldn't help but watch to be honest. It was limp when he first touched it and now suddenly it was starting to grow. By the time it was horizontal it was massive and then it grew a little more and stood up straight like a metal post. He seemed to be taking pride in it as he carried on stroking its length.

"You are unwelcome here, but I would be remiss if I didn't show you the hospitality that this house is famous for," said the demon as he drew nearer.

I tried to move, but ghostly hands were pinning me down. The demon walked around to the end of the bed and then grabbed my ankles. I tried to kick out but it was useless, he was far too strong.

He suddenly pulled me down the bed with ease and then ripped my panties off, before spreading my legs apart.

Then he deliberately moved the bulbous end of his cock through my pussy lips, without pushing inside me. I could feel the huge head passing over my clit repeatedly and couldn't help getting wet from the sensations it was causing.

"I see by your body's reaction that you are excited over the prospect of feeling this inside you," he said mockingly, as he stroked his huge cock once more.

I turned to face the ghosts, trying my best to ignore him.

"How can you allow him to do this, he's used you from day one to get everything he wants. If you allow this to continue, you will be his slaves for the rest of eternity!" I shouted.

I didn't know whether I was getting through to them or not and was interrupted by the demon, when he suddenly parted my pussy lips with his cock and I felt it penetrating me.

'Oh god, it's too big,' I thought, as only the first three inches got through my defenses.

I then felt hands massaging my breasts and my nipples were being pulled this way and that. The demon withdrew and then entered again. The more he did this, the wetter I got, until finally he was pushing nearly all of it inside me. I'd never been stretched so much in my life and although he repulsed me, I couldn't help react in a sexual manner. Within seconds, he seemed able to move faster and I was feeling incredibly hot as his cock repeatedly violated my pussy. My nipples were rock hard and I could feel one of them being sucked on.

"You may not want this with your mind, but your body is telling a different story," he said as he pulled me onto his cock with ease.

It was true, I would've done anything to be able to stop him, but the more he fucked me the more I succumbed to the pleasures that were now taking over my body. His cock was making me more excited than I could ever have imagined and suddenly I knew that I was going to climax. Before I did, he turned me around and gripped my butt, before placing his cock back inside my pussy and going deeper than before. I gripped the bedcovers as it slid all the way inside me. He then picked up speed and I started to cry out as I had my first orgasm.

I was climaxing around his cock, but he didn't slow down or stop. He kept fucking me harder and harder, until finally he grunted aloud and I could feel his seed exploding inside me. Still, he didn't stop, even as his seed began to run down my thighs along with my own juices.

"You certainly have a tight cunt," he said as his cock entered me for the umpteenth time.

I looked up and saw the person in the picture above the mantel and he saw my tears. He looked up at the demon and then suddenly I couldn't feel any ghostly hands touching me anymore. Then the demon pulled out, or at least I thought he did. In reality, the ghosts were pulling him away from me.

"What's this, you dare to disobey me?" said the demon.

They didn't answer him. Instead, they pulled him out of the room. I followed them as they took him to the secret room down stairs and watched as they placed him onto the pentagram. Then a card was handed to me and when I tried to read it, it was in Latin. I couldn't speak Latin, or at least I couldn't understand what I was saying, but I read the words out as loud as I could.

"Genitus everto of abyssus, ego iacio vos tergum ut vorago of abyssus," I said.

The demon screamed as flames engulfed him and within seconds, he was gone.

"Thank you, you saved me," I said to the one person I'd felt any sort of connection with.

He just smiled and then they all vanished. I didn't think they'd gone, I just think they'd seen and done enough for one day. I went back up stairs and got all of my cameras together and after looking through them, I found some great footage of the demon as well as the ghosts. I now had all the evidence I needed, so I packed everything up before going to sleep.

In the morning, I felt refreshed and eager to go. I'd ordered a taxi and it was going to be there in ten minutes, so I took my bags to the front door. Before I left, I turned to face the inside of the house. I couldn't see or feel any presence, but I hoped that they could hear me.

"If someone ever comes to live here, please don't hurt them. It's nice, being watched over and it's good that someone can look after the house for you. I'm glad that I met you all and I wish you well. I also wish that I could help you pass on to the other side, but I think the deal you made is binding and there is nothing I can do about that."

Then I heard the taxi sounding his horn and picked up my bags.

"Farewell," I said as I closed the door behind me.

****

I watched Angela leave, although I knew that she couldn't see me. There were things I would've told her, such as the fact that we were compelled to seek out those that could provide sexual gratification, at least while we were under the same roof. The hold that this house had upon us was absolute, and I couldn't see us ever being free of the demon's deal. In hindsight, making a deal with a demon was probably the stupidest thing I've ever done, but what was done was done, there was no point in crying over spilt milk, as it were.

At the time, we all thought it was a great deal. We thought the idea of being able to enjoy sexual pleasures throughout eternity was a fantastic deal, provided we were inside the house. We simply didn't know that after our deaths, we could no longer interact with one another. We could talk to one another, but we couldn't indulge our fantasies. The only ones we could do that with, were humans that lived under the same roof.

It was a month after Angela had left that the two new arrivals appeared. They were both female and in their twenties. I found out quite quickly that they were following up on Angela's investigation as they mentioned her name a number of times. Their names were Carol and Beth, which I assumed was short for Elizabeth. We watched them as they set up cameras around the home, but we didn't interfere. They seemed to be having a disagreement after the first two hours of being there.

"I really don't believe any of this, you know?" said Carol.

"Well, you saw the video evidence and you know Angela isn't the kind of person who would lie about something like this. What do you think happened? Judging by what you saw on that video?" replied Beth.

"I don't know. I'm just having trouble believing that spirits can interact with us on a physical level."

The conversation went on like that and after they'd set up their equipment, they made themselves something to eat. They decided to sleep in the same room as Angela had slept in, and I found out that Angela had told them about the full moon. For some reason, we could be seen, at least partially, during a full moon. Even we didn't know why that was true. When they retired for the evening, we watched them and waited until we were sure that they were both asleep.

I was the head of the household when I was alive, so I still had a certain authority during my death. The other's, which included two maids and several other servants and friends of the family, all followed my lead. Therefore, when I suggested that we take the skeptical one first, they all agreed. I always started the proceedings off, as it was expected of me.

They were both asleep when we entered the bedroom and I headed straight to Carol's bed. She looked serene as she lay there. It made me wish I'd known her when I was alive. I reached down and pulled the covers down the bed, until she was lying in just her panties and a skimpy nightie, which barely reached her hips. I heard the camera switching itself on and found myself wanting to give it a good performance. Just as I reached for her legs, the clouds broke and moonlight poured into the room. I could see my hands becoming visible in the light, which was a bit disconcerting as normally we were shapeless.

I was lucky that she was in a deep sleep and lying on her back. I reached down and gently rubbed the lips that were a thin outline beneath her panties. She moaned quietly in her sleep and spread her legs a little. I guessed that she thought she was dreaming and as I rubbed a little more, I began to see a wet patch appearing.

"Mmm...mmm...mmm," she murmured.

I pulled her panties to one side and began to stroke her skin, concentrating on the clit that was now protruding. Her friend Beth turned over in her bed but didn't wake up, so I indicated to the other's that they should start on her. Looking back to my own target, I could see that she was now squirming on the bed as I kept stroking her bud. I stopped briefly and then leaned forward and started to lick her pussy, as I did so I grabbed her thighs with both hands and lifted her butt off the bed.

She woke up and looked me in the eye as my tongue entered her. The fact that she could see through me, probably escaped her attention at first, as the feelings from my tongue doing its work were distracting her. I saw her looking over to her friend, only to see her being taken by two other ghosts and enjoying every second of it. Then, as I carried on licking a couple of my servants began to fondle her breasts, while another floated above her face and presented his cock to her mouth.

I looked up to see that Beth was being fucked at both ends and groaning aloud with pleasure. I then decided to fuck Carol, so I let her back down to the bed and spread her legs. This all sounds easy, but the fact is, we had to concentrate to keep the parts we wanted to stay hard, solid, otherwise, we couldn't affect the living. Until now, my cock was merely vapor but because I wanted to use it, it was now solidifying and I was able to interact with it. I guided it into Carol's opening and then pushed it in easily, as she was very wet.

"Oh god, this can't be happening. God help me though, I don't want it to stop," said Carol as the ghost in her mouth lost concentration for a moment and allowed his cock to vaporize.

I was able to feel from the end of my cock and around the ridge, which was all part of the deal with the demon. However, in order to satisfy my targets I had to move fast. Their stimulation came from the entry point, so it made more sense to concentrate on that area. As I picked up speed, I could see that my servant was spent already as he was now pulling out of her mouth and the vapor of his seed was exploding onto her face. She didn't feel anything, but in the moonlight, she could see the vapor and knew what it must be.

I carried on fucking her and watched as two other servants massaged her breasts. I always considered myself a breast man when I was alive, so I enjoyed watching her nipples being poked and pinched as I fucked her. She reached her orgasm before me and screamed with pleasure as I began to move faster. Her mouth was filled again by one of those pulling her breasts around and she suddenly went quiet. I looked up to see large amounts of seed vapor coming from the direction of Beth's bed and knew that they had finished with Beth.

I then started to cum myself and pulled out to watch my seed covering her stomach as it vaporized around her. When the servant pulled away from her mouth, I watched his seed do the same and then we let her go. We stepped out as they recovered, but I listened to the conversation that followed.

"I would hazard a guess that you no longer have any doubts?" said Beth knowingly.

Carol sat up on the bed.

"I can't believe what just happened, yet I know it did. Did the camera get it all?" replied Carol.

They both got off their beds and recovered the film from the camera. Beth reached into her rucksack and took out a small DVD player. Once it was hooked up, they played the disc and saw it all from the very beginning.

"Angela said we could communicate through the laptop, as they can read and type. What should we ask them?" said Beth.

"Ask them if there's a way that we can send them across to the other side."

Beth turned the laptop on and typed that question. I came in again to see it on the screen, knowing that now the lights were on in the room, they wouldn't be able to see me. I could still reply though.

"We are trapped here, destined to seduce any that stay within these walls. We know of no way that the deal we are bound by, can be broken," I typed.

"I thought that the demon was sent back. If that is the case, what is holding you here?" typed Beth.

"He was sent back, but that didn't break the contract, it merely freed us of his influence."

"I see, well in that case perhaps we should summon the demon again and make another deal," typed Beth.

Carol quickly read what Beth had written.

"Are you crazy, I want no part of that shit," she said.

"Carol is right, you cannot trust a demon. They will promise you whatever you desire, but there will always be a catch," I typed.

"If we do nothing, you and your friends will be destined to remain here for all eternity," typed Beth.

"That may be true, but we deserve our fate. We were fools to ever make the deal in the first place and now, we are paying the cost."

Beth sighed and sat down heavily onto the bed and started to talk with Carol.

"I hate the thought that they are trapped here forever. Everyone should be able to move on when they die," said Beth.

"I don't care for it either, but I see no way to help them," replied Carol.

****

In the morning, I watched them leave, but before Beth closed the front door, she turned to speak.

"I will be back in a few months' time, as I have a plan," she said.

I didn't think any more of it until six months later. It was just before Christmas when Beth walked through the door once again. She looked incredibly sick, in fact, she was coughing something terrible. The first thing she did was to set up the laptop and type something.

"I want to contact the demon. I wish to get your curse lifted. Can you help me?" she typed.

I typed, "We could contact him again, but for what reason?"

"I have a plan to set you all free," she typed in reply.

She coughed again, only this time I saw blood in the palm of her hand.

"You're not well Beth you need to find a doctor."

"It's too late for me, just take me to the secret room and the pentagram," she replied on screen.

I didn't question further, instead, I opened the door and she followed. I opened the other doors for her to follow, until finally I was opening the secret passage and she was walking inside. There on the floor was the pentagram and I handed her the parchment that would summon the demon. She followed the instructions on the paper and after lighting the candles, she spoke the words aloud. Within seconds, the circle filled with a dark foreboding smoke, that couldn't escape the circle it emanated from.

Moments later, the same demon I'd come to know for all those years appeared and the smoke dissipated. Beth stepped forward, and I could see that she was struggling to stand, let alone speak.

"I wish to make a deal with you demon. I wish to give my soul in order that all the ghosts within these walls can go on to the afterlife and not be bound by these walls," she managed to say.

The demon looked her up and down and could see that she was close to death. His eyes seemed to light up, as if to say, my master will be pleased. We then, witnessed a parchment of paper appearing in his hand, along with a quill and inkpot.

"Sign this paper, and the deal will be struck," he said gruffly.

Beth reached over and took the paper she then took the pen and dipped the quill into the inkpot that the demon held. She turned to look around the room and although she couldn't see me, I smiled and mouthed the words, thank you.

She signed the paper and suddenly a magnificent light appeared on the far wall. The light lit up everything in the room, including me. I turned back to Beth and she was looking straight at me.

"Go...take your people and go. Find out what awaits you on the other side," she said.

Just then, Angela and a priest walked into the room.

"Beth, what on earth are you doing?" she said.

Beth ignored her for a moment and turned back to the demon.

"I cast you back demon, until such a time that my soul becomes available to you," she said.

The demon vanished with a smile on his face, as if he knew that that wouldn't be long. Beth then turned back to Angela and greeted her with a hug. As they hugged, she looked up at the priest.

"Did you bring the note?" she said to him.

"Yes, I brought it," he replied.

"Beth, what is this all about?" said Angela.

At that moment, all of my friends and servants were crossing over to the other side and although I was compelled to join them, I had to see what Beth had planned.

"As you know Angela, I have cancer and have known that I was going to die for some time now," said Beth.

"But...you were in remission; I thought that you were recovering?"

"My doctor told me a year ago that there wasn't much hope for me, even though he tried everything within his power to make it not so. When I came here, I knew I had a chance to do some good in my life, something that would make a difference. When I left here the last time, I wrote a letter to the priest and well, Father, if you could read it out, they will understand," she said and then fell to the floor.

The priest ignored the request, instead he ran to her aid only to discover that she was dead. Angela held her close, openly crying until suddenly Beth's spirit rose from her body and hovered above it.

"Don't cry for me Angela, I'm going on to a better place," said Beth.

"No...she gave her soul to the demon, in order to set us free," I said, only then realizing that they could hear me.

I guessed it was God's heavenly light, which gave me my voice back and turned to see Beth smiling at me.

"Read the letter Father," said Beth.

The priest took the letter out of his jacket pocket and opened it.

"When I was handed this letter, I didn't fully understand the significance but it reads as follows: I, Elizabeth Fox, do pledge my heart and soul to almighty God on high. No one other than God can redeem such an offer for I give no permission for others to do so," he said.

Beth turned back to me.

"I'd already given my soul to someone else, so I can't give it to the devil," she said with a smile.

I threw myself into her arms and was surprised that we could touch one another. I kissed her cheek and then we both turned to Angela and the priest.

"It's time to cross over Angela, but before I go, I want to thank you for being such a good person. You have brought happiness to many people and judging by your friends, I would say, you will bring happiness to many more. God bless you," I said.

"Goodbye Angela, I'll look out for you when it's your time to cross over," said Beth.

With that, we both turned towards the light and walked through. I turned back as we entered and could see the tears streaming down Angela's face. I smiled and then looked to my future.

The End

www.ingramcontent.com/pod-product-compliance
Lightning Source LLC
Chambersburg PA
CBHW031052110825
30930CB00013B/39